# Something on the Inside

# T. N. Williams

URBAN
CHRISTIAN

*www.urbanchristianonline.net*

URBAN CHRISTIAN is published by:

Urban Books
1199 Straight Path
West Babylon, NY 11704

ISBN-13: 978-1-60162-952-4
ISBN-10: 1-60162-952-4

First Printing December 2007
Printed in the United States of America

10  9  8  7  6  5  4  3  2

*This is a work of fiction. Any references or similarities to actual events, real people, living, or dead, or to real locales are intended to give the novel a sense of reality. Any similarity in other names, characters, places, and incidents is entirely coincidental.*

Submit Wholesale Orders to:
Kensington Publishing Corp.
C/O Penguin Group (USA) Inc.
Attention: Order Processing
405 Murray Hill Parkway
East Rutherford, NJ 07073-2316
Phone: 1-800-526-0275
Fax: 1-800-227-9604

# DEDICATION

In loving memory of:

Louis 'Killer' Green
Jeffrey 'Bam' Shelton
Antwan 'Twan' Keyes

If I could reach into heaven and touch you one last time,
I would hold onto your essence
with my fingertips,
let unrestrained words flow
from these lips;
show the appreciation I didn't give
when you were on this earth.
But unfortunately I can't put life in reverse,
so now I do
what I didn't then.
I honor the lives of you unforgettable three young men.

# ACKNOWLEDGMENTS

First, I have to give God His due, because my steps are ordered by my Heavenly Father. I thank Him for allowing me to do His will with my imperfect little self. I don't know why You chose me, but I accept it and hope I do You proud.

Next I want to say thank you to my husband, Shun, I am who I am, because you are who you are. To my three babies, Jackie, Jordan and Xavier, I want to thank you for being understanding during my new juggling act. You inspire me daily. My parents, Cynthia and Greg, my step-parents, Harriett and Cotton, all my sisters and brothers whether step or biological, but especially Gretta Brown and Brandy Jackson; I thank you two for being rock solid during my transition. To the rest of my crazy extended family, I have nothing but mad love for all of you. Your nuttiness keeps me grounded.

To Carl Weber, for your vision, I am honored to be a part of it. Joylynn Jossel, my editor, I thank you for your patience through my chaos and your humility during my learning process for the completion of this project. It has been a true labor of love. Kendra Norman Bellamy, I am in awe of all the hats you successfully wear. You give a new meaning to multi-tasking.

To Taisha Cullum and May Furlough, who read the story as I created it, gave me honest feedback and encouraged me to not quit when I didn't believe in myself. I am forever grateful to have you in my life. I have to give an extra special acknowledgement to Pastor Nathaniel Moody, the Only Lady Laura Moody, and the entire

Brown and Hutcherson Ministries in Grand Rapids, MI. You have shown me what true leadership can do and what positive fellowship can change. I have never seen a more unified and positive church family. Iron sharpens iron. May God continue to use you for his mighty work.

For all the readers who will purchase this book, I thank you in advance. In order to be a writer I had to be a reader first. I value you and hope you receive a blessing between these pages.

If I forgot anyone, please blame my head not my heart and know it wasn't intentional.

# CHAPTER ONE

"Hey, Celia, we are heading over to TGI Friday's for a bite to eat. Do you want to ride with me?" Shannon cheerfully asked as the team from SecureTech exited the *Strategies for Management* Seminar.

Shannon slipped off her tan suit jacket and tossed it over her shoulders, walking side by side with Celia towards their rooms on the third floor. They were both Directors at the Detroit division in the international high tech alarm security company. Shannon was in Product Development and Celia in Marketing. Shannon had spent the last few days showing Celia the sites in the city of Orlando after each night's workshop ended. She had been to the annual event four years running, while this was Celia's first time attending.

"No, I think I will pass. I'm pretty beat," Celia wearily responded.

"Are you sure? That sitting all day is what probably made you tired. Once the blood starts circulating through your veins the fatigue will wear off. This is our last night to enjoy the beautiful surroundings. We will be eating

here for dinner before the award ceremony tomorrow."
She flicked a stray blond hair from her face.

"I know. Do you think I will be missed if I forego the
award ceremony and leave for Detroit early?" Celia asked.

"You want to leave this gorgeous weather and scenery
to get back to the gloom and doom of Detroit?" Her brow
lifted above astonished blue eyes.

"Detroit is not a bad place to be, even without the
palm trees. Some of us like living there."

"Homesick." Shannon hunched her shoulders, "It's up
to you whether you go early or not. There are enough of
us here that we won't run out of people to accept our
award."

The Detroit branch of SecureTech had snagged the
Triple Achievements award for the first time. The Corpo-
rate office was acknowledging not only the doubling of
profits, but also the outstanding teamwork and innova-
tive marketing approach that Detroit operations had ex-
celled at in the previous fiscal year. Things were
definitely looking up for the branch once considered the
underdog; that is until the Board of Directors imple-
mented the training programs. SecureTech wiped out all
the low performing divisions and hired new people.

Celia was relieved to say the least. "Good. Have fun at
TGI Fridays."

"I will and you have a safe trip if I don't see you before
you leave."

Celia walked to her hotel room more exhausted than
she had been the entire week. Thankfully the conference
was ending that day. Celia wasn't interested in staying at
the resort any longer. All she wanted to do was get home
to her husband and two children.

She slid the card key into the door and dragged herself
into the deluxe suite with its thick purple and sage
stripped drapery and gorgeous view of the waterfall

pool area. The warm colors gave it an inviting ambience. Celia kicked her pumps off as she entered the room. The king-size bed had been made up by room service earlier, and instead of sandwiching herself between the cozy folds of fresh linen, she fell full body in her black Prada suit on top of the bedspread. Warding off the drowsiness that plagued her, Celia reached over and grabbed the telephone off the nightstand pulling the phone cord until the phone lay next to her. From the many overnight flights she had taken over the past year, the airline's number was embedded in her brain.

"I'd like to change my flight to an earlier time please," she mumbled after dialing and being greeted by an airline representative.

"Excuse me?" a southern drawl asked.

Celia turned her voice up a notch, "I need to exchange my ticket for an earlier flight."

"Well, alright Ma'am, I can help you with that. What is your flight number?"

"Hold on."

Dang it. That meant she had to collect her purse off the television stand. She forced the weight of her body from the bed, rolling over until she made it to the edge. Celia snatched the purse from the stand, made her way back to the foot of the bed and crawled up to the receiver.

"Flight 1107 out of Orlando to Detroit for Saturday."

"Thank you, ma'am," the operator said, cheerfully clicking away at her computer.

Celia yawned then rubbed her eyes. She stuffed a pillow under her head and waited for a response. She had to count the pleats in the curtains just to stay awake.

"There is a flight leaving Orlando at 11:50 a.m. tomorrow morning. Do you want to take that one?"

Celia considered the option of falling asleep and resting until around ten in the morning; heading home completely refreshed. She entertained the idea for several seconds before deciding against it. Her desire to sleep in her own bed next to the man she loved overruled any other necessity. She could always get some shut-eye on the plane.

"Do you have anything going out tonight? Preferably before eight o'clock?" Celia asked.

"No, sorry we don't." The operator paused. "We do have some open seats for a 10:30 p.m. flight tonight."

That meant she would get home before sunrise. Not what she was hoping for, but it would be good enough. A couple hours wouldn't make all that much difference anyway.

"I'll take it." The anticipation of seeing her family made her slightly more energetic.

"Wonderful. All I need is your name and credit card number to process this and make the changes."

Celia quickly gave the operator all her company information and then wrote down her new flight departure and arrival time.

"Mrs. Alexander you are all set. Is there anything else that I can do to help you?" the woman asked.

"No. I think that is all I'll need. I appreciate all your help."

"Great. Thank you for doing business with our airline and I hope you have a safe trip."

Celia felt revived with excitement about getting back home to her family as she jumped from the bed and sauntered to the closet. She pulled out her suits and laid them flat on top of each other inside her garment bag, smoothing out thin wrinkles as she went. She then zipped up the garment bag and gently placed it on the back of a chair. Her makeup case and toiletries were on the counter in the bathroom. She tossed those in her overnight case along side her pantyhose and slippers.

By the time Celia had finished examining the room for articles of clothing and packed all her belongings, it was almost seven o'clock in the evening. Scared that if she lay down she would fall asleep and miss her flight, she opted instead to get the Bible out of the top drawer of the nightstand and read a couple chapters. She usually tried to devote some time to absorbing God's word, but found that her hectic schedule made it difficult to maintain any form of consistency.

Celia plopped down in a chaise lounge by the window and turned on the light placed on the console. She read about Joshua and how he ordered soldiers he trusted to seize Jericho because God had declared that land for the Hebrews. She thought about Joshua's obedience to God and how much trust it took to carry out the task. Deep; it must have taken deep-rooted trust.

She flipped through her Bible and found her favorite book, the book of Solomon. It was the only place in the Bible that spoke of the beauty of love and sensuality, which her own marriage was full of. Celia sat the Bible in her lap and glanced at the phone still lying exactly where she left it in the middle of the mattress. Maybe she should call Khalil and tell him to be naked and ready. She smiled at the image of him spread seductively on their Egyptian cotton sheets surrounded by the petals of freshly picked African violets. Arousal heated her body as she reminisced about the morning of her trip.

*"Khalil have you seen my garment bag anywhere?"* Celia asked as she searched underneath the bed.

*"I think I saw it folded up on the top shelf in the closet,"* he said from the master bathroom, shaving hair off his smooth mocha skin.

*"Are you sure, because I just came from there?"* she questioned uncertainly. Celia sashayed into the walk-in closet. The

*stepladder was propped up against a box of winter clothes. She used it to reach around on the shelf above the clothing rack.*

*"I'm sure." Khalil's late reply came as he entered the closet behind her.*

*She grasped the edge of the garment bag from under a stack of towels; straining to pull it out as she balanced her body on the ladder.*

*"Um . . . um . . . um. What a beautiful sight," she heard him say as she shimmed the garment bag loose.*

*He slid his hand under her sheer nightie. He hooked his fingers around her panties, pulling them down around her ankles.*

*She wrapped the garment bag around her fingers and grabbed the pole of the clothing rack as the weight of his body caught her off guard. "What are you doing?" she asked, even though the answer was obvious.*

*He scrunched her gown around her waist, holding it in place with firm hands as he bent and brushed his lips against the flesh of her bottom.*

*"Let's do it right here," his sexually charged voice requested.*

*"Right here?" she repeated turning sideways to gaze into his passion glazed toffee colored eyes. Her nightgown dripped over his hands at her hips.*

*He nodded his head smiling at her as he mouthed, "Right here."*

*"What about the kids? They are wide awake and there is no telling if they may need us." Both their thirteen-year-old daughter and ten-year-old son were downstairs in the kitchen eating breakfast.*

*"They won't." He pulled Celia down to the floor of the walk in closet and made love to her.*

*Afterwards Celia drew bath water in their garden tub. The smell of lavender bubble bath aromatically infused the air in the bathroom. Khalil got into the tub first. Celia stepped in next, sitting between his legs.*

*"Aaaaaaahhhhh,"* she sighed as the soothing water hit her skin.

Khalil wrapped his arms around her shoulders, kissing the back of her neck.

Celia leaned against his chest and relaxed. *"This is going to be a long week."*

*"Yes. The kids and I are going to miss you,"* he said, stroking her breast.

*"The kids aren't going to miss that,"* she joked.

*"No, I'll be the only one missing that part of you,"* he laughed.

*"I'll miss you too. Hopefully the days will go by fast."*

*"Um . . . Hmm,"* he said, laying his head on top of hers.

It seemed that Khalil's job as an Aerospace Engineer would be more stressful than her position, but he had established himself to the point that he didn't have to do the grunt work that she had to do. This was the first year that she was mandated to attend the annual conference. Since her recent promotion to District Manager, company activities had become company requirements. She knew that with her new job title, changes would occur, but she never imagined her family responsibilities would take a back seat to long hours in the office and over night stays across the country. She would have to learn to delegate authority to get some of the work done. Give duties to employees that she outranked in seniority. Relieve the load a little.

They soaked in the tub while Khalil soaped her body then his, cleaning the both of them simultaneously.

*"I got to finish packing,"* Celia explained, tying the knot of her robe after stepping out the water. She pattered to the adjoining bedroom feeling like her day was starting perfectly.

Khalil had put his t-shirt and pajamas back on. He was in the kitchen washing breakfast dishes when she came down fully dressed with her garment bag in tow.

*"Make sure Caleb goes to children's church today. Last week*

*he was booted out of teen ministries." She discussed their rambunctious son.*

*A car horn blew outside. Khalil peered out the kitchen window. A yellow cab had pulled up in front of the house.*

*"I know. Remember I was there too," he told her before drying his hands off with a paper towel, grabbed the garment bag out of her hand, and carried it to the door. "Hold on," he hollered out the door to the cab driver as he embraced Celia in a bear hug. She wrapped her arms around his neck.*

*He began to pray "Father God, please protect my wife as she heads out on her journey. Bless her with your almighty grace. Anoint her with your boundless mercy. Cover her, Lord, that she may return home safe and sound. Amen."*

*Khalil lightly kissed Celia's lips gently sucking the soft skin in his mouth. "I love you with all my heart. I promise to hold down the fort while you are gone, but you hurry up and come back to me."*

*Celia kissed him again as her eyes smiled at him. "I will definitely be back; nothing but God himself can keep me from it. I promise you."*

*He escorted her to the cab with his hands full, garment bag in one, her hand in the other. Opening the car door he placed the bag on a hook and pulled her into his arms, inhaling the mango scent of her hair crème.*

*"Until Saturday," he said.*

*"Until Saturday," she responded, sitting in the cab. He closed the door and backed up the walkway.*

*As the cab drove away she watched her husband slowly stroll backwards up the steps of their gorgeous modern Spanish-style home. She waved once more before the cab turned the corner, leaving her Farmington Hills suburb.*

Celia missed Khalil in the worse way. She hesitantly snapped back into the present, as she placed the Bible back in its drawer, set the phone on the stand and lifted her belongings as she went to check out.

* * *

The airport was more deserted than Celia expected. When she initially came to Orlando, the walkways were filled with business people trudging luggage and parents dragging their children on route to their destination, but now it was fairly quiet.

"Maybe Thursdays are slow travel days," she mumbled to herself as she searched for her terminal after picking up her ticket from the service booth. Her stomach growled. She couldn't believe she had forgotten to eat. As beautiful a city as Orlando was, that just proved to her how badly she wanted to leave it. Hunger couldn't even keep her there.

Celia changed course from heading towards her terminal to search for a food court. Her mouth salivated from hunger as soon as she found the area comprised of different restaurants. The various aromas made her stomach growl even louder. She stood in the middle of the aisle surveying her options. Burger King, Wendy's, Taco Bell, nor Pizza Hut appealed to her craving. She finally decided on a turkey sub sandwich from Subway. After her food was prepared, Celia placed her garment bag over her shoulder and her overnight case on the floor in order to get money from her purse. She should have turned in the garment bag with the rest of her luggage, but she noticed that her garment bag had several small rips in the plastic seam after the flight to Florida. It appeared like someone had hastily thrown her belongings on the storage floor and she didn't want her nice suits mishandled any further on the return home.

She went to a table in the center of the airport food court. Celia lifted the sandwich like it was about to be her last meal and rolled her eyes in the back of her head as she enjoyed the flavor. That sandwich was hitting the spot. She had gotten through half the sandwich before she noticed a man the color of dark Belgian truffles in a Kenneth Cole business suit staring at her from a nearby table. As soon as her eyes made contact with his, he stood and strolled her way. He sat in the chair across from her without asking. His eyes lingered on the movement of her lips. She stopped munching.

"Excuse me for staring, but you are an exceptionally exquisite beauty," he spoke with a Caribbean accent as his white teeth gleamed brightly. His skin was flawless and his evenly trimmed goatee accentuated strong bone structure.

"I'm flattered," Celia said as her cheeks warmed.

"I couldn't help wanting to get to know you." He leaned forward and placed his hands in front of hers, barely touching her fingertips.

"I'm sorry, but I'm very happily married," she informed him, twirling her platinum gold wedding band around her finger.

He didn't blink or break his gaze as he spoke in a husky baritone voice. "Your husband has nothing to do with us."

His buoyancy took her aback. "I . . . um, have to catch my plane." She took a napkin and wrapped her sandwich in it.

He leaned back against the chair and swept his fingers down his goatee. Amazement danced in his eyes as he watched her.

"Excuse me," she said, reaching for her garment bag.

"Do you need me to carry your things for you? It looks like you could use the help," he offered, standing up.

"No, thank you. I think I got it." She nervously struggled to hold the sandwich, the overnight case, her garment bag and purse.

"Are you sure?" he asked as he observed her fumbling.

She dropped her purse and sat everything down, rearranging the way she was carry them. "I'm positive."

"Well if you won't let me assist you then at least accept my card. You may change your mind about allowing me to get to know you." He pulled a business card from his suit jacket and gently pushed it into the fold of her purse's side pocket.

"You have a nice night," she said as she left the food court. She could feel a trail of heat tingle the length of her spine.

When she got to her gate area, she placed her belongings in one chair and sat in the next. She pulled the business card from her purse and read the name. Maliq Nwosu. He was intriguing but she was committed to Khalil; couldn't ask for a better husband or marriage. She would never jeopardize her marriage for any man, no matter how charming or debonair, and especially not a man that didn't value the sanctity of marriage. She tossed the card in a trash bin thinking about her family. She wondered what Khalil was doing and if the kids had taken their baths or brushed their teeth. She pulled her cell phone off the clip attached to her hip and started dialing; just to check on things. She would love to hear Khalil's velvety voice and listen as her children explained their day with excitement.

"Flight #787 to Detroit now boarding. Those with first class tickets please come forward," a male voice came from the airport intercom system.

Celia hung up before the call connected and put the phone back in her purse. She removed the ticket from the section of her overnight case and got in the short line. It was a relief to know in a few hours she would be home. She thought of her husband's words.

*I promise to hold down the fort while you are gone, but you hurry up and come back to me.*

She boarded the plane and settled her garment bag and overnight case in the overhead compartment and sighed as she got comfortable.

The flight attendant came through with a tray of beverages and snacks after lift off. "Would you like anything to drink?" she asked Celia.

"Yes, could I have a Sprite please?" She still had her sandwich to finish. The flight attendant handed Celia a napkin with her drink. She set the pop and her food on the tray. This time when she bit into the turkey sandwich it tasted like warm rubber and cardboard. Celia chewed anyway, washing it down with her Sprite. She balled up her napkin and laid her head against the mini pillow the airline offered.

Four seemingly short hours later, Celia woke up to the pilot stating, "It is now 2:48 a.m. We will be descending into Detroit Metropolitan Airport in about ten minutes. The temperature in Detroit is currently 68 degrees. Please check your tickets for any connecting flights. If this is your final destination, welcome home."

*Home. Home sweet home.* A smile formed on her lips and spread across her face.

Celia didn't want to call Khalil. Phone contact wouldn't suffice. She could imagine the look of elated surprise her husband would have at her early return. She needed to see him and feel his enthusiasm with a welcoming embrace. She could imagine his playful seduction as he undressed her with his eyes, then undressed her with his hands. Celia could just imagine the passionate things they would do before the sun kissed the sky. Reality would soon change all that she imagined, because Khalil had an unimaginable surprise of his own.

# CHAPTER
# TWO

Celia's cab pulled up in front of her home. She entered the tepid breezeless night air. Celia paid the driver, who was kind enough to place her luggage on the doorsteps while she gathered her remaining items. The street light glowed on the pavement. She pulled her house keys from her purse and laid the overnight case on the front steps while she pushed open the door. She heard the alarm system twerp. She was surprised that Khalil hadn't turn on their security alarm before he went to bed, but then again she was always more adamant about protecting their home then he was. Creating safe home environments came natural to her as part of her profession.

She picked her luggage up from the front steps and closed the door. She then tiptoed on the marble floors from the foyer into the family room where she dropped her garment bag, purse and overnight case on the ottoman. She slid her shoes off and rubbed her feet in the thick plush carpet. It was like walking through heaven. Heaven on earth.

Celia sashayed in the dark to turn on the alarm. She

quickly typed in the code and watched the alarm light turn from green to red, indicating that her home was secure. Excitement accelerated each step as she bounced up the spiral staircase. Looking down the dark hallway at their doors, she considered checking on her kids first before abruptly dismissing the idea. Khalil took excellent care of their babies. She would talk to them in the morning. Celia unbuttoned her shirt and bit down on her bottom lip as she turned the knob to the master bedroom. She envisioned him as she gleefully peeked her head into the room.

Loud grunting noises greeted her. The smile faded as confusion crossed her face. She moved into the room listening harder. Her eyes were unable to focus on her husband in the darkness. Celia stood still, adjusting her vision, and within seconds she could discern the familiar sounds as sexual moans. Her voice was caught in her throat. Her air supply seemed to slowly dwindle. Shock enveloped her body, cementing her feet to the carpet, holding her hostage in a horrific movie that she didn't volunteer for.

Celia could swear she heard a male voice repeatedly calling out her husband's name, but that possibility wasn't something that she could accept. She forced the lead in her legs to move forward, her mind determined to see what her heart wouldn't believe. Celia squinted her eyes at the people lying in her bed, disrespecting her home. Neither noticed the silhouette hovering next to them. She tried to blink away the reality as the male voice became much clearer. The name being called was not that of her husband. Dread crept into her brain and seeped through her whole being like a rapidly spreading cancer.

Celia voice found words. "Oh my God."

To her ears it sounded like a whisper, but to Khalil it must have come out loud and clear.

"Celia," The man she knew as her husband fell from the bed onto the floor with a thud.

She found the strength to hit the lamp button on the nightstand, flooding the room with light. She stared at the wall as she took in shallow breaths. Celia refused to pass out from being lightheaded.

"Celia?" Khalil called her name again as he sat on the floor covered with the comforter he had pulled with him. She couldn't bring herself to look his way. Instead, her eyes locked with another pair of eyes. Eyes that were full of fear. Eyes more familiar than she would like to admit. Yes the same color and shape as hers. The eyes of her child stared back at her.

"Kaleia." Her husband had moaned the name of their thirteen-year-old daughter. The depravity of the situation hit her in the face. She felt like she had just been pimp slapped on a street corner. Too stunned to respond, she was still unable to believe what her eyes had seen. She scanned the room while the rest of her body remained motionless and her arms dangled to the sides; a paralyzed being propped up by contradiction.

Her bedroom.

Her husband.

Their daughter.

She visually brushed the ebony wood furniture that sat in its original place. The armoire was still in the left corner next to the sitting area of the bay window. The custom-made dresser with matching mirror was on the sidewall closest to the bed. The original Jacob Lawrence painting centered by candle sconces above the headboard. The warm color of butternut squash covering all the walls accented the authentic pieces, which she had picked out with Khalil.

*This wasn't happening.*

The wails coming from Kaleia slowly broke her trance;

anger was replaced with numbness as she absorbed the perversity. She needed to get out of this room. Celia needed to get out of the house. She looked at her offspring and then her husband and wanted to leave both of them there together as a disturbed memory, but her motherly instinct wouldn't allow that.

"Put your clothes on Kaleia" Celia stated through clenched teeth. She closed her eyes and inhaled deeply several times, blowing fury from her nostrils, before taking that first step. She was trying to contain the rage building in her system.

Khalil grasped her hand as she strolled by him. "Baby, hear me out," he pleaded.

The fury took over as her leg lifted and the sole of her barefoot made contact with his eye. She reeled her leg back with all her strength and kicked him again. Over and over again she tried to stomp him into the carpet. He put his arm in front of his face to block the blows. She didn't care. She aimed wherever she saw skin exposed, wishing she still had her pumps on so she could see blood.

"Stop Momma. Please stop," Kaleia screamed.

Celia looked up and saw her daughter balled up in the corner of the room with her ears covered crying. She was dressed in the Sponge Bob nightgown that Celia had bought her. The nightgown that Kaleia had complained she was too old to wear.

Celia set her foot on the ground determined to compose herself. She looked at the doorway and noticed Caleb staring at her with wide-eyes. She wondered how much he had seen. She clutched her open shirt together and calmly said, "Caleb go get your shoes on. We're leaving."

"Mom, what's going on," Caleb asked, his voice shaking.

"Don't worry about it. I want you to hurry up," Celia replied.

He nodded and obediently went towards his room, glancing back numerous times before he made it to his door.

"Kaleia, you get up and do the same thing," she ordered.

Kaleia stayed in the corner with her head between her knees.

"Shoes. Now!" Celia's voice rose with firmness.

Kaleia stood up and darted eyes from her mother to her father as he laid in a crumpled mess by the bed.

Celia waited until Kaleia left the room before sauntering back over to Khalil. She bent down next to him as he flinched, expecting her to do more bodily harm. She made sure his eyes matched hers before hissing, "If you ever try to touch me or either of my children again, I will kill you. I will take your sick, perverted, worthless life without blinking an eye."

He opened his swollen mouth then closed it again, realizing the severity of her words.

She walked into the hall, taking another deep breath, sucking in air as if she was coming out of an inferno of fire. She glanced down the hall to see whether the children were still in their rooms but the lights were off. Each step was harder than the last as she went down the stairs.

Caleb was standing in the family room. Kaleia was sitting on the sofa. Celia reached into her purse and handed Caleb her keys.

"Sweetheart, go start the Jag for me and take my overnight case with you."

His eyes got big. He cautiously asked as he picked up Celia's overnight case, "For real. I can get in the driver's seat of the Jaguar?"

"Do not get too excited. Turn the car on, but don't

leave the driveway," Celia said as she watched Caleb. Her face smiled even though her heart was dying. "Kaleia."

The alarm from the security system went off as Caleb exited to do as he was told. She lost her train of thought amongst the noise. "Never mind, let's go."

Celia waited until Kaleia stood and she then walked behind her as nausea overcame her with the full magnitude of her unnatural situation. *Khalil would never . . . could never . . . but he did.* The room seemed to spin in rapid rotation as dizziness seized her mind and her legs turned to warm Jell-O. She got to the front door and braced the doorframe. The taste of bile stung her tongue as she regurgitated her turkey sub all over her marble floors. She wiped her mouth with the back of her hand as she noticed Khalil standing at the top of the stairs dressed in the same t-shirt and pajama pants she has seen him in the last time she left her home. Celia pulled the door closed on the echo of the alarm and her family's security.

Both her children were in the backseat when she made it to her Jaguar. The Yolanda Adams *Day by Day* CD was playing. She pushed the off button of the stereo, shook her head, and stared at the three-stall garage before pushing the gear into reverse and backing out.

She didn't know where she was going as she cruised the quiet streets. She refused to go to family or friends. She wasn't ready to explain why she and the kids were out in the middle of the night. She drove forty miles to Lake Superior. She often found peace by water. Celia sought calmness as she stopped her car several yards from the sandy beach. The parking lot was dimly light and deserted. She got out the car and leaned against it as a slight breeze brushed across her face. She capped her mouth with her fingers and blew out air into her hand.

Celia slogged up the pier and stood against the railing, wrapping her fingers around the cold metal. Waves crashed on the wall below her. She listened to sounds of the night as the wind howled. Celia gazed at the full moon partially covered by clouds. The sky, an oasis of color, indicated daybreak was approaching.

The pictures of her husband and her daughter doing unspeakable things in her bed flashed through her mind in instant replay. She tried to block the memories, but the visions remained. She tightened her grip on the railing and looked up into the sky. The first tear dropped from her eyes onto her hand.

"Why me Lord?" She cried allowing tears to freely stream down her face and fall in to the water. The pain was so great, she felt her legs would cave from beneath her. Celia's shoulders heaved up and down as she pleaded for an explanation.

"What did I do to deserve this? I've been obedient to you, how did I lose your favor?" She couldn't imagine this being her life. Not after fifteen good years of marriage. No human being should witness what she had seen; feel what she was feeling—unbearable grief. She cynically laughed at the absurdity of it all. She had felt every emotion known to man within a twenty-four hour period.

She waited for an answer that didn't come. She released the railing and went back to her vehicle gazing at her children before stepping back in. Caleb had fallen asleep. His head was pressed against the window. Kaleia stared straight ahead looking disconnected, as if her emotions had shut down. Celia wanted to talk to her child, but couldn't think of anything to help the situation. She was unsure of what would come from her mouth if she started a dialogue. A part of her wanted to hug Kaleia. Examine her for bruises or marks, anything that would indicate that she didn't enjoy what Khalil did to her. Celia wanted to make sure she was okay; if it was possible to be okay after something like that. Another part of her was itching to slap her daughter until her fingers went numb. She wanted to shake her. They had talked about sex and Celia thought her daughter was clear about what that involved. Celia wanted to ask her how she could let any boy or any man touch her intimately like that, let alone her own father. Too many emotions were running amok for her to trust herself. She may do more harm than good to the both of them. So instead, Celia got back into her car, buckled her seatbelt, and silently prayed to God for guidance, because understanding wasn't a possibility.

# CHAPTER THREE

"Can I get a room or suite with two double beds and a sofa?" Celia asked the front desk clerk.

A Hispanic man in a polo shirt with the Holiday Inn logo clicked buttons on his computer before answering in a thick Spanish accent, "Yes, we have a few suites available. How long will you be staying?"

Celia hadn't really thought about it. She knew she wasn't going back home; didn't know if she would ever walk through her house again. It was a home that no longer existed. A residence full of memories and material possessions.

"I'm not sure, but if I could reserve a room for the next couple of days and get back to you on an extended time frame that would be greatly appreciated." She wearily dug through her purse for her wallet.

"Not a problem. I booked you for checkout on Sunday at noon. Just let us know if you need the room for a longer stay. That will be one hundred and seventy-nine dollars per night."

Celia nodded her head and gave him her MasterCard.

He took it and went to scan it.

"Hold on. I need that card back. Let me give you a different one." She and Khalil shared that charge account. The last thing she wanted was him tracking her down with a card number. She might be acting paranoid but it wasn't a chance she was willing to take. She pulled out her own personal Visa.

The clerk took the second card and rapidly ran it through. Celia tapped her fingernails on the counter while she waited. The disturbing pictures of what she'd seen kept flashing in her mind. He came back and handed Celia her Visa and the card key for the room. Celia was starting to feel nauseous all over again. She stuffed the cards in her wallet and began fanning her face. She didn't want to spill the remainder of her stomach contents in the lobby.

Kaleia and Caleb were in the lounge area. Caleb had laid out on the hotel loveseat, placing his feet on top of Kaleia's lap who was at the opposite end.

"Caleb, wake up," Celia lightly patted his face. He looked so much like his father.

"Mom, I'm tired," he said, stretching as he stood up.

"I know you are." Celia let him lean his weight on her. "You can go back to sleep as soon as we get in the room."

"But why can't I sleep in my own bed?" he complained.

" 'Cause you can't." She didn't have a better answer than that for the time being.

"But why?" he whined.

"Caleb," she warned him with her tone.

He instantly got quiet as he yawned and rubbed his eyes.

Caleb jumped into bed as soon as they entered the hotel room. Celia's head was pounding, her stomach queasy. She ran into the bathroom, jerked up the toilet seat and fell to her knees. Her head was swarming, but there wasn't anything coming up, not even the clear liquid she expected. She crawled over to the sink cabinet and rested against it. The dizziness remained. She tucked her knees against her chest and crammed her head between her thighs.

"Breath in through the nose, out through the mouth," she told herself as she followed her own advice.

Tears fell down her cheeks; tears filled with sickness, grief and disgust so intense that she thought she would die from misery right there on the tile in the bathroom. After a while the dizziness was replaced by exhaustion. She became besieged with tiredness. She used the toilet to anchor her weight as she stood up. Celia walked over to the sink and glanced in the mirror but the image of a broken woman stared back at her. Puffy red eyes accompanied her eyeliner, which had left streaks of black down her face. Her spiral curls turned into a frizzy halo. Celia turned the water on and soaked a towel in sudsy water. She swirled the towel around in the sink as steam fogged the mirror. She stared blankly at the towel grateful that the pictures had stopped rotating in her mind.

The heat was soothing as she pressed the towel to her skin and washed the make-up from her face. She brushed her hair into a ponytail and reexamined the view. Better. Couldn't change what was going on inside, but at least on the outside she looked better.

Both her children were knocked out when she left the bathroom. Caleb lay sprawled out on top of the bedspread, one arm dangling over the side. Kaleia had cocooned her body within the blanket. Celia shut the lights off and went to sleep on the sofa by the closed curtains.

It was still dark when Caleb shook her awake.

He was on his knees next to the sofa. "Mom, I have to go to school. You got to get up so I can go home and change clothes."

The poor child had no clue. Celia wasn't taking him back home, at least not yet. Her brain was in a fog as she tried to rationalize with him.

"Son, you aren't going to school today and we aren't going home right now."

"But you don't understand. My class project is due today. I worked really hard on it with my friends, and if I'm not there, I won't get credit for it. Please, Mom, I want to go to school," he pleaded.

"You're not going to get in trouble. I will call your teacher and let her know you won't be in today. I promise."

"Can't you and Daddy work this out while I'm at school?"

"No, we can't, and stop bugging me." Her irritation was showing.

Caleb looked miserable as he sat on the floor next to the place where her head fell on the sofa.

"Honey, mommy's sorry for being rude. I just got big stuff to take care of before you go back to school. Bear with me." She patted his shoulder from her resting position.

"Okay," he said sounding dejected. She felt his confusion touch her bafflement. She had no explanation for herself let alone one that would make sense to him.

"Now go back to sleep and I'll take care of things in the daylight."

She could hear his feet shuffle across the floor and the bedsprings squeak slightly as he lay down. She could also hear him mumbling under his breath although she couldn't make out his words. Celia felt bad for him. Felt terrible for all of them as she dozed back to sleep.

\* \* \*

"Turn the television down. You're going to wake Mom up," Kaleia said.

"No. I can't hear the cartoons if I turn it any lower," Caleb refused.

"You're not deaf. Give me the remote," She demanded.

"I don't have to. Leave me alone," he hollered, wrestling with his sister.

"Caleb, I'm not playing with you!"

Celia sleepily listened before saying, "Both of you stop. I don't want to hear anymore fighting."

Her head was still pounding and the noise level didn't help. She opened one eye as light beams streamed through the beige curtains. She sat up and looked around the room confused. The memories of the night before flooded her conscious.

"Ugh," she said, shaking the images away. She wasn't about to be tormented. "Help me, Lord. I need you to cleanse my mind and bless me with your anointing. I won't be able to make it without you today, Lord," she whispered the prayer to herself.

Another thought formed in her head as she looked at her wrinkled clothing. She didn't bring any clothes. The kids were in their pajamas. They didn't even have clean underwear. She watched her children debate with each other as she figured out her next course of action. She wasn't going home, not for bare essentials, not for anything. Maybe she should call her parents and have them pick some things up. Then again, they would ask questions. No, she would have to come up with another solution. She should have booked a room at the Hyatt Regency, in an area where she was more familiar with the shopping venues, such as Greenfield Village.

She went in the bathroom and did her morning routine mechanically. Celia took a shower and could feel when the hot water cascaded down her body. She brushed her teeth and tasted the toothpaste on her tongue, then combed loose strands back into a ponytail, pulling her hair tight, until her eyes slanted. A ritual of necessity and of faked normalcy. Just like the rest of her life.

She remembered seeing a Wal-Mart on the way to the hotel.

Celia decided to go ahead and get going. "Kids, I need to buy us some things. I'll be right back. Do not leave this room and do not call anyone," she told them. Caleb gave her a look like she was crazy. Kaleia stared at the floor.

"Am I clear?" she demanded to know.

"Yes," they said in unison.

"That's better."

After leaving the hotel room, Celia drove to the Wal-Mart on Middlebelt in flurry snow. The weather was a complete contrast to the fair temperature the night before when her plane landed. Even though she was only ten minutes from the hotel, anxiety wrenched within her insides. Snowflakes dusted the parking lot where she pulled into a space. She gave herself an hour to get what she needed and return to the hotel.

"Excuse me, could you tell me where the Junior Miss department is?" Celia asked the Wal-Mart greeter who was handing out carts.

"Yes, go down the center aisle and turn left past the magazine rack." The greeter pointed out the directions.

Celia had been to Wal-Mart a few times with her twin sister Alicia before. Usually it was to pick up bathroom or cleaning products because they had such good prices. She couldn't get it out of her head; that house will never be the same again.

The Junior Miss section was exactly where the employee had said it would be. Rows of shirts, sweaters and various pants filled the area. She felt terrible for bringing her kids out the night before without a stitch of warm clothing. Michigan winters could be bitterly cold and she hadn't even considered them getting sick with those thin pajamas on. She grabbed packs of thermal underwear, bra and panty sets, long johns, and tube socks off display capsules. She searched through a rack for a pair of jeans to fit Kaleia's petite frame. Celia found a burgundy sweater and wondered if Kaleia would like it. Her daughter was a picky dresser. Except for pajamas and underwear, she hadn't worn anything that didn't have a designer label attached to it since she was two-years-old, back when FUBU was popular. Caleb was just the same. He has a pair of shoes for every name brand outfit in his closet. Khalil and Celia spared no expense regarding their kids. Khalil's six-figure salary as an Aerospace Engineer allowed them that privilege. Her children were about to have a culture shock. The clothes in the store actually weren't as bad as she presumed they would be. Hopefully, she could convince the kids of the same thing.

Standing by a display of jeans was Michelle, one of the members of her church congregation. Celia tossed the sweater into the cart and tried to make a quick retreat. It was too late, she had been spotted. Michelle smiled and pushed her cart towards Celia. The bulge of her over-sized tan winter coat swished as she moved. Michelle was a heavy set light-skinned woman. She often wore clothes that tented her figure.

"Well, what a surprise," Michelle said.

"Same here," Celia said, pasting the biggest smile she could muster on her face.

"God bless, it's good to see you in my neck of the woods." Michelle hugged Celia

"Yeah, I know. It's always good to see you as well. I

was stopping to grab a couple things before I head over to the Gospel Music Hall of Fame with the kids," Celia lied.

"Oh you have the kids with you," Michelle began searching the area.

"Um. Well actually they are in the car," Celia said, pointing towards an exit sign.

"Okay, I'm surprised they don't have school on a Friday," Michelle commented.

"It was half a day; teachers in-service or something. Then they didn't want to get out the car because it's so cold out. I was walking to the music aisle when I saw this adorable sweater for Kaleia." She changed the subject and held the sweater in front of her to show Michelle. Celia was ashamed at how quickly the lies were coming out of her mouth. She'd have to repent later.

"That is a cute sweater," Michelle agreed. "Just between you and me, some of these clothes need to be permanently taken off the racks. It's a disgrace what I see these teenagers wearing nowadays. A shirt so thin that you can tell what color the girl's bra is; if they are even wearing a bra. And then those jeans called hip huggers. Have you seen them things?"

Celia nodded her head.

"Sista girl, now those things need to be straight up outlawed. You see more crack than a drug addict with a social security check. You know what I mean?" Michelle questioned as she pursed her lips into a frown.

Celia bit on her bottom lip listening; she wasn't going to respond to that.

"Plus, if you ask me, Pastor needs to address that issue in church. Parents should be monitoring their kids better. Walking in the house of God with some party clothes on. It's ridiculous."

Celia interjected, "Kids have their own sense of fashion."

"Yeah, fashionably naked. Now you're raising those two kids you have right. They're always nicely dressed with impeccable manners. Plus you have that extra fine husband to boot. It is a blessing. I bet you thank God everyday."

Michelle's compliment stung Celia like a swarm of bees escaped from a beehive and assaulted her head. "Thanks. I do have to go. I'm sure the kids are getting restless and I need to buy some more stuff." She pushed the cart past Michelle pacing herself so it didn't appear like she was running away.

The abrupt end to the conversation surprised Michelle. She called after Celia, "I'll see you on Sunday."

Celia waved goodbye as she headed to the Boys department. She picked out a set of gloves, three jogging suits, some thermal underwear and tube socks for Caleb. She went to the grocery section for quick fix meals and perishable items before checking out. The snow was pelting the ground as she got into the car. It looked like two more inches of snow had accumulated while she was in the store. Celia made sure to drive slowly back to the Holiday Inn.

She was relieved to see both kids sitting on the beds peacefully watching a movie when she entered the hotel room.

"I'm back," she proclaimed as if they didn't see her standing there.

She sat the plastic clothing bags in a chair by the dresser and took the rest into the kitchenette. She had bought a box of cereal, half a gallon of milk, popcorn, a loaf of bread, two packs of turkey ham and a large bottle of V-8 Splash. That should tide them over for the time being. She would order room service for dinner.

"Mom, you bought us clothes from Wal-Mart." Caleb sounded offended.

Celia poked her head around the corner of the kitchenette. Caleb and Kaleia had spread the clothes in front of them on the bed. Kaleia wrinkled her nose and scrawled at the burgundy sweater.

Caleb was a little more vocal. "Mom, we never shop at Wal-Mart."

"There is nothing wrong with shopping at Wal-Mart," Celia told him.

He cocked his head to the side. "Since when?"

Celia went back to the kitchenette and ignored his dramatics.

She had never shopped for the children's clothes at Wal-Mart. Then again, there were a lot of things she hadn't done before. But things were about to change.

# CHAPTER
# FOUR

On the third day she rose just as confused and distraught as when she initially signed. Celia had been hibernating in the hotel. She and the children sheltered from the rest of the world. It was the only thing she could think to do when nothing else made sense. She knew eventually she would have to come out of hiding. All that isolation wasn't healthy for the kids.

Celia looked over at her daughter sitting Indian-style on the bed near the window. A teen magazine remained in front of Kaleia's face. It didn't look like she had turned a page since she picked it up.

Celia knew she couldn't avoid the conversation she dreaded. The unpleasantness of asking Kaleia about the other night popped into Celia's mind frequently since they left the house. Every time she thought to ask about what happened, fear and guilt held her back. Maybe it was her fault that her child was violated. Maybe she should have a job that kept her home more. Celia had been away on fourteen business trips in the past year alone. During all those trips Kaleia and Caleb were left in

Khalil's care. Fourteen opportunities for Khalil to molest his child. Fourteen times that he could do whatever he felt like doing; fourteen times too many. What about when Celia wasn't out of town, but out of the house? Was Kaleia safe then? Or when Celia was in the home, but soundly asleep and clueless? Was he bold enough to leave their room and slip into his daughter's bed and steal her innocence? It was enough to make Celia want to drive back to Forest Hills and slit his throat from ear to ear. She would gladly watch Khalil bleed to death for what he did.

*No . . . Don't think like that.*

The focus needed to be on Caleb and Kaleia. Celia needed to know what Kaleia knew, without the speculations and assumptions. She would find out what Kaleia had to say before she brought Caleb into the conversation. Maybe God would show mercy and she wouldn't have to ask Caleb about his father's immoral and crazy activities. At the very least, Celia needed to get Caleb out of the room so she and Kaleia could start a dialogue.

"Caleb, pick out some clothes and go take a bath. Brush your teeth while the water runs in the tub," Celia instructed Caleb as he lay immersed in the Play Station II game supplied by the hotel. He seemed hesitant to take his eyes from the screen as his player on NFL Madden ran the ball towards the 100 yard line.

"Okay," her son responded when his player was tackled. Caleb turned the game off and set the controller in the cabinet under the television console. He went to the closet where Celia had placed all the outfits on hangers. He pulled out a navy blue hooded jogging suit.

Celia watched him get a pair of tube socks and underwear. She didn't speak again until the bathroom door closed and she heard water running. Fortunately, Kaleia had dressed earlier and Caleb took long baths so hopefully he would be in there at least an hour. Starting the conversation would be the hardest part. Celia didn't know how else to begin except to speak from her heart. "Kaleia, you know I love you, right? You and your brother."

Kaleia peeked atop her magazine and slowing nodded her head in acknowledgment.

Celia continued on, "I would give my life for either of you without a second thought. I remember carrying you in my stomach and loving you before I ever saw you. When you were born I had this super intense desire to shield you from the harshness of the world and guide you through life. I don't know how else to explain this but, parenting is different than any other responsibility in existence. I value you and Caleb more than anything else on this earth. More than anything I own. If the heel of my shoe broke or if I burned a hole in my shirt while ironing, then I would go to the store and get news ones. I could quit my job today and feel pretty confident that another position somewhere else would be available or I could sell the house and buy one just as nice somewhere else. Kaleia, what I mean to say is that much in life is expendable. I can replace many things and I might feel an inkling of sadness for the loss of my clothes or job or house, but I would eventually get over it. I could never replace you or Caleb. I brought you into this world. We . . . Khalil and I created you."

Kaleia pressed the magazine against her chest and straightened her legs out. Celia swallowed a lump in her throat as she felt herself stumbling for more words.

"There is no greater responsibility than parenthood and I can't help but feel like I failed you as a mother and Khalil . . . well . . . your father shouldn't have done what he did. What I saw him do the other night, that's not parental love. I really need to know if that happened before. How long has your father been touching you like that?" Celia finally asked.

The magazine dropped onto the bed. It looked like the color drained from Kaleia's face as her caramel skin turned ash beige. Her eyes bulged, and then Kaleia shook her head rapidly as words tumbled from her mouth. "Mom, please don't make me talk about that."

"Kaleia, I don't mean to make you uncomfortable, but we have to talk about what happened."

Kaleia continued to shake her head with her lips pressed into a tight line. She gripped the covers of the bed as her erect posture went into defense mode. Celia was shocked all over again. She didn't know what to think about Kaleia's response.

Celia had to continue on with the conversation, no matter how painful, "We're going to have to go to the police. Kaleia, your father will be arrested and—"

Kaleia cut in, stunned, "Arrested? We can't have Daddy put in jail. Why would you even say something like that. My daddy doesn't deserve to go to jail."

Celia tried to remain calm. "Your daddy committed a crime. He committed a crime against you. Sending him to jail is the least that should happen."

"Mom, you don't understand. I love my daddy. I won't have anything to do with sending him to jail. I just won't do it," Kaleia stated emphatically trying to sound grown-up, although her squeaky voice represented a scared little girl.

Keeping her composure was becoming more difficult for Celia, but she had to keep going. She didn't want to badger Kaleia, but she also didn't want to let the subject go. Celia had come too far to back down now. "Then make me understand, because I don't get it. You are right, I don't understand." Celia threw her hands in the air; she admitted her confusion. "I completely and ut-

terly don't understand. None of it makes sense to me.
That is why we need to talk about this. I know I'm not
blind, your father molested you. He committed the crime
of incest. I need you to make me understand why that is
alright or why that is acceptable. Why did you let your
father get intimate with you? Are you scared of Khalil?
Did he threaten you or what? In God's name explain it to
me." Celia felt flustered.

Kaleia kept shaking her head, but words weren't coming out of her mouth. Celia wanted to scream, shout, cuss
and cry. She wanted to force a confession or admission
from her daughter's lips, but what would that prove.
Celia silently prayed that if she couldn't get through to
Kaleia then maybe somebody else would.

The bathroom door open as Caleb came out fully
dressed, his pajamas balled up in the fold of his left arm.
"Are we going anywhere today?" Caleb asked as he
stuffed his dirty clothes in a tote bag.

"Maybe." Celia got up from the sofa feeling defeated.
Celia turned the television on with the remote control.
She scrolled for kid friendly channels.

"Watch TV while I make a phone call." Celia briefly
glanced at Kaleia who looked relieved that their conversation was over.

Celia threw the remote control on the bed and turned
her cell phone on. She waited for the signal to clear. Immediately the message server clicked on. The kids watched
*That's So Raven* on the Disney Channel. Celia took the
phone in the hall to hear over the show's theme music.

"You have twenty-two messages," the electronic voice
informed her.

"Twenty-two?" she muttered, not expecting to have received that many calls since Friday. Guilt tugged at her
for not letting anybody know her whereabouts. She held
her breath as she listened to the messages.

Friday, 7:03 a.m.: "Celia, it's Khalil. We need to talk about what happened. Give me a call when you get this message."

Friday, 7:34 a.m.: "Baby, it's not what it looked like. I can explain everything. Just give me a chance. I know it looks bad. Worse than it actually is. If I were in your shoes I would probably be thinking the same thing you are thinking, but I would never do what you think I did. I forgive you for attacking me too. I know you were not yourself when you left the house this morning. "

Friday, 7:38 a.m.: "I'm not going to work today. I called in sick. I was afraid you might call and not be able to reach me at the office. You can reach me at home though. I'll be waiting by the phone until you call me back."

Friday, 8:19 a.m.: "Celia, please, please, please call me back."

Friday, 9:50 a.m.: "I'm worried about you and the kids. I can't believe it started snowing again. It's getting pretty slippery out. You didn't have a coat on when you left. Let me know you are okay. If you want to come home and change into some warm clothes I promise to let you vent. You're going to get sick out in this weather without a coat on. Come home. Celia I beg you to come on home. Let's work through this."

Friday, 10:25 a.m.: "Caleb's teacher called and left a message, because he isn't in class today. I didn't answer. I'm screening calls, but you might want to phone the school and tell them something."

Friday, 10:27 a.m.: "Mrs. Alexander. Good Morning this is Ms. Wilkes, Caleb's teacher. He wasn't in class and I was concerned that he might be ill. He never misses school and has a group project presentation today. If you could give me a call, I would appreciate it. Thank You."

Friday, 12:40 p.m.: "Baby, I'm praying for your safety, but I want to hear from you."

Friday, 2:57 p.m.: "Celia, if you don't call me back, I'm going to start calling all the people you know. This is ridiculous. You are making a mountain out of a molehill. Blowing what you think you saw way out of proportion. I know that if you aren't speaking to me that you have called your parents or somebody to let them know where you are."

Friday, 4:03 p.m.: "I haven't called anyone yet. I don't want them worrying unnecessarily like I am right now; you know I don't like putting people in the midst of our problems. We are good at solving things without adding extra feedback to the mix, but baby you're torturing me. I'm getting to my wits end. Alright. Bye."

Friday, 6:12 p.m.: "I'm going out of my mind. At least hear my side. You are making this bigger than it should be. There really is a logical explanation."

Friday, 7:33 p.m.: "It's obvious that you don't want to talk to me. Let one of the kids call me. All I want to know is that you are safe."

Friday, 9:25 p.m.: "Celia, honey I love you . . . sniff . . . sniff. I love my kids. I will do anything to hear your voice. Call me."

Friday, 10:49 p.m.: "This is your mom and Khalil just came over. He is here now. He's very upset and said you two had a big fight. I'm not sure what is going on but call us or call him as soon as you get this message."

Friday, 11:52 p.m.: "You must have your cell phone off 'cause I know you would answer the phone when your parents called. I'm going to stay at their house just in case you do decide to call them back."

Saturday, 3:38 a.m.: "I can't sleep. I wanted to hear your voice. This is the only way you will let me be close to you. I didn't expect you to answer though. Love you."

Saturday, 8:04 a.m.: "I know you're mad at me, but the only way to work through this is if we have a civilized conversation. That would require us to talk to each other. I'm sorry that you are so upset that you have cut off the rest of the world. Maybe I deserve this, but baby I need to speak with you so we can come up with a resolution. We have been together for fifteen years. Fifteen years is too long to stop talking now. We promised each other that nothing would be so big that we couldn't work it out somehow. Remember that. I see you need some space and I'm willing to give you all the time you need, but I am scared that something awful or tragic has happened to all of you. I love you. I love you so much that this is killing me. I'm dying on the inside without you and our kids. You have taken them away from me like I don't care about them just as much as you do. That is not fair. That is not right."

Saturday, 1:16 p.m.: "Your parents and I are praying for you. I believe that God is keeping you safe. That's all I have to hold on to. My only hope is that you are okay. Talk to you soon."

Saturday, 8:03 p.m.: "I'm not going to keep calling you if you won't answer your phone. Tell my kids I love them. I won't call again till you return my call."

Saturday, 9:22 p.m.: "Hey my twin. I hear you and your husband are having issues. Call me when you need to talk."

Sunday, 9:06 a.m.: "Celia, this is your father. You need to let us know what's going on. Whatever it is can't be worth all this drama. I don't know what's wrong with you young lady, but this is totally out of character for you. If we haven't heard from you within the next couple of hours, we will call the police and file a missing persons report on you and the kids."

Celia began to panic. She looked at her watch. It was a quarter past ten in the morning. She had no idea that her whole family was involved. They were more worried than she had thought. If her father was threatening to call the police, then he would make good on that. He didn't play with that kind of stuff.

Khalil had run to her parents of all places. He had some audacity to bring them into it. He was acting like her anger was trivial; like she had sent him to the store for milk and he brought back ice cream instead. No matter what he said or did, she knew without a doubt that she wasn't out of her mind. Maybe she shouldn't have gone into seclusion without telling her family but that didn't make her insane. Not insane, dumb or blind. What she saw was exactly as she saw it, him molesting their thirteen-year-old daughter.

Her anger revived itself as she paced the hall floor with the cell phone clutched in her hand. She formed a circle with her mouth and blew air from her lips as the veins in her forehead thumped rapidly.

"Oh all the nerve," she said to herself infuriated. The more she thought about it the hotter she got. Khalil had reached a whole new level of sickness. She forced herself to calm down. Celia dialed her parents' phone number, shaking her agitation off as she waited for someone to pick up.

"Celia?" her mother immediately said.

"Hi, Mom," Celia tried to sound upbeat.

"Are you okay? How are the kids? Are they alright?"

"Yes, we are all fine."

"Good," her mother paused. "Now have you lost your mind, young lady? Didn't you get our messages? We have been sitting on pins and needles over here."

"I'm sorry. I never meant for you to worry like that. I had my cell off; otherwise I would have called you sooner. I didn't get my messages until right before I called you."

"We didn't know what to think when Khalil first

showed up. You two never involved us in your personal business before, so your father and I had reason for concern."

"I'm sorry that Khalil put you in the middle. I had no idea he was going to do that and it was totally uncalled for."

"I'm just glad to know you all didn't get into a car accident or something. The weather changed so quickly the other day. I called all the hospitals this morning. You have no idea what it is like to try to get information from a morgue."

"Mom, you should have had faith that we were alive at least."

"I would have had more faith if you'd picked up a phone and called to let us know where you were at. That would have settled everything."

"You are absolutely right."

Celia heard voices in the background before her mother spoke again. "Your husband wants to talk to you."

"No!" she shouted emphatically.

"Celia. You should speak to Khalil. He has been going crazy over here."

"He was already crazy before he got there" Celia wanted to say, but instead replied, "Mom, if you give him the phone I will hang up and I am not calling back."

"Fine, but you are acting real touched right now."

"I might be touched, but I refuse to say anything to him."

"What do you want us to do?"

"Send him home."

"That's awfully insensitive. Eventually you will need to work things out with Khalil. The sooner the better," her mother advised.

"This isn't fixable with one conversation." Celia had

no interest in arguing with her mom. "Look, Mom, I just wanted to let you know the kids and I are fine. We are safe. I can't talk to Khalil and I don't want to talk about this situation right now. Please understand that I am doing what I have to do. We are staying in a hotel but I will let you know when that changes."

"You have us; you know you don't need to waste money at a hotel."

"As you see, Khalil would have followed me and there is too much going on as it is," Celia sighed.

"Well, we are here for you when you're ready."

"Thank you. That is all I'm asking for."

"Take care of those grandbabies of mine."

"Always." *Just like Khalil was supposed to do.* "Talk to you later."

"Okay, Celia. Bye," she said hesitantly.

"Mom?"

"Yes, Celia?"

"I love you and Daddy. I really appreciate your concern."

"We're your parents, it's our job to look out for you. We love you too."

"Goodbye." Celia choked back tears and hit the end button on her cell phone.

She stared at the phone in her hand then reached for the doorknob to the room. She released the knob and dialed Alicia's number. If there was one place she could go that Khalil wouldn't show up at it would be Alicia's place.

Although Alicia was indifferent to Khalil, he, on the other hand, barely tolerated her twin sister. He said that she rubbed him the wrong way with her poor attitude towards the male gender. Alicia often spoke her mind and didn't care if she offended anyone. Celia would call her out-spoken. Khalil thought she was tactless. Khalil stayed away from Alicia even though she never put him down personally. Maybe he was scared that Alicia could read him and would vocalize his flaws; serious flaws that Celia wasn't privy too before now. Alicia vocalized every flaw of the men she encountered.

Years before, Alicia did tell Celia when they got engaged, that Khalil was too good to be real and to watch her back for any shadiness, but Celia hadn't taken the comments seriously. Never had a reason to think that her husband was less than honorable. She simply chalked it up to Alicia being her usual opinionated self.

"Baby Sista, what is going on in your world," Alicia asked as soon as she picked up the phone. Only thirteen minutes separated them, but nobody could tell Alicia that.

"I can't say much over the phone. Do you mind if I come to stay with you for a little while?"

"You know you don't need to ask, just show up."

"I know. I had to clear the cobwebs in my brain. Actually, I'm still trying to get a grip, but I think I'll go crazy if I stay in this hotel room with my kids for one more night."

"Must be serious."

"Yeah, it's pretty serious."

"Are you on the way?"

"Uh, huh. I have to checkout, but I'll be there in less than an hour."

"Which hotel are you at?"

"The Courtyard in Livonia."

"You made sure to go where he wouldn't look for you."

"Basically."

"I'll be here."

"See you in a few."

If Celia couldn't depend on anybody else, she knew

Alicia would always be there in her time of need. They were as close as siblings could be without being conjoined. Their personalities may be as different as winter and summer, but their hearts were one and the same.

Celia walked back into the hotel room and stuffed the cell phone in her purse. "Caleb. Kaleia. We're going to Aunt Alicia's house."

Caleb ecstatically jumped up and down on his knees in the bed. "We are finally leaving this room. Thank goodness!"

Kaleia didn't comment, but instead stuffed the domino game into an empty Wal-Mart bag as she looked around the room for her belongings.

Celia took a couple of the bags and went into the kitchenette to get their snacks. She felt like she was being pardoned from prison after serving time for a crime she hadn't committed. She had no idea what the future held, but she wasn't going backwards and Khalil would pay.

# CHAPTER
# FIVE

When Celia pulled up to her sister's home in East-pointe, Alicia was standing in the doorway wearing a gold crew neck sweater and dark blue jeans that had a gold inseam. Her arms were crossed to ward off the chill of the weather. The kids got the bags out of the car as Celia walked up the driveway.

As soon as Celia stepped in, Alicia extended her arms. "You look like you need a hug," she said as they embraced.

"I don't look that bad. Do I?" Celia asked her identical twin.

Every time Celia saw her sister it was like looking at a reflection of herself. From chocolate dipped almond shaped eyes and the fullness of their lips to the straight angle of their noses inherited from a mixed blend of African and Indian ancestors. Their hair was the only thing that set them apart. Alicia's was in a short pixy cut that barely grazed her ears, which were adorned with large hoop earrings, while Celia's was pressed and curled down the middle of her back.

"Like a Mack truck hit you head on and then ran you over again in reverse to make sure you wouldn't get back up." Alicia guided her to the guest room in the back of her brick ranch home.

Celia chuckled, "And I thought you were happy to see me."

"Of course I am. Just because you look like road kill doesn't mean I love you any less."

"Whatever. Where's Taija?" Celia asked when she realized her niece hadn't made her appearance.

"Around the corner braiding her hair. She is becoming quite the little stylist," Alicia stated proudly. "I told her when she starts making more money than me, she's going to pitch in on rent. Share the wealth."

Celia laughed again as they walked through the living room and down the hall where there were three bedrooms and an office. It felt real good to laugh. Her sister could always help lift her spirits.

Celia and Alicia were pregnant with their girls at the same time. Taija came three days before Kaleia. Alicia believed that to be an omen for them to raise their daughters like siblings. Celia tried her best to make that happen even when Khalil made it difficult. He complained that Alicia would pass her negative attitude towards men down to their daughter. Despite his objections, most of which Celia ignored, Taija and Kaleia shared every birthday together and the girls were indeed as close as their mothers had been when they were growing up. No one would be able to tell that they came from twins. Even at an early age people could tell the difference in the girls' genetics. Where Kaleia was petite, Taija was big-boned.

The guest bedroom was simply decorated no frills. An old tattered oak dresser and a bed were the main features, specifically for sleep, not comfortable lounging. It would be home for the interim. Kaleia would bunk in

Taija's room and Caleb could sleep in the den of the furnished basement. Caleb walked into the bedroom and set his mother's overnight case on the mattress. "Mom, can I go down the street to the school and snow slide on the hill?"

"Did you ask your Aunt Alicia if you could take Taija's sled out the house?"

He turned his attention to Alicia smiling and politely asked, "May I use the snow sled please, Aunt Alicia?"

"Yes, you may." She rustled his curly mop of hair.

He bound out of the room with the speed of lightening.

"He needs a hair cut," Alicia said.

"He's determined to have an Afro. I tried explaining to him that he doesn't have the right texture of hair to grow an afro. But you know how boys are. Hard heads and harder bottoms."

"I'll have Taija do something to his head when she gets home. Do you mind if I drop Kaleia off to where Taija is at?"

Celia was reluctant. The thought of letting Kaleia out of her sight made her stomach drop. She didn't know if she could do that under the circumstances.

Alicia noticed her reservation. "We can talk uninterrupted. Kaleia will be fine with Taija."

"Okay. Go ahead and take her," she said playing in her hair. Celia pulled her ponytail loose and racked her fingers through the thick course fibers. She needed something to do with her hands as anxiety stabbed at her resolve. "How long will they be over there?" she asked as she walked to the bedroom window and stared out at the fenced in the backyard. Celia hoped the emotions reeking havoc on the inside weren't as evident to her sister.

"Who knows? Shouldn't be too much longer. If I had

to guess I would probably say two or three hours tops."
Alicia spoke to Celia's backside, knowing whatever was
wrong had to cut deep. She had never seen Celia look so
tortured. Her baby sister couldn't hide the pain, though
she was desperately trying to appear in control.

Alicia wasn't going to ask questions until they were
entirely alone. "You want anything while I'm out?" she
asked.

Celia shook her head, but didn't turn around to respond. "Thanks, but no thanks."

"Okay. I'll be returning in a few. If you think of something just hit me on my cell. I'm going to stop at the
liquor store while I'm gone." Alicia wanted to hug her
sibling again but left her alone.

Celia folded her arms across her chest and stared at the
wooden jungle gym in the backyard as the winter breeze
swayed the chains of the swing set. The kids had out-
grown that set years ago. Alicia should have gotten rid of
it. Celia remembered when it was installed. Taija and
Kaleia were only four, but they tried to stay outside until
the night turned pitch black. The girls cried when they
were forced to come inside, like the jungle gym would
disappear overnight and they'd have to find something
else to entertain them.

Caleb was a baby who could barely stand, let alone
walk, but he was fascinated by the slide. He used to
climb up the stairs with his chubby unsteady legs and
would look around for somebody to rescue him when he
made it to the top. Khalil waited to see how far up Caleb
got before he went to get him, pushing him down the
slide while holding his little body in both his hands.
Caleb's face lit up and he giggled every time. So many
memories.

Celia left the window and walked through the living
room into the kitchen. Just as she suspected, the bags

from the hotel were stacked on the island. Celia began taking items out of the bags and putting the food in Alicia's pantry. She twirled the lazy Suzy several times trying to locate space in the packed cabinet. Alicia obviously wasn't lacking for food. Her kitchen was fully stocked. She balled up all the empty bags and tossed them into the trash bin under the sink. She turned around and examined the pristine white kitchen with its hunter green ceramic floors. The area was small, but Alicia always kept it spotless and well organized.

Celia was starting to get restless amongst the solitude of the house. The pictures still flashed in her head. They had become less frequent and less vivid, but the fact that she couldn't permanently expel them from her thoughts was frustrating. She walked into the living room and opened the CD compartment of the black lacquer entertainment unit. Alicia had an extensive collection of oldies but goodies music; from back before hoochie videos were created. She pulled out a Donny Hathaway case, read it and smiled. She loved Donny. He was a deep brotha with songs that massaged the soul. She set it back in the compartment. It wasn't the time for Donny. His words would depress her already fragile disposition. She searched until she found a *Best of Boney James* Jazz CD. The instrumental serenade would be perfect. Celia dropped the disc into the player and turned the volume up. Music filled the entire room.

She hadn't noticed that Alicia was back until she heard her voice over the music. "I'm going to put up this stuff and I will be right in there."

Celia sat on the black sectional sofa. A large print of an African couple wrapped in each other's arms on the grass of a forest was right above her head behind the sofa. She cushioned her back with one of the checkered black and gold throw pillows. A gold valance hung over the vertical blinds of a picture window where sparks of light gleamed through from across the room. She picked up the current issue of *Essence* that was on the coffee table.

The click clack of glass on glass hit the table as Alicia sat down an unusually shaped aqua bottle with the name Hypnotiq on the label. Next to that she had a pint of Hennessy and two highball glasses.

Celia looked at the table then frowned at Alicia. "You know I don't drink alcohol," she stated.

"Yes, I know that, but today you might consider making an exception. I wouldn't normally try to get you to cast aside your beliefs, but a little poison won't kill you. It will take the edge off. Numb the ache a little."

"I've been numb enough for the past three days. I doubt this stuff will make me feel better." She watched Alicia bust the caps on both drinks as she created a mixed concoction. The blend of the two drinks created a green fluid.

She lifted the glass in front of her examining the strange color. It looked harmless enough. She held the glass under her nose and quickly recoiled from the smell. "Ugh. That stuff is toxic. Whatever it is I'm not drinking it. I don't know how you do it."

"Girl please, this ain't nothing. I've had much stronger. I was being conservative for your sake. This is called an Incredible Hulk. Sweet and potent, just like me." Alicia gulped down the liquor and smacked her lips.

"You can keep the Incredible Hulk. God got me."

"God got me too. God got me this drink," she lifted the glass of green liquor in the air. Alicia continued on, "Now tell me what's going on. From what I can tell when I left earlier, somehow the problem with Khalil also involves Kaleia."

"Why do you say that?" Celia asked, fidgeting with the magazine she had placed in her lap.

"For one, when Caleb left the house you didn't have a second thought about him going. Yet after I asked if I could take Kaleia with me, you just about jumped out of your skin. It was ridiculously obvious that Kaleia was mixed up in the drama between you and Khalil. Plus, when we were in the car she barely had two words for me the whole trip. That girl sat there like her lips were zipped closed. Kaleia wasn't her usual talk-until-you tune-her-out self."

Celia sat the magazine back on the table and folded one leg underneath her bottom. Alicia had always been extremely observant. She should have joined the Detroit police force as an officer instead of becoming a records clerk in the homicide department.

"Don't tell me. Kaleia has a drug dealing boyfriend and you found a stash of marijuana in her bedroom," Alicia concluded.

Celia furrowed her eyebrows, "Where would you come up with some nonsense like that?"

"Am I close?"

"Kaleia isn't like you were as a teenager."

"She doesn't have a boyfriend."

"No."

"A drug problem?"

"Unh, unh. I think I might be able to handle a drug problem better than I'm handling this."

"No drugs and no boyfriend so she can't be pregnant. I'm tapped out of earth-shattering crises."

*Pregnant.* Celia hadn't even thought of that possibility. Kaleia did start puberty when she was eleven. She was as capable of making a baby as any other fertile human. But her father's baby, that idea was too much to stomach. No. Her daughter couldn't be pregnant.

Snap . . . Snap . . . Snap

Alicia popped her fingers in front of Celia's face. "You going to tell me what is up or what?"

Celia turned her attention to the popcorn ceiling. "I want to tell you. I don't know how to say it."

"Blurt it out. Quick and painless."

"If only. I doubt it will be quick or painless." Celia rubbed her forehead.

"I'm listening."

"I . . . um . . . well, uh . . . I caught Kaleia in my bed naked with someone," she gulped then bit her lip as she willed strength to speak the words.

Alicia frowned. "I thought you said she didn't have a boyfriend?"

"She doesn't." Celia put both legs on the floor, instinctually ready to bolt.

Alicia jerked her back down on the sofa asking, "Then who?"

Celia stared into Alicia's eyes. Still unable to say the words; putting those two names together was like bringing life to the unspeakable.

Alicia stared back. "Who?" she asked again.

"Khalil." The statement was barely a whisper.

Alicia narrowed her eyes as she strained to comprehend what Celia was saying. "What?" she scrunched her shoulders up.

Celia sighed, closed her eyes and said the name again, "Khalil."

Alicia's gasped. As her eyes grew the size of paper plates, they almost bucked out of her head. "Khalil was naked with Kaleia?"

Celia nodded as she cast her gaze at the bumpy pattern on the ceiling.

"In your bed?" Alicia questioned.

"Yep." Celia cringed from the memory. She relived the

incident like it was happening all over again. She didn't want to see, didn't want to feel.

"You can't be serious."

"I would never play like that. To be honest, I'd give a limb for this to be a hoax."

"*Hell naw*," Alicia shrieked angrily. She turned up the glass until the contents were gone. Then she took the drink that she made for Celia. "You sure you don't want some?"

Celia tilted her head to the side, and then rolled her neck around like she was trying to get rid of a muscle spasm. "I'm sure."

"I hope you don't mind, because I'm going to drink for the both of us. God may have you, but I don't know how you manage to stay sober after seeing that craziness."

Celia didn't comment. She didn't feel like preaching about how alcohol never solves life's woes. Intoxication only slows the process of dealing with the ugliness of reality. Halts progress. Faith had taught her to trust in God at all times. Good or bad. If her mind were in an alcoholic fog, then she wouldn't be able to hear the directions God was going to give her to make it past the perverse drama. She wouldn't hear his answers that would surely come.

"When did all this happen?" Alicia asked.

"Thursday night, or rather Friday morning."

"I thought you were in Florida then."

"I was. I missed my family, so I came home early hoping to get a warm welcome. I wanted to surprise them. I had no clue that I would be the one in for the biggest surprise of my life."

"Unbelievable. Khalil needs his tail kicked. I've heard of stories like this down at the precinct. Usually about stepfathers though. I never would have taken Khalil for a pedophile. Most of the degenerates that we book look like they're into illegal or insane activities. I must be losing my touch. I can usually identify a pervert."

It hurt to hear Alicia talk about the man she was married to like that; like they were discussing a newspaper article. Somebody else's dysfunctional life.

"Do you know how long he has been doing that with Kaleia? You realize that just because he got caught doesn't mean that was the only time it happened."

"Alicia, I have no clue. I didn't know what to say to Kaleia. What question am I to begin with? How do you start a conversation around that? I don't know. I don't blame her though. Her daddy is sick. She probably couldn't tell him no. That's her father. Oh my God, how can a man have sex with his own flesh and blood? It doesn't make sense."

"Most of the silly stuff men do make little sense."

"I suppose." Celia gazed at the empty glass her sister held in her hand. "There is a big difference between silliness and sickness. Something is not wired right in Khalil's brain. No man wakes up one morning and decides to get intimate with his child or any little girl for that matter."

"I told you he was too good to be true. It's the ones you least expect that do the most dirt," Alicia said matter-of-factly.

"Why couldn't I see? I keep replaying our life together and I didn't see it coming. There should have been signs. A lingering hand. A hug that lasted too long. Something. I should have seen something."

"Sometimes people are too close to see what's right in front of them. Preoccupied. So busy driving ahead that they don't bother to look at the danger in the rearview mirror and see that they are about to be sideswiped from the back."

Celia began crying as emotion wielded up in her chest. She felt like a faucet with a broken washer inside, unable to control the leak because she couldn't see all the damage. "You know what is even crazier than this whole situation?"

Alicia shook her head and took Celia's trembling hand into her own.

"He didn't acknowledge doing anything wrong. Even told me that he forgave me for hitting him that night. Can you believe that? He forgave me, like I had something to be guilty about."

"Baby Sis, when have you ever known a man to automatically admit to any wrongdoing? His response was normal."

"I don't know what to do," she sobbed fitfully.

Alicia picked up the phone and began dialing. "You crazy for not calling the police already. It's alright though, I got some friends in blue that would have no problem making him permanently disappear."

Celia gasped, "We are not having Khalil killed." She snatched the phone out of Alicia's hand.

"You're right. We need to keep him alive and make him suffer. How about I get him roughed up a little? Make him wish he was dead?" She looked like she was enjoying the idea way too much.

"Alicia, you're starting to scare me." She balled up the sleeve in her fingers and wiped her eyes. "Causing him bodily harm isn't the answer. I kicked him plenty of times that night. Those blows didn't make me feel any better or him any saner."

Alicia filled another glass to the rim with her liquid potion. "Maybe you didn't kick him hard enough or maybe you didn't kick him in the right place. You should have destroyed his genitals, so he wouldn't be able to assault another little girl. Sick puppy."

"You know I'm not a violent person."

"You don't have to be violent by nature to have violent tendencies. We all have a breaking point. If it was me," she pointed an unsteady hand at her own chest, "and that was Taija being abused, we would be having this conversation during my arraignment on murder charges." Her speech was beginning to slur as she used her index finger and thumb like she was pulling a trigger.

Celia believed her. She knew that her sister had a wicked temper and had gone off on Taija's father, Eric, on more than one occasion for far less.

Alicia had been bitter since Eric exchanged wedding vows in Key West while they were still dating. To add insult to injury Alicia was in the hospital on bed rest with toxemia. He didn't tell her about the nuptials until three weeks later when he came back from his honeymoon. By then Taija had arrived prematurely but healthy. Eric waltzed in the hospital room like he was about to receive a Newborn Father of the Year award. He began apologizing that he had left his pager at work accidentally. He set a flower vase with a single "I'm sorry" balloon attached to it. He couldn't have been thinking to confess to her that he had gotten married and then stay within hands reach, because she grabbed the balloon cord, wrapped it around his neck and tried to choke the life out of him. It took half the nurses in the baby ward to get her to loosen her grip before his lips turned purple.

Alicia was on a man hating war path from then on. It was also around that time she began drinking heavily.

Celia hadn't been there that day. She had recently given birth to Kaleia and didn't want to bring her outside. She was forever annoyed with people putting their dirty hands on her baby. She kept a wash cloth in a baggie and insisted that anyone touching her baby needed to wash their hands first or forget about getting close, spreading germs.

They had totally separate philosophies for dealing with life's problems. Alicia lived by the eye for an eye rule. Celia was the peacemaker. They seemed to balance each other out though.

Alicia eyes began to close as her head fell back on the armrest. She still held the full glass upright in her hand. Celia removed it from Alicia's grip and slid the half empty bottles of Hypnotiq and Hennessy off the glass table. She stored them in the cabinet above the kitchen sink. After thinking about it, she reached back up and took them out, unscrewing the aqua liquor and pouring it down the drain. She did the same thing with the other bottle. Alicia wouldn't be too happy about her dumping her alcohol, but she would have to get over it.

Celia went to the hall storage closet and pulled out a down coverlet. She took it back into the living room with her. Alicia was lightly snoring as a sliver of drool dangled from the corner of her open mouth. She smelled like a wine refinery. Alcohol emanated from her pores. Celia lifted the dead weight of Alicia's legs onto the sofa and tucked the blanket around her body.

She grabbed a Bible off the bookcase shelf of the entertainment center and walked back to the guest bedroom. If she were going to get drunk, it would be off God's word. That's the ultimate intoxication.

# CHAPTER
# SIX

"She's beautiful." Khalil removed the pink blanket and counted the newborn's tiny fingers and toes as he sat on the edge of the hospital bed. He smiled admiringly at the infant in his arms.

"I agree. I can't decide whom she looks more like, you or me. She's going to have your thick long eyelashes, although she won't keep her eyes open long enough for me to tell what color her eyes are. Look at my baby picture though . . ." Celia slid a photo off the table next to her. "Doesn't she resemble me when I was a baby?"

"Yeah. She does sort of remind me of you. Wow, I know she's ours but it just doesn't seem real. Until I saw her I never could imagine this kind of love. We still need to narrow down names for this precious little one."

"I'm still stuck between Aaliyah and Jasi'lyn. Both are pretty names. What do you think?"

"Hum . . . I think that since she is the perfect unification of you and I that maybe we should combine those two names. Spelled J-a-s-i-l-e-y-a-h." He ripped up an envelope and wrote the name out.

*"That's different, but how about K-a-l-e-i-a, a mix of your name with mine."* She took the same piece of paper he had and rewrote the name.

*"Kaleia . . . I like it."* He pulled the little knit cap down over the baby's head. He repeated the name, *"Then there it is, our perfect union. Kaleia."*

*"Kaleia is our perfect union."* Celia agreed.

There was no doubt about it. Khalil loved his daughter. Maybe he loved her too much. Could that be it? His love for Kaleia had turned bad like a carton of spoiled milk left out and looked over. Celia felt like she had looked over something that should have been obvious.

The shadows of life had snuck up and swallowed her whole. Chewed her up and spit her out. She wanted to wallow in the numb pain of it. Numbness she could understand. Pain she could identify.

"Breakfast is ready. I fixed you a plate. You are going to have to wake up." Alicia's demanding voice disturbed Celia's thought process. She could feel her feet being nudged by Alicia but she didn't want to move.

"I'm not sleep. I am thinking with my eyes closed," Celia murmured as she covered her head with the sheet. She had hoped Alicia would take the hint and leave her alone.

"Now you know I am not big on cooking. You should come get it while the getting is good."

"I'm not hungry."

"Everybody is already in the kitchen waiting for you. Please, get up."

"I'm not hun-gree."

"Celia, you will not stay in this bed and sulk all day. You still have two children that need you to pull it together. Now you better get up before I make you get up."

As if her threats meant something. Celia's problems were ten times bigger than Alicia's feeble little threats.

Alicia must have thought she was talking to Taija. Celia twisted her body in the bed away from the annoyance that Alicia was becoming. She covered her head with a pillow to drown out her sister's babble.

"Oh, so you are ignoring me now?"

Celia let her silence do the speaking for her.

"Don't say I didn't try to be reasonable."

Celia tried to grasp the mattress as she felt her body swiftly jerked down towards the foot of the bed. "Heeeyyyyy," she shouted as her butt hit the floor with a thud.

"Get it together." Alicia picked up the pillow that Celia had dragged with her and threw it on the mattress.

"What happened to all the sympathy?"

"It's sitting at the kitchen table with my niece and nephew. Now I'd appreciate it if you don't take all day coming to breakfast with us."

Celia grabbed the pillow from the mattress and flung it at her sister's head.

Alicia appeared unmoved by the action as the pillow skimmed the top of her head and fell in the hallway. "Cute . . . now get it together," she said as she left the room with the door slightly ajar with the pillow in the way.

The kitchen was silent as Celia tied the knot of her robe and approached the small white pinewood dinette set. She looked at the nice arrangement of food. Alicia had gone all out buffet-style with an assortment of hash browns, eggs, pancakes, bacon and sausage patties. The mixture of smells tickled Celia's nostrils, but didn't entice her appetite.

Taija, Kaleia, Caleb and Alicia had prepared plates sitting untouched in front of them. The table was only made for four people. A black mesh swivel chair was squeezed between Taija and Caleb's seats.

"Morning," Celia muttered plopping down in the office chair that must have been pulled from the computer area.

Caleb immediately forked his eggs and began to shovel food in his mouth.

"We didn't pray," Celia said more from habit than anything else.

Caleb moved his attention from his plate to a bowl of cereal.

"Boy, put that fork down and pray." Alicia slapped his hand in mid air.

"Oh," he responded like the food would leave the table if he didn't rush through his meal.

Celia would usually reprimand Caleb herself for acting like he didn't have manners, but all she wanted was to go back to bed.

"Since you so hungry go ahead," Alicia said, pointing to Caleb. "Say grace."

He clamped his hands together, bowed his head and paused like he was deep in thought, then he pronounced, "Jesus wept."

He looked up for approval as his hand lingered over a piece of bacon.

"Fine. Eat." Alicia poured herself a cup of coffee. The imprint from the pillow where it flattened her curls showed as she dipped her head to drink.

Celia had a plate already made for her, but she was unable to make herself eat it. She pushed the hash browns around, but when she noticed everybody staring at her, she decided to stab an egg and pop the food in her mouth for show.

"Aunt Celia," Taija said like she was repeating herself.

"I'm sorry did you say something," Celia replied.

"Yeah. I was asking if Kaleia can come see our new dance routine after school."

"Oh. I don't know. Let me think about it."

"If it's okay with you, I can drop everybody off this morning and get off work a little early to pick them up this afternoon." Alicia stared at the lint balls on Celia's blue robe. She was the only one still in pajamas.

"You don't have to do that. They aren't going to school today." Celia put the cap back on the milk.

"Man, not again." Caleb dropped his spoon in the empty bowl.

"Watch it," Celia said.

"Mom, please let us go to school," Kaleia pleaded. It was the first complete sentence that Celia had heard her speak.

They just didn't understand. She didn't want to keep them out of school. She didn't want to miss work either. Celia couldn't risk Khalil unexpectedly showing up at their schools or at her job. Avoiding Khalil until she could get things figured out was at the top of her to do list. After Alicia asked if Kaleia was pregnant, it made the possibility real. She had to get Kaleia to a physician and have her checked out. It was probably too late for a rape kit to be done, but a doctor may still find signs of trauma. Celia's insides churned. Reality could sure be like hell. It was all too much to bare. It was too much for one pair of shoulders.

"Hey, how about you three clear the table and wash the dishes real quick. Celia, can I talk to you in my bedroom?"

"Sure." Celia hoped that Alicia wasn't going to give her another lecture. She pushed the chair back with her towards the computer area.

Alicia whispered as soon as she closed the door, "What is wrong with you? Are you trying to traumatize them some more? Don't you think they have been through enough already? School will get their minds off this crap."

Another lecture.

Celia lay back on Alicia's bed and used her forearm to cover her eyes. She would have plugged her ears but knew the response from Alicia wouldn't be good, so instead, she tuned her out . . . again.

Sleep was calling Celia's name. It was amazing how a person could function on a few hours of sleep with an adrenaline rush, but could barely make it through the day any other time.

"What are those herbal supplements people use? Gingkoba? No, I think that is for memory loss. Or is it Ginseng? I can't remember. Maybe I need both." Celia spoke to herself.

Alicia stopped talking about whatever she was saying, "Huh?"

"I'm sorry, continue on." Celia waved her free hand in the air.

"You're not even listening."

Celia sat up on her elbows and scowled. "Listen, Alicia, I'm tired and I have enough on my plate. I need to call my job to take the remaining three weeks of my vacation time off, and then call the kids' school to let them know Caleb and Kaleia may be absent for awhile. I have to go to the bank to transfer funds so that I'm not completely broke, and that's just the beginning. My daughter needs to be seen by a doctor. I don't know what time it is, but I'm sure you have to get your daughter off to school and get to work yourself. I am going to 'get it together,' so stop worrying. And for God's sake stop fussing. I've been a mother just as long as you."

Alicia stood there a moment before grabbing her keys off the dresser.

"Okay." She hesitated. "I will be back at around three so you can get some stuff done without dragging Kaleia and Caleb around with you."

"Thanks."

"Bye."

"Unh, huh." Celia lay back covering her face again. Her head and heart were disjointed. The struggle to maintain was greater than she could handle. She had faith, but strength was nowhere to be found. Her life had crumbled under the pressure of Khalil's deceit. Somehow, Celia had to find the strength to keep going despite the destruction.

# CHAPTER SEVEN

The clock on the wall in the clinic said it was eleven twenty-seven in the morning, but it was five minutes slower than the watch on her wrist. They were scheduled for eleven forty-five and the time couldn't come quick enough. It was a Godsend that Celia was able to secure a same day doctor's appointment. Alicia had come home on an early extended lunch to watch Caleb while Celia took Kaleia to the clinic. Celia felt terrible about calling her sister at work for more help, but she didn't have another option on quick notice. She had apologized repeatedly for her poor attitude towards her sister during breakfast and for disrupting Alicia's life. Alicia had said she didn't take it personally and was willing to help anyway she could. Celia didn't know how she would get through the messiness of her situation without Alicia by her side. Fortunately she wouldn't have to.

Consent and confidentiality forms, HIPAA laws, genetic history, and health insurance, Celia leafed through each page, examining the paperwork thoroughly down to the small print at the bottom of the page. She felt like she was signing Kaleia's life away as she added her signature to the carbon copy sheets. It was all repeat information that she had filled out at her regular physician, but she was too uneasy about the specifics to discuss the nature of Kaleia's visit with a doctor that knew her family for the entire span of her marriage. Dr. Corbin had delivered both her children, gave them their immunization shots, distributed spring allergy pills and performed hernia surgery on Caleb when he was eight months.

Celia took Kaleia to him when she first started her menses and Kaleia was convinced that she'd die from the onset of cramps. She believed nobody had endured pain as great as her pain. She had even told Celia she would never have children naturally if periods were even close to labor pains. Dr. Corbin gave her a small prescription for Vicodin, which Celia thought was a little extreme for cramps, but Kaleia was more than grateful for the relief. Eventually she became satisfied with Motrin and learned to adjust to her monthly cycle.

Dr. Corbin also saw Celia for her annual breast and pelvic exam. Dr. Corbin consulted Khalil on a strict 2000 calorie healthy diet plan when he decided to bulk up his muscle mass, because he felt his body was too thin. It was a food plan that the entire family could adhere to, so Celia wouldn't have to buy or cook separate meals to aid Khalil in his pursuit for LL Cool J's physique. Celia feared what her doctor would think if she divulged that her husband had molested their daughter.

Kaleia sat slouched next to her mother in the Women's Health Clinic. Her arms were crossed as she bounced her left leg. She had bought a lavender Baby Phat jersey set before the appointment. The key chain inside her pants pocket jiggled with the movement.

"It will be over before you know it," Celia told Kaleia, although the statement was more for her own benefit than that of her child. Kaleia had been informed about the appointment as soon as Celia got off the phone scheduling it. Celia had tried to explain why Kaleia needed to see a doctor on the drive to the clinic, but Celia still didn't feel prepared for it. She didn't know how to adequately prepare Kaleia either.

"Unh, huh," Kaleia answered reaching into her compact purse, taking out a piece of Doublemint gum and folding it into her mouth. She made popping noise with the gum on the back of her teeth. Her gaze fixed across the waiting room.

Celia followed her gaze and saw a tawny brown-skinned girl holding a newborn baby. Her freckled face gave the appearance of innocence and youth. Auburn bangs almost covered the girl's eyes. A ponytail sat lopsided atop her head. She tried to coax the hollering baby as she patted his back in a rapid motion. She pulled out a tiny container with a pacifier in it from a bag placed between her feet. She quickly pushed the pacifier in the infant's mouth, while she continued to dig through the navy blue and white koala bear-covered bag. The pacifier dropped to the floor and she picked it up sanitizing the ring with her tongue before cramming it back into the baby's mouth.

His tiny head bobbled freely like a car dashboard ornament from the lack of neck support as she dug through the baby bag. She finally had a diaper and flannel blanket in hand. She flattened out the blanket in the chair next to her. She gently laid the infant down and changed his soiled diaper, unconscious or uncaring of the attention that had been drawn to her.

"Kaleia Alexander," A nurse called out from inside a doorway by the reception area.

Celia handed the nurse the clipboard of finished paperwork as Kaleia stood apprehensively behind her.

"It's not necessary for you to go in if she is comfortable by herself. Our physicians see young adults by themselves on a regular basis," the nurse informed Celia.

"That may be true, but my daughter will be seeing no one without me. I hope that will not be a problem," Celia responded kindly.

"I just wanted to make you aware of procedure. You are more than welcome to accompany your daughter. Please come with me."

The nurse checked Kaleia's weight, height, temperature and blood pressure before saying, "I need you to get undressed from the waist down. The doctor will be in shortly."

Celia sat holding her purse clutched in her lap as she waited for Kaleia to undress, still unable to believe they were in such a crazy situation. She had to accept things as they were and was running on fumes to cope. Worse case scenarios routed in her brain, even though she was praying for divine intervention. Her ideas of the best situation had changed over the past few days from her being able to provide emotional, physical and financial support for her family, and her children growing up in a healthy Christian two-parent household, to getting through another day without a nervous breakdown. She no longer valued the car she drove, the beautifully decorated home she used to live in, the international trips twice a year her and Khalil took or the costly private schools her kids attended. It all seemed material and insignificant in the great scheme of things and less and less important with each passing hour.

"Mom, can I get some privacy to take my pants off," Kaleia said, pointing towards the door.

"No." Celia was anxious for the exam to be over with, but she wasn't moving from her seat until it was done.

Kaleia begged, "Please. This is hard enough without you watching me get undressed."

"The answer is still no. I gave birth to you. You don't have anything that I don't have. If you can let your daddy see your naked behind, then this should be a walk in the park."

Kaleia winced.

Celia apologized, "I'm sorry that was uncalled for, but I won't be leaving this room until we make sure there isn't anything physically wrong with you. I'm looking out for your best interest. You might as well close your eyes and act like I'm not here if you feel it's going to be that hard to have me in the room."

Kaleia quickly took the pants off her petite frame and jumped up on the examination table, not removing her underwear until the thin sheet of paper covered her lower half.

Celia unconsciously rolled her eyes and pursed her lips at Kaleia's bashfulness as she tried not to be angry that her daughter felt more comfortable with a man seeing her unclothed than her mother who had the same body parts as her. What made it okay for her father but not for her? Celia thought about Kaleia's declaration of love for Khalil when Celia talked to her at the hotel. She wondered if Khalil had somehow brainwashed Kaleia into acceptance of male attention. Anything was possibly at that point.

They sat in silence until the physician entered the room. Celia had requested a woman doctor when she called to make the appointment. The last thing she wanted was another man touching her child's intimate parts, which was another reason she couldn't see their family physician. Her ability to trust any man was compromised by Khalil's perverted deception. All men with the exception of her father and oldest brother were considered suspect until further notice as far as she was concerned.

A cinnamon-complexioned woman with long golden dreadlocks that draped her shoulders entered with a warm smile. "Good morning, I'm Dr. Williams. You must be her mother, although you look more like sisters. I can tell you take great care of yourself. Your skin is very healthy." She shook Celia's hand.

"Thank you very much, and yes, I am her mother. The one and only," Celia replied with a small smile.

"And, young lady, I will be examining you shortly. I love your name; do you pronounce it Ka-lee-ah?"

Kaleia appeared to become more relaxed in the doctor's presence as she beamed from the compliment, "Yes, that is exactly how it is pronounced. Thank you."

"I see this is your first visit to the clinic. Is this your first Pap smear?" Dr. Williams asked.

"I think so," Kaleia said, unsurely.

"Yes, it is her first one," Celia quickly interjected.

Are there any questions or concerns you have before I begin the Pap smear?" Dr. Williams asked the both of them.

Celia looked at Kaleia expecting her to say something that would save her the trouble of facilitating the conversation, but Kaleia was suddenly wearing a blank stare.

"My daughter was inappropriately touched by someone and I want to make sure she isn't pregnant or has any other detectable medical problems."

"When you say inappropriately touched, do you mean sexual contact that wasn't consensual?"

"Yes . . . um . . . she was molested by a family member." Those words were becoming easier to say as she acknowledged the circumstances.

"Do you feel you have been violated?" the doctor sympathetically asked Kaleia.

Kaleia shrugged her shoulders, "I guess."

Dr. Williams gently patted Kaleia's shoulder. "I won't ask any more questions. If you do feel like you have more to say then I'm all ears. What is discussed in this room will stay in this room. I don't want you to be afraid here."

"I'm not scared. I don't have anything to say."

"Alright. Let me go get the nurse to assist me. I will be back very shortly." Dr. Williams left the room, closing the door behind her.

"She's nice huh?" Celia said to fill the silence.

"Yeah."

"It's wonderful to see a black woman doing her thang as a physician. One hundred years ago that was almost unheard of, you know. Unless she was a midwife, because back then, black families weren't allowed admittance in many hospitals, so somebody had to be skilled at delivering babies. There were a lot of midwives that were black. People didn't believe black women were smart enough or skilled enough to be doctors and take care of all their health needs. Things have definitely changed for the better." Celia knew she was nervously rambling, but couldn't help it.

"It's cool, but our family doctor is a white man."

"True. Maybe it's about time that we look into getting a new physician."

Kaleia shrugged her shoulders indifferently.

Dr. Williams came back in with the nurse that had taken Kaleia's blood pressure. They had a tray of instruments with a bottle of clear gel on a blue sterilization sheet.

She sat in a chair between Kaleia's legs and pulled out the stirrups. The nurse added gloves to the doctor's hands as she spoke, "This is a relatively simple procedure. We are going to get a few vaginal cultures to run some test and make sure you don't have an infection; we will also draw blood from you. It shouldn't hurt, but try not to tense up while I insert the spectrum."

Celia couldn't bear to watch. Instead, she stared down at her chest with her arms crossed, watching the rise and fall of her breast. She wished she could warp into another time in an alternate universe where daddies would never touch their little girls and she could make the current situation disappear.

"All done. Told you that I was quick," Dr. Williams said cheerfully, taking the gloves off and pushing the stirrups back into the examination table.

Celia finally looked up as Kaleia scooted back into a sitting position as she held the paper sheet in place. Her legs dangled in front of her over the edge of the table.

"Nurse Judy will get a little blood work. I'm going to check these out in the lab while she does that and you should be all set after that," Dr. Williams said, then left the room again. The nurse tightened a rubber rope around Kaleia's arm and felt around for a vein. Kaleia scrunched her eyes closed until Celia could see lines form at the corners as she waited for the nurse to finish. Nurse Judy quickly cleaned the area, left the room and Dr. Williams returned right after.

Celia was relieved when the doctor came back with the results. She braced herself for potential bad news.

*Prepare for the worst but expect the best. God please allow her to give us something good.*

Dr. Williams scanned Kaleia's chart in a folder she was holding. "All of her tests came back clear. She is definitely not pregnant. No infections or diseases. A physically perfect bill of health from what I can see."

Celia released a sigh of relief. "Thank you God," she said loudly.

"Mrs. Alexander if you don't mind, I would like to talk

to you for a minute while Kaleia gets her clothes back on."

"Sure," Celia stood up and put her purse strap on her shoulder. She felt like an elephant had been lifted off her body as she glided out of the examination room.

When they got into the hallway the doctor whispered, "If she has been molested, then I suggest you get her psychological counseling to deal with the trauma. The physical exam only tells so much. There may be much more damage mentally than you or I can tell from looking at her. From her response, when I asked her if she had been violated, I would say she is still in denial about what happened. I can give you a list of credible psychiatrists that we are affiliated with. I personally suggest Dr. India Malawi. She has extensive experience with child molestation cases and has written several books on the subject."

"This whole thing has been very difficult for the both of us," Celia replied. "I have no idea of how long it's been happening or how often. My entire family as a whole has been affected. I want to reach out to her and comfort her, but I really don't know what to say to her. Basically everything that comes out of her mouth is a one word syllable. She went from being a talkative and vivacious young lady to this quiet withdrawn little girl. It's like her personality has dissolved into this shell of the person I knew. I would do anything to help my little girl, and although I believe God can deliver you from anything, if you feel Dr. Malawi can help Kaleia, then I want to at least try counseling."

"She's good. I don't think you will regret it. She specializes in African-American families. She is also well respected in the professional community. I think you will be putting Kaleia in extremely capable hands. I will go get her business card and refer you over. The sooner you get your daughter in to see Dr. Malawi, the better off she will be."

"Thanks."

Celia walked back in the room to check on Kaleia. "Are you ready?" she asked as she noticed Kaleia sitting on the table fully dressed staring at the palm of her hands.

"Yeah," she said pushing a tress of silky black hair behind her ear.

Celia watched her daughter hoping that Dr. Malawi would be able to get through to Kaleia; crack the wall Kaleia had built around herself. The wall which her own father caused her to build.

# CHAPTER EIGHT

Celia tied her tennis shoes and did stretching exercises while she waited for Monique and Justice, her walking buddies to arrive at the church. They had been faithfully meeting every Thursday evening to power walk before Women's Fellowship. The group initially started with seven ladies but for various reasons had dwindled down to the three of them. The only time they didn't get together was if there was a church conference, family obligations, or business trips.

A week ago to the day, her life as she knew it, vanished. Celia needed to do something to occupy her mind. To keep her heart from hurting. Exercise was usually a great stress reliever.

"My Sista in Christ, glad you could make it Celia. We missed you last week. I know all that traveling you do has got to be a beast." Monique set down her portable CD player as she entered the gym.

Greatness in Faith was a massive church. The gym was right behind the church. They had built the recreation center and two level gym three years ago, when the congregation reached four thousand members. Pastor Nathan Daniels, the head of Greatness in Faith, wanted to give the youth of the community something fun to do during the week in God's house. The gym was equipped with an interactive computer system in the weight room, a rock climbing wall, two lap pools, a shower room and a full-size sound-proof basketball court on the second level. It was mainly intended to keep kids off the street. Their pastor also encouraged healthy living for all the members of his congregation. The gymnasium became so popular that members had to sign up in advance to use it.

Monique frowned. "You don't look well. Are you sick?"

Celia thought she had done a good job of hiding her anguish within, but evidently not good enough. She tried to play it off. "I'm okay. Extended jet lag. Don't worry about it. Once I get to walking I'll be just fine."

Justice came running in as she tossed her shoulder-length light brown hair into a ponytail. "Sorry I'm late. Richard and I are sharing a car this week."

"That's okay. I haven't done my warm-ups yet." Monique straightened her thick thighs and bent down to touch her tennis shoes.

"How about you, Celia?" Justice asked.

"I did some stretching before you both got here," Celia replied.

"Are you okay?" Justice also frowned with worry. "You don't look like yourself today."

"I'm fine. Monique asked me that already. I'm going to walk around the track while you two get your stretches in."

"You sure?" Monique asked with arched brows.

Celia nodded as she stepped in the lines of the track.

She didn't know if she would make it through fellowship after the walk without breaking down.

"This is a test. This is just a test. Greater is He that is in me than he that is in the world. I'm going to be alright. I got to be alright," she spoke as she clamored around the track and focused on breathing instead of thinking. "Breathe in . . . one . . . two. Breathe out . . . one . . . two."

Monique and Justice joined her on the second trip around the church gymnasium's track as Tye Tribbett blasted from the CD player plugged into the loud, wall speakers.

"We closed on our house yesterday," Justice said, grinning as she did a two step. "Richard and I have been married eight years and finally we bought our first house. Can you believe it? God is so faithful. I don't think we were ready before now, as bad as we wanted to stop paying rent. We weren't ready mentally or financially. We prayed hard for this house. So I know it was the right time to make our dream of homeownership a reality." Justice's dimples sunk into her caramel face from excitement.

"That is great. You deserve a house. Let us know if you need help moving. I can get Eric and my two little brothers to pitch in," Monique said as her round chocolate face beaded up with sweat.

"I will let you know. I will probably take you up on that offer. With four kids under the age of seven, you would be surprised at how much stuff we accumulated. I started packing last week and I don't feel like I have accomplished a thing. Celia, your house is a mini-mansion. I feel for you if you and Khalil decide to sell that house, but then again, you probably won't ever move, as beautiful as it is."

Celia pressed a fake smile to her face. She wanted to say it was just a house, a house that didn't mean a whole lot anymore; that she had already moved out and left everything she owned in it. Khalil had called everyday, sometimes several times a day for the entire week. Each time she saw his phone number it was like a stab to the heart. Celia wanted to share her troubles, but airing out her dirty laundry with people she went to church with wasn't something she could do.

Monique poked her lips out, "I have to actually get married in order for us to buy a house. Jason wanted us to stay engaged for two years. He said it was for us to appropriately plan our wedding out and to make sure we are compatible, because we had only been dating six months when he popped the question. I personally think he is getting cold feet."

Monique wiped her forehead with the sleeve of her purple jogging suit as they began to pick up speed.

"I don't need two years to know he is the man I want to spend the rest of my life with. I can feel it in my heart that he is my soul mate. I hope he doesn't change his mind before we make it down the aisle." Doubt formed in Monique's pretty dark brown eyes.

"It would be better that he changed his mind before the wedding as opposed to after. As long as you believe God blessed the relationship, you shouldn't have anything to worry about," Justice said as they made their last lap around the track.

"Our black people don't know how to date anyway. We jump into committed relationships before we know if our partners are worth committing to. Richard and I grew up down the block from each other and we still dated for three years before we got married. It wasn't easy, but I'm glad we did it that way. I appreciate my husband that much more."

Celia met Khalil at a frat party she was talked into going to by Alicia. He asked her to dance and they became inseparable from then on. Celia had gotten married a little over a year after they first started seeing each other and even then she didn't know much about his family history. She knew his father had died when he was young and that his mother gave him to his father's sister, Aunt Cheryl, a week after the funeral. Celia only met his aunt one time and that was at the wedding. He wasn't close to her and refused to talk about his mother. Celia didn't inquire because she was in love. He wasn't involved with his family so she didn't bother trying to get to know his Aunt Cheryl or anybody else. Besides, he fit perfectly within her family, with the exception of Alicia, and Celia was perfectly content with that.

Justice, Monique and Celia headed towards the shower room. Fellowship was going to start in half an hour.

Celia stopped walking as the pictures of Kaleia and Khalil popped into her head from out of nowhere. She felt like she couldn't run from them no matter how hard she tried.

"Celia, you look pale. Maybe you should go home." Justice's eyes filled with concern.

Monique agreed handing Celia her duffel bag. "Yeah, go home. Get you some rest. You look like you're about to pass out. Do you need one of us to drive you home?"

"No, I don't want to leave my car here over night. They may come tow it. Talk to you later," Celia said weakly as she waved goodbye.

"Drive safe and we will be praying for you," Justice told her.

On the drive home, Celia couldn't shake the despair and loneliness. She was too embarrassed to talk about it with her church friends. They believed her life and marriage were without blemish. She didn't want to see a look of pity from Monique and Justice or worse, she didn't want to see judgment. Celia knew it wouldn't be intentional for them to judge her situation, but it was a human response. If she couldn't stop judging herself, she couldn't expect them to react any different. She would rather suffer in silence than be judged.

# CHAPTER
# NINE

A stampede of children flooded the hallway of Greater
Grace Christian Elementary that Monday afternoon
as Celia walked to the school office. Caleb hadn't been to
school at all the week before. She had left a message on
the voice mail of Caleb's teacher earlier in the day, requesting to pick up his homework assignments from the
days missed and for the upcoming week. They were
playing phone tag as Mrs. Wilkes then left her a message
saying that she would have a folder prepared. She mem-
orized responses if certain questions were asked so she
wouldn't have to be overtly dishonest about disturbing
her children's educational process.

Mrs. Wilkes was sitting at her desk reviewing class
work. Her layered brown hair stiffly hung on her bowed
head and glasses perched the bridge of her nose. She intently scanned the pages with her finger before marking
the top with a red ink pen.

"Good afternoon, Ms. Wilkes," Celia said, making her
presence known.

The teacher's head snapped up as she realized she

wasn't alone in the room. "Good afternoon, Mrs. Alexander. Nice to see you again." She straightened her glasses then clasped her hands on the desk in front of her.

Celia nodded. "Caleb loves your class. He's always talking about how you make school more fun."

Ms. Wilkes grinned proudly, "That's wonderful to hear. Makes my job enjoyable to know my students appreciate me. I try to incorporate activities that require student participation. We have a lot of visual learners and I find that young children need to see evidence to understand it; tap into the creative enzymes of the brain."

"Kids are sponges. They soak up information. I'm glad that he has you as a teacher. I've seen other teachers that were only in class to make a paycheck. You can tell when an individual isn't passionate about their job. Under those conditions students struggle the whole year without guidance and those teachers don't even realize that their attitude is the problem."

"Teaching can be a thankless occupation. I think some people come into the profession with the best intention, but find it was a greater challenge than they signed up for. I was a substitute for a public school while I finished my graduate degree and I must admit that I saw disrespectful actions by teachers and students alike. When children come from poverty, have limited parental support and a shortage of school supplies, well, they can test your ability to be productive. Private institutions operate differently than the public schools. Greater Grace is an awesome place to work. Most of the teachers and students are here because they want to be, not because they have no other option."

"My husband and I chose private education because we wanted our children to grow based on a Christian foundation. We toured quite a few public schools that had excellent educational programs. I don't think there is a public school problem but rather a multi-layered poor school problem. When parents can barely provide a roof over their kids' heads, then the need to survive may overshadow monitoring homework assignments. Kids can get lost in the shuffle; become damaged by their environments." Celia wanted to scream at her own irony. Kaleia had been damaged without the excuse of poverty. Dysfunction crossed class and affluence.

"I can tell that Caleb comes from a great home environment. He is such a joy to have. He is a little gentleman. He's always eager to help out too. It has been strange not handing him homework to pass out to the other children. I didn't realize how consistent our routine was until he was absent. You said on your message that there had been a death in the family. I want you to know that I deeply sympathize with you through your time of need."

Celia didn't want to have an extended conversation about the demise of her marriage. She didn't want to mingle grief with public shame. She felt as if her situation was probably worse than physical death. If Khalil had been killed in a car accident she would have been able to understand that, but she didn't know if she'd ever recover. Betrayal magnified her pain.

"Thank you very much. I appreciate that," she said, wrapping her arms around herself and examining the displays of children's art placed on the windowsill.

"My mother died from breast cancer three years ago and I still miss her terribly. There is no greater grief than the loss of a loved one. You and your family have my condolences."

"We're maintaining. All of us are doing the best we can to adjust under the circumstances."

"It takes time to adjust. Let me know if there is anything at the school we can do to help your family."

"I will. For now if I could make sure Caleb is able to complete all his assignments so he doesn't fall behind the rest of the class, that would be the most important thing for us."

"Of course. He is a bright young man; with a little help from you he should have no problem finishing his work. Most of it is fairly easy and self-explanatory. You can also call me if something doesn't make sense. I will try my best to explain over the phone if necessary, but I doubt it will come to that."

Celia walked over to the display of red clay faces. Detailed artwork with varying faces. She looked for Caleb's name; interested in what he created.

Ms. Wilkes pointed out the one that was his. Celia lifted the heavy object and ran her fingers over the curves. It was barely bigger than her hand, but she could clearly see the eyes, nose and mouth within the oval shape.

"That was a project we did last month. We were focusing on the image of God. We all know that God molded and shaped us. I asked the children to think about their ideas of God's features and for them to mold the clay according to that mental interpretation into a physical form. I chose gray clay so they wouldn't be concerned with ethnic background. At least that was my hope. Anyway, I was amazed by the imagination of my students. They were extremely detailed in their creations."

"Beautiful. They are absolutely beautiful. Can I take Caleb's with me?" Celia asked, still admiring the artwork.

"Of course you can. Initially the kids were going to bring them home right after they finished the project, but I was so impressed that I wanted to hold on to their images until after parent-teacher conferences. If I could get away with it, I would take them all home with me and put them in my china cabinet. That's how much they touched me," Ms. Wilkes confessed as she moved several other clay faces down a few inches to fill the space where Caleb's artwork had laid.

"Kids can have such a clear idea of life. Sometimes their interpretation is more on point than us adults. Probably because their minds aren't cluttered with the baggage we collect when we are grown."

"You could be right. It says in the Bible that God values the innocence of a child. If we can always see the world through the eyes of a child, maybe the world wouldn't be full of chaos."

Celia sighed and then smiled although joy didn't reach her eyes. "Once again, I want to thank you for taking out the time to put together all of Caleb's homework. I will try to get it back to you before the end of the week."

"Don't worry about it. Take your time. I understand the circumstances and I can make an exception. Get it back when you can." Ms. Wilkes patted Celia's shoulder.

"I still plan to have it turned in by the end of the week."

"When do you think Caleb will be returning back to school?"

"I can't answer that. I wish I knew. Ideally, it will be in less than a week or so. There is a great deal going on though, but as soon as I know I will let you or the school office staff know. I have every intention of keeping you informed. I do ask that when he does get back you don't ask him about what happened. It was pretty traumatic."

"That's fine. Please tell Caleb that we miss him and look forward to having him back in class with us very soon."

"I promise to pass the information on to him. I'm sure that he will be glad to hear that. I'll be talking to you Ms. Wilkes. Have a good evening." Celia tucked the large envelope under her arm and went outside.

She blinked at the mirage, as she got closer to her vehicle in the school parking lot. It looked like someone was sitting in her driver's seat from the side angle of the building she was exiting. She was imagining things. Nobody besides Khalil even had keys to her Jaguar.

"Khalil," she said as she recognized him, not knowing if she should keep walking or dodge back into the school for safety. People would think she was crazy running from her own husband. She continued forward as her heart beat rapidly against her rib cage. Khalil rolled down the window as he noticed her approaching. "Get in," he told her pointing to the passenger seat as she lagged by the driver's side.

"But . . ." It felt like stomach acid was rising up into her chest, suffocating her heart and lungs. She stood still searching the area for assistance as if she was being carjacked or kidnapped.

"Celia, I'm not going to hurt you. Please get in." He spoke softly as he reached over the armrest and pushed the passenger door open.

She dropped the folder of Caleb's homework from her arm. Papers scattered on to the ground. She quickly tried to recover them before the gust of wind blew them away. Her hands shook vigorously. She could barely grasp the pages and stuff them back into the folder. Celia's breath quivered in her throat as she sauntered to her passenger door.

*Stay calm. You can do this*, she told herself before sitting next to Khalil.

She listened to the quiet hum of her vehicle as the engine vibrated to life.

"What are you doing here, Khalil?" Her voice trembled although she spoke lightly in hopes that he wouldn't pick up on the fear.

"I followed you from Alicia's," he calmly stated as his

eyes focused ahead as they drove out of the school parking lot.

"Why are you following me?"

"I followed you for the obvious reasons. You wouldn't accept my phone calls. We need to talk. I missed you." He removed one gloved hand from the steering wheel and clasped her clammy one. He caressed the back of her hand with his thumb, stroking it like he had a right to.

Celia felt tainted by his touch. Uncomfortable in his presence. She desperately yearned to snatch her arm away from Khalil, but couldn't tell the capacity his mind was in. Not triggering some kind of psychotic reaction was foremost in her thoughts.

She had no control as he weaved in and out of traffic, driving the regular speed limit, forty-five miles per hour. He merged onto I-696 on the Walter P. Reuther Freeway, keeping the pace of the car steady. He pressed buttons on the car radio. He stopped at a gospel station as Byron Cage sang, "Presence of the Lord is Here."

From his physical appearance Khalil looked normal. His hair had a closely cropped curly texture. There wasn't a mustache, beard or goatee covering his smooth expressionless baby face. He was dressed in khaki pants and a cream turtle neck sweater underneath his brown bomber jacket.

He glanced at her staring at him. "We haven't spoken in eleven days. I gave you ample time to contact me, so we could open up a discourse. I'm in our house alone. There is no reason why you shouldn't be there with me. We should be getting up in the morning together, planning our day over breakfast, just like it has always been."

She wanted to holler that life is nothing like it used to be. That it will never be like it had been before. That it was his fault not hers. He was to blame for them not being able to get up in the morning together. He was the reason breakfast didn't taste the same. Everything that had transpired over the past week and a half was because she had no other choice. He left her with no other realistic options.

"Khalil, sometimes space is better for resolution. I can't pretend that everything is all good. I needed space to think. I still need space."

"I have given you plenty of space. I haven't tried to crowd you. You could have at least talked to me over the phone, if you didn't want to see me. I didn't sleep more than three hours for the entire week after you left. I was worried sick. Literally, worried sick. Do you know what it is like to be so consumed with worry that you can't eat or sleep or do anything but stare at the phone?"

She absolutely knew what it was like, but evidently he didn't see that. "You were at my parent's when I called. I assumed you knew we were fine."

"You spoke to your mother. You didn't speak to me though. Your husband, who had left many messages. There is a difference."

He exited off the highway into an unfamiliar destitute part of the city. Old abandoned buildings and several small boarded up houses lined the street. Wet trash scattered the lawns of brown dry grass where snow had begun to melt. He turned a corner past a junkyard filled with scrap piles of rusty beat-up cars.

"Where are you taking me?" Celia anxiously asked.

"You'll find out soon enough."

Her heartbeat quickened as fear crept into her spirit. Anxiety clung to her like a leech under water. It was sucking calmness from Celia as she wondered why he would bring her to a deserted area. If he wanted to have a conversation, there were a million and one other locations throughout the city that would have sufficed as neutral ground. People don't usually frequent isolated areas with good intentions.

It was unsettling to sit next to the man she'd loved for most of her adult life and not be able to trust him. Her image of him was drastically altered by his recent actions. Years of trust were destroyed in a matter of minutes; minutes that still didn't feel real, even though she had witnessed it. Witnessed her happiness dissipate as if it never existed in the first place.

He stopped the car on gravel in front of an enormous old rickety warehouse. Celia rubbed the ring finger where her band used to be. She anticipated his next course of action; wondered if she would have to out think him.

He turned the ignition off, got out and strolled around to her side. She looked at her purse, which held her car keys, before looking at the steering wheel. She thought about jumping into the driver's seat and riding off before he made it to her. She calculated the time it would take to do that and leave him stranded. Just like her he had a remote key though and she didn't have anybody to rescue her if he was faster than she and became angry.

As he opened the door, she realized that she hadn't thought or moved swift enough. "Come on," he said, reaching for her hand.

She looked at his extended hand and picked up her purse. She got out of the car trying her best to avoid purposely touching him. The putrid odor of urine and stale air slithered up her nose like a venomous cobra ready to attack. She wrinkled her nose, offended by the overpowering odor. The smell singed the hair of her nostrils as she cautiously stood next to Khalil.

He looked annoyed. "Celia, you are acting real strange."

He wrapped his fingers around her wrist and tugged. Her hands were balled up in a tight fist. He began walking, but Celia's erect stance prevented him from moving farther than three steps.

"I told you that you don't need to be scared of me. I just want to show you something." He tugged again and she hesitantly relented.

Regardless of what he said, it felt like she was being led to her death and executed without the courtesy of a last meal. She shrugged the feeling off. Celia wasn't claiming her termination from a life she still had to repair.

She shuffled her feet against the gravel and pebbled ground. Chipped shipping crates, scrap metal and black plastic barrels surrounded the red brick building. A cesspool of garbage that the city must have dismissed sprayed the ground.

Khalil pushed a button and a metal gate creaked open allowing entry into the building.

"Khalil, I don't understand why we are here," Celia stated.

"Baby, this was the foundry that my father slaved at for twenty-five years." He pulled a flashlight out of his coat pocket and turned it on as they stood in the entry-way.

She held her hand over her nose to lessen the stench after unsuccessfully breathing through her mouth. The smell was intensified by the dank enclosed space.

"What are we doing here?" she asked again.

"My father spent sixteen hours a day in this place during my childhood. I barely saw him because he worked so many hours." His eyes glazed over as he spoke. "I despised my father's job for taking him away from me. First for the nights he didn't make it in until well after my bedtime and then when he died of black lung disease after years of inhaling toxic chemicals during brass extrusions. I was only eleven-years-old with no father. No man to answer my questions about life. No man to attend my basketball games. No man to explain the birds and bees. I had no one to teach me all the valuable things a little boy should know in order to become a man. I learned by trial and error because of this building."

Celia wasn't vaguely interested in his story as she slid her hand in her purse and held onto her keys, preparing to run if necessary.

"Can you imagine this place alive with activity? Machines operating and production lines of employees laboring away in hot conditions as molten specks of chemicals sprayed the air? They were breathing in toxins that were slowly killing them," Khalil's voice echoed as he stepped further inside and used the flashlight to motion around the dingy concrete and up a metal railing that extended from the stairs all the way up to a second and third floor.

No, she couldn't imagine what he was referring to. What she could imagine was him inappropriately fondling a child he helped create. What she could see was him stripping away the virginity of their daughter with no remorse while Celia walked around totally unaware that sick wickedness dwelled in the confines of their home. She could see plenty that she'd prefer not to. The history of that old building that they were standing in didn't even register on her I-give-a-care scale.

"Khalil, the smell in here is starting to make me ill. If you don't mind I'm going back to the car," She turned to leave.

"Wait!"

She abruptly stopped, but she didn't turn back around.

"The reason I brought you here is to show you the place I want to buy."

She slowly rotated her body until she was looking at him again. "Excuse me," she said.

"I want to purchase this building. I want to start a

business for us . . . and for our children's future; to compensate for my father's death." He spoke like the conversation was logical, although it sounded like a bunch of gibberish to Celia.

She continued to stare at him, outwardly confused but inside bubbling over with annoyance.

He continued explaining himself. "I've been an Aerospace Engineer since before we were married. In the beginning, it was thrilling to go in and create mechanisms for airplanes. Lately it's lost its challenge. I don't look forward to going in anymore. I need something to spark that drive again. I want to use this place to manufacture child size flight vehicles. Not toy models that sit in a display case, but rather planes that small children, and maybe even teenagers, can get in and learn to fly. Kind of like those remote control cars? You remember we bought one for Caleb when he was in preschool? There could be a children's flight school held in one of the airfields for private lessons," he said excited.

She tilted her head to the side and put her hands on her hips, listening to his banter about creating toys. He had destroyed their family, but wanted to create miniplanes.

"I can get the property virtually tax-free because of its location. Plus, I would have no problem getting a loan for the start-up cost. I could connect with some community leaders to buy other pieces of this land for dirt cheap and bring life back to this area. The possibilities are endless."

Celia was infuriated. "You have some nerve."

She stomped back to the car, seriously contemplating him being left behind with his toy project. The only thing to stop her was her desire for answers. She wanted to know why he did what he did to their daughter. How could he taint such a beautiful young lady? What made

him take her virtue and innocence, when fathers are supposed to be the main ones to protect their offspring?

"You don't like the idea?" he followed closely on her
heel, moving past her towards the driver's door.

She shouted across the Jaguar's top, "Have you lost
your mind? You damaged our daughter and screwed up
our family. Our lives together are gone. And you want
to plan a future of toy planes? That's nuts." She was too
heated to care if he did try to harm her.

He hollered back, "I did not screw up our lives together.
You walked out on me, with our children nonetheless. I
have done nothing but try to fix things between us."

"You sexually molested our daughter. That's called incest and you think you can fix things? You think it's that
easy? Then you bring me out here, to God knows where
and I'm suppose to act like nothing happened. You want
me to be excited over this?" She furiously thrust her
hand towards the warehouse. "This place is supposed to
make me forget you were in our bed screwing our little
girl?"

His face became angrily twisted. "Screwed our little
girl? What are you talking about? No, I did not. How
could you even insinuate something like that? Where did
you get that idea from, Celia? Kaleia was in our bed because she had been crying about a boy harassing her at
school. She told him she wasn't old enough to date, but
he didn't like her answer. I was planning to go up to the
school on that Monday to handle things. How could you
think I would ever . . ." he didn't finish the sentence.

"You both were naked."

"Like hell. No, we were not. I had on boxer shorts.
Kaleia wore underwear. You must have been hallucinat-
ing. What kind of mushrooms did they have you eating
down there in Florida, that would have you imagining
things?"

"Kaleia was naked. She was in our bed, as naked as a jaybird. I know what I saw. I know what I heard. You are not going to make me think I'm crazy."

"Obviously, I don't have to make you anything. You're doing a good job of it by yourself. Delusional! You know, I thought you were mad because I was babying Kaleia in the middle of the night and I let her sleep in our bed, but now I see you are a different kind of mad."

Celia got in the car and slammed the passenger door shut.

Khalil jumped in and slammed his door. He jammed the keys into the ignition, before tightly grasping the steering wheel with both hands.

"Look. Honey, I think this is a simple misunderstanding. Screaming at each other won't solve anything. I want my family home. All of us back together. I'm willing to do whatever is necessary to make that happen," he calmly told her.

Celia sat in the car fuming as she purposely replayed that night over again in her head. Confirmation of her own sanity.

"God would want us to work this out," he said, stroking the side of her face with the back of his hand.

She didn't comment. She didn't move as she concentrated on the crates placed against the warehouse. There was no point in debating biblical principles and holy doctrine with a lunatic.

He put his key in the ignition and drove away from the building without saying another word. The silence was louder than any discourse they could have exchanged.

Khalil whizzed through highway traffic as night began to fall. Other cars became blurs as his speed steadily increased. He drove as if he no longer cared about being pulled over by state police. Celia held on to her seat belt strap as her body jolted every time he changed lanes.

They seemed to get back to Caleb's school in half the time it took to leave it earlier.

Khalil quickly pulled up in front of the school and stopped next to his white Durango. He turned and cupped Celia's face in his hands as he forced his tongue past her tighten lips. He rolled his tongue with hers trying to evoke passion. It only revolted Celia more. He leaned back and held her chin. "I love you, baby. No woman could ever take your place."

"Of course not, you're into little girls," she whispered.

He took her hand and placed it on the bulge of his lap. "You feel that," he moaned. "See how you make me feel. I can't control how much I miss you."

She jerked at her hand, but he locked it underneath his strong fingers.

"I'll give you more time to think things through; let you come to your senses. Don't take my patience for granted. I know where you are staying at. If you refuse to come home, then sooner or later I'm going to knock on Alicia's door and get my kids. Let's not make this ugly." He rubbed her hand up and down his harden bulge.

Her skin crawled with disgust as he released her hand and kissed her cheek lightly.

"I'll be talking to you," he smiled as he opened the door.

Celia remained glued to her passenger seat staring at nothingness until he drove away.

# CHAPTER
# TEN

"I need a gun!" Celia exclaimed, walking in the side door of Alicia's from the garage.

Alicia dropped the porcelain platter she was holding to the floor. It shattered into tiny pieces on impact. "You need a what?" she asked as she spun around from the dishwasher.

"A gun. Khalil followed me to Caleb's school from here." She ran into the living room peeking out the vertical blinds of the picture window at the empty street.

Alicia guardedly watched Celia from the kitchen entryway as she held the broom.

"I'm checking to see if he's out there, still watching the house," Celia answered her sister's question before she could ask.

"I'm not giving you a gun," Alicia informed her.

"Alicia, you said that you have friends that can make him disappear. I don't want him to disappear literally, but I do need to protect my kids from him."

"Girl, I was drunk when I said that. You know not to listen to me when I'm inebriated." Alicia bent down with the dustpan, sweeping up the mess from the kitchen floor.

"As I said before, I don't want to hurt Khalil. He drove me into the middle of nowhere to talk. I can't tell if he was trying to manipulate me or if he is in denial about what he did, but something ain't quite right in his brain. He is not the man I married and I can't be sure what he is capable of doing. I'm not risking my children's well being. You should have seen him. He tried to convince me that I made up what I saw that night I got in town. That I was seeing things that don't exist. No, no, no, he won't be coming up in here and taking my babies," her voice escalated.

"Celia, you need to calm down before the kids hear you talking like that," Alicia murmured.

Celia had forgotten that they weren't alone. "Where are they at?"

"Caleb is in the basement's recreation room, probably playing football on the Xbox. Taija and Kaleia are locked away in Taija's room. Don't you hear the music?"

Celia hadn't noticed, but could clearly hear bass bouncing off the thin walls once she paid attention.

"You are right. They've seen and heard enough already," Celia agreed.

"Exactly."

"I still need that gun."

"I can make a couple calls, but I'm telling you I don't agree with the idea of a gun in my house."

"Would you prefer to confront Khalil without one?"

"I would prefer not having to confront Khalil at all. We both know there is no love loss between us."

Celia was determined. "I have to protect my kids."

"Okay," Alicia hesitantly agreed. She removed the phone from the console attached to the kitchen wall. She shook her head as she waited for the person she was calling to pick up. "Hey Ruben, how's it going? Uh, huh. I'm doing okay." She twirled on the stool and propped her elbows on the island. "Remember when you told me that you would do anything for me and that all I had to do was say the word?"

Celia walked over to the other side of the island so she could hear the conversation.

Alicia continued. "Yeah. I believe you. Ruben, look I have to cut the small talk. I need a favor." She lowered her voice and whispered in the phone, "I need a piece."

Celia's forehead began to bead up with sweaty tension.

Alicia rolled her eyes exasperated, "Not that kind of piece. I don't need a booty call. This is serious business I'm talking about. I need a real piece."

As she listened to his response, Alicia settled her chin in her propped up hand. "I hear all that, but can you help me or not? I'm not going over details by phone. We have to meet in person. Yeah . . . um, tonight in two hours will be fine. Give me your address." She covered the mouth piece and asked Celia, "Can you hand me that pen and notebook pad on the counter behind you?"

Celia looked to her side and grabbed the metallic blue ballpoint pen and a yellow pad. She placed it in front of Alicia. Alicia quickly wrote down his information and hung up.

"We can't leave the kids here by themselves. I don't trust Khalil not to show up while we are gone," Celia said.

"You don't have to go. I can pick it up for you."

"No, this is my drama. I need to be with you. Do you think Aunt Lee May would watch the kids?"

"Yeah she would watch them, but with her mighty mouth I don't know if that is a good idea. That would look suspicious. We never leave our children with her.

Plus Dad would be ticked if you took them to his sister's house instead of him and mom's. We might as well take the kids to them. They would love to have Taija, Kaleia and Caleb over."

"Well, I can't lie to our parents, so you are going to have to take them in."

"Fine. I'll come up with a story, but I don't see the difference between you lying and me lying for you."

"None," Celia admitted.

"Let's get the kids and make that move," Alicia said, getting up from the stool.

Celia touched Alicia's shoulder, "I don't want to take the kids to our parents. I can't face them yet with the news about Khalil." Celia had spoken to her mom and dad at least five times since taking refuge at Alicia's house, but each time they asked about Khalil or why she left home, she found an excuse to end the conversation.

"Eventually you are going to have to talk to them about this. They shouldn't be in the dark."

"It was hard enough telling you, let me decide when I'm ready to bring Momma and Daddy in."

"Well, what do you want to do with the kids?"

"Can your friend come to us? I mean, do you think that would be an inconvenience for him to bring the . . . um . . . gun here?"

"I guess he can bring it here. You want me to call him back?"

"If you could."

Alicia sighed. "Girl, I'm used to creating my own drama. I don't know if I can handle all the extra."

"I'm not trying to make life difficult"

"I know you're not. I can see how hard this is for you. Baby Sis, I got your back." She hit redial on the phone.

Celia zoned out while Alicia was conversing. She knew a gun was extreme, but didn't extreme situations call for extreme solutions? She hated guns passionately though. Didn't want to see one let alone have to use it. She had to do what she had to do. It wasn't like she'd actually have to shoot him. Just seeing the gun would probably be warning enough for Khalil, if it even came to that.

She left Alicia in the kitchen and went to knock on Taija's door. When she didn't get a response over the loud music she cracked the door open and poked her head in.

"Hey ladies," Celia said.

Kaleia and Taija were both sitting on the furry white area rug ripping pictures out of magazines and placing them on the floor. Swatches of flowered fabric, a glue gun and a white poster board covered most of the space next to them.

"Hi, mom," Kaleia said.

"What's up, Auntie," Taija followed.

"That's a lot of pictures. What are you doing with them?" Celia asked.

"We are attaching them to this piece and making a wall collage. I want to place it above my computer desk," Taija said, gesturing to the poster board as she trimmed the edges of her picture with shears.

"Sounds interesting," Celia picked up one of the pictures out of Taija's lap.

"That is Omarion, my future husband. Well, as soon as I meet him. He can sing, dance and he's fine. Talk about a package deal. It doesn't get any better than him. Ah Auntie, he is da bomb. I'm in love. Fo' real!" Taija went on and on.

Kaleia admitted, "He is kinda cute."

"Pssst. Kinda! No, he is fine. Can't nobody touch my man in the looks department," Taija corrected her cousin.

Celia listened to Taija ramble on about her fantasy relationship. Last week she was in love with somebody else that was famous. Luckily, that was the extent of her interest in boys. Taija hadn't mentioning liking anybody that was more attainable. Teenagers grow up so fast; it was refreshing to see that neither girl was crumbling under peer pressure yet.

At least that was Celia's impression, before she knew what Kaleia had experienced. She wondered if Kaleia had spoken with Taija about the incident or if there was more to the story and she just didn't know it yet. Celia would prefer for Kaleia to confide in her, but she was realistic about that not being the case. It was much more likely that Taija would hear the sordid details if Kaleia was telling anybody.

Taija lifted the board and started explaining some of the photos already glued to the center, "See this is Ne-Yo, Lloyd, Bow Wow and my brother-in-law, O'Ryan."

"How is that your brother-in-law?" Celia asked.

"He is Omarion's younger brother. See the family resemblance to my husband? Work with me Auntie."

Celia put her hand over her heart to feign sympathy, "Oh, well excuse me. I digress."

Alicia walked in and grabbed Celia's arm and began dragging her from the room. "I hope I'm not interrupting, but we got something we need to take care of. Ya'll keep doing what you doing," Alicia told the girls.

Celia said to the girls as she was pulled, "We'll talk later."

When the two women got to the living room Alicia whispered, "He's on his way. I don't know what kind of weapon he is bringing, I just told him to give me something that is easy to handle. Now are you sure that you want to follow through on this? Guns are not toys. They kill."

"Alicia, I am not Caleb's age. I am as sure as sure gets.

We need protection around here and that gun is definitely going to give us that."

"Alright, Baby Sis. If you are sure, then I am surely
with you. It's just awkward. This will be the first time
I've invited Ruben to my home and I wish it was under
different circumstances."

"So what kind of friend is this Ruben? Friend with
benefits?" Celia asked her sister as they both sat on the
sectional and waited for his arrival.

Alicia almost looked like she was blushing, but said
non-chalantly, "He is a co-worker. An officer of the law.
We've been working together for three and a half years
now. He thinks he's in love with me."

"Is the feeling mutual?"

"Girl, naw. He's Puerto Rican."

"So?"

"I ain't ready to go international. I want to stay close to
my roots. I'd rather wait for a strong black man."

"Unh, huh," Celia smirked.

"I know I don't always have the best things to say
about our black men, but that doesn't mean I have cut
them off. When I decide to step outside, you will be the
first to know. Ruben is good peoples, but he's the wrong
shade of brown. Give me a Hershey cocoa brotha, hold
the whipped cream," explained Alicia with assurance.

Celia smiled. "Yeah okay."

"Hey, don't act like you don't know my taste. I've been
loving chocolate since we were in high school."

"I remember." Celia reminisced back when they were
young. "You know what . . . You would have loved the
chocolate brotha I met in the airport while I was down in
Florida."

"You met a man? Shut up! Baby Sis, you've been holding out." Alicia furrowed her eyebrows and placed her
hands on her hips.

"It's not like that. Some real estate developer named Maliq Nwosu. He was Jamaican or Haitian or heck I couldn't tell you. I'm sure he had an accent like he was from the islands. Anyway, he invited himself to a seat at my table while I was eating and started hitting on me. I've never meet anyone so bold in their approach."

"Maybe you should have hit back."

Celia gasped, "I would never cheat," and bit her bottom lip at the meaninglessness of her statement, "on Khalil."

Alicia read Celia's face. "I bet you wish you had taken that brotha up on his offer now that you know."

Celia rubbed her ring finger before sadly saying, "No I don't regret not talking to him. When I married Khalil I made an oath. I take my vows literally. For better or worse, that doesn't change my responsibility or my loyalty to the sanctum of marriage. It wouldn't have been right. Even knowing what I know, I still can't justify that. Not in my eyes. Not in God's eyes. I don't want a foul pass. Not ever."

"I guess I can understand that. We are so different, Baby Sis. I'd need some retribution. I still can't believe Khalil. My own brother-in-law is a pedophile."

The ringing of the doorbell interrupted their conversation. Alicia and Celia stood and looked at each other as nervousness filled the room.

Alicia said, stuffing her hands in her pants pockets, "You sit back down. I'll go get the door."

Celia nodded her head in agreement and plopped on the sectional sofa as anticipation entangled itself with fear. She convinced herself that this was the best solution. A gun had to be the answer. She didn't want to kill Khalil. She wanted to protect her kids like a lioness defending her cubs.

A tall muscular man the color of warm butterscotch strolled into the living room behind Alicia. His solid frame strained against the fabric of his long sleeved shirt as he loosely swung a black briefcase. He didn't look like any police officer Celia had seen. He seemed more like a linebacker for a professional football team.

"Ruben, I would like to introduce you to my twin sister. Celia, Ruben. Ruben, Celia." Alicia pointed to each of them.

Celia felt like a midget standing next to him. She extended her hand, "Nice to meet you, Ruben. Thanks for coming on short notice."

"Anything for Alicia." He gazed at her sister intently.

Alicia didn't acknowledge his comment. "I don't want to do this out here. Let's take this into my bedroom." Alicia led the way into her room with Ruben and Celia padding in close proximity. She stopped at the hall closet to hang up Ruben's Burberry coat. She turned the dial on her mood lighting as they entered.

"So this is what your bedroom looks like? Very frilly and feminine," Ruben said observing the canopy bed and mauve décor.

"I enjoy it, but don't you get too used to being in my private space." Alicia eyeballed him suspiciously.

"It's not like that. You know me better than that. I would never invade space I wasn't invited into," he said sincerely.

"Yeah, whatever," Alicia chuckled, fluffing the cream lace covered pillows on her bed.

"Where would you like me to place the briefcase?" he asked her.

"Right on top of the bed is fine," Alicia replied. "Did you bring a selection of arms for us to choose from?"

"First I need to know why you need this." Ruben braced his fingers on top of the briefcase.

Celia glanced at Alicia, "Um . . ."

Alicia glanced back before directing her attention on Ruben. "We need to protect this house and the people in it. There have been some recent events that call our safety into question," Alicia answered for her sister.

"Has somebody threatened you?" Ruben asked both Alicia and Celia with concern.

"Yes, in not so many words."

"I need you to be a little more specific if you want me to hand over a weapon." Ruben waited patiently.

"My sister's husband has been getting his freak on with their daughter. After Celia found out and left him, he threatened to come take the kids from her if she didn't come home," Alicia blurted out.

Celia just about melted in her skin from humiliation. She couldn't believe how quickly those words flowed from Alicia's mouth into the ears of a stranger.

Celia spoke almost scolding, "Alicia."

"Well, that's what happened," Alicia exasperated.

"Yeah, but did you have to throw it out there like that."

"I don't see a reason to beat around the bush."

Celia began nervously playing in her ponytail as she watched Ruben rotate numbers on the combination of the briefcase. His fingers worked steadily before the lock clicked open and the lid rose into the air.

Ruben pulled the revolver out explaining, ".357 magnum. Standard issue. It is great for self defense."

Celia stammered, "Is it legal?" Adrenalin rushed through her system like she had just taken a sixteen-mile run. She knew that all cops weren't law abiding. She had heard stories about some officers that keep evidence such as unmarked guns, money and drugs for themselves instead of reporting it.

He looked questioningly at Alicia before explaining to Celia, "I am definitely not dirty. This is from my private collection."

"I didn't mean to offend you," Celia said apologetically. She wanted to put her foot in her mouth for questioning his character. She should have known better than to think her sister would have shady friends assisting them, cops or not.

He pulled the clip out of the gun and examined it. "You have twenty-four rounds, although I doubt you will have to use that many to stop him. Now have you thought of other options instead of using a firearm to protect yourselves? You might want to consider pressing charges against your husband."

"I can't send him to jail," Celia quickly said, thinking about Kaleia's response to that very thing back at the hotel.

"You don't want to send him to jail, but you don't mind shooting him?" Ruben asked.

"I've already asked her the same kind of questions," Alicia piped in.

"I will repeat . . . . I have no intention on shooting him. This is just a precaution in case there is a confrontation. I will feel better if we had a weapon for safeguard in the house. It will be no different than anyone else that has a gun in their house for protection. I don't know the first thing about buying a weapon, which is why I asked for help. Now if you don't want to help me, then that is fine. I understand your apprehension, but I'm not changing my mind," she said defensively.

"Let me show you how to use a Magnum." Ruben gave her instructions on proper gun use.

Celia paid close attention to how he held the gun, the method for replacing a clip, taking the safety off and aiming. She practiced several times as Ruben stood next to her watching.

"Mom, Caleb's getting on our nerves," Taija hollered as she tried to come into the bedroom.

Alicia was nearest to the door and banged it closed with her behind before Taija could get it open good. She hadn't thought of locking the door.

"Hey," Taija said, offended from outside the room.

"Work it out," Alicia shouted through the door, leaning her weight on the frame.

"But he won't get out of my room."

"Work it out," Alicia repeated louder still.

"Now if you're missing a nephew when you come out, Kaleia and I aren't responsible because you told us to work it out." They could hear Taija stomp off mumbling.

"See that's why I only have one child," Alicia scowled as she put up her index finger.

"I think we are done here. Celia, if you need some more instruction I can meet you and Alicia at the firing range for more practice." Ruben set the gun back inside the case and shut it closed.

"That won't be necessary," Celia said, confidently taking the briefcase from him. She had the basics down and that should be enough.

"Alicia, call me if you need anything else." He walked towards her as she opened the bedroom door.

"Will do," she said, escorting him out the room.

Celia sighed as she fell onto the bed. The weight of a weapon in the house anchored her body to the bed. She thought that she would feel lighter having protection, but sadness still consumed her.

*It shouldn't be this way*, she thought as she knelt on the floor and shoved the briefcase under the bed.

While she was still on her knees she prayed "Lord, I know that I don't always listen when you speak, but let me do your will and not my own. If this is not what you want, if you have a better solution for the protection of this house, let me know."

She stood grateful for the relationship she had with God, but the heaviness remained.

# CHAPTER
# ELEVEN

The praise dancers formed a circle in the front of the sanctuary. Seven ladies in white angel-sleeve dresses and matching slippers stood linking arms together. Their heads were bowed as music began to fill the church. Parishioners sat in silence watching as lyrics emerged from the hidden speakers.

"Imagine me, being free, trusting you totally."

Celia recognized the song from a recent Kirk Franklin album and began to smile. It was a favorite of hers. She loved all the music that Kirk Franklin had made though. She scooted back in her seat and strained her neck to see past the heads of people in the pews in front of her. The Praise Team spiritually hypnotized the congregation as they slowly released each other's arms and swayed in sync across the sanctuary. Celia temporarily closed her eyes absorbing the emotions that were taking over.

"Imagine me, being free, trusting you totally."

Her heart began to swell from their prophetic expression. Their dresses swung freely in the air as the dancers flowed back and forth across the floor. They put their all into the lyrical movement as they exalted God. Celia cleared her mind of every negative thought and just listened. She felt like God was wrapping his arms around her and hugging her tight. Telling her that everything was going to work itself out as long as she believed in His power. She asked for His mercy. Her head swayed to the music as her eyes followed the dancers. She wanted to absorb the intensity displayed. As she cleared her mind, all the worries washed away. Tension left her body as she exhaled. Celia gladly inhaled the calm, but overpowering presence of God.

*Imagine me, being free, trusting you totally.*

She sang to herself the lyrics of the chorus being played. She sang as tears clouded her vision. Celia held on to the feeling like it was a life jacket out of a sea filled with quicksand. The spirit consoled her with unexplainable grace. Several of the dancers also had tears in their eyes as they twirled with hands raised up high. Celia lifted her hands to honor God as well. For the first time in weeks she felt like her load of grief and shame lifted. Like she was protected from her circumstances.

*Imagine me, being free, trusting you totally.*

An usher came down the aisle with a Kleenex box in hand. Celia waved her hand for a tissue. Her chin was dripping with salty tears and her nose had began to run. She pulled several tissues from the box as it was passed down the pew.

"Thank you, Lord for your mercy. I know you are with me. I can feel you all over this place. Stay with me Lord. Guide me in my storm, because I can't see right without you. Only you can bring me through," she whispered, wiping her nose.

The praise dancers moved back into a circle, uniting hands on bended knees as the chorus of music faded.

\* \* \*

Celia saw the reflection of her face as she looked into the rearview mirror at the girls chatting away. She had serenity and peace of mind. Things were finally starting to improve. Church had revived her energy. Her children were safe and sound in the car with her. Kaleia was laughing like her old self. Celia was glad that Taija attended Teen Ministries with Kaleia.

"Caleb get your seatbelt on," Celia said, looking out the corner of her eyes at Caleb in the passenger seat.

"Oh, I forgot" he said, clicking the belt into its chamber. "Mom, can I ride on the bus this summer when we go down to Atlanta for Megafest?"

"You want to ride a bus?" Celia asked surprised.

"Yeah. The church is getting those cool buses with the televisions in them and the kids get to have a bus all to ourselves."

"Hum. I don't know, Caleb. That is a long ride from here to Atlanta. Almost a seventeen-hour drive. You sure you gonna be able to hang and behave with minimal supervision?"

"I can hang. I'm a big boy, Mom. You don't have to worry about me. Minister Scott was telling us about all kinds of fun stuff they have planned for us during the trip. He told us it was a surprise and that we would just have to be on the bus to find out. He also said that if we raise enough money, then we can also go to Six Flags while we are down there."

"Sounds exciting."

"So can I go? Please can I go?" Caleb begged.

"Let me think about it. It sounds like a good idea, but I have to find out who is chaperoning."

Celia slowed down as the traffic light turned red. She glanced in her rear view mirror again as she noticed a white Durango on her bumper. Her heart jerked in her chest as she peered into the window of the vehicle behind her. The joy she just had seemed to be exiting her body as she blew air through clinched teeth. Her day had been going good. Why did he have to pop up and ruin her peace of mind?

She drove towards the Dearborn Heights area hoping that eventually he would turn off and go in a different direction. Celia turned right past a corner convenience store. He turned right, following close behind. She pulled into a gas station and used an automated pay machine to have the car washed. Khalil did the same.

"Mom, can we stop and get some food to eat? I'm starving." Caleb rubbed his stomach.

"Didn't you eat this morning before we left?" she asked Caleb as she kept her head forward but stayed focused on her husband's vehicle. She tried not to look obvious and have the kids realize their father was behind them.

"Yes. I had a bowl of frosted flakes, but that was before Sunday school." He raised his hand and began counting fingers. "That was almost five hours ago."

Celia's stomach was in knots, but she couldn't blame the kids for her loss of appetite.

"We will have to get something that everybody can agree upon," she said.

"Pizza Hut," Caleb said before Kaleia and Taija could respond.

The girls looked at each other shrugging shoulders. "Pizza works for us," Kaleia answered.

Celia silently thanked God, because she could rarely get them to agree on anything. She exited the car wash and turned on the street in the opposite direction of where she had intended on going. Maybe if she got out of sight before his car was clean, he would leave them alone. She drove in a residential area of colonial homes for awhile before heading back to the business district.

She breathed a sigh of relief when she didn't see his Durango. Another confrontation with Khalil wasn't something she was up for, especially not with the kids in the car. Celia was still trying to get them adjusted to his absence from their life.

She saw the red sign for Pizza Hut and pulled into the parking lot.

"Auntie, can we get that one pizza that has the four separate sections? I don't remember the name, but wasn't it on a commercial?" Taija asked.

"I know which one you're talking about. What do you ladies and gentleman want on your section?" she asked the kids as she reached for her purse off the mat on Caleb's side.

"Meat Lovers," Caleb grinned emphatically while rubbing his hands together and licking his lips.

"Auntie, I want mushroom and sausage."

"Veggie Lovers," Kaleia said.

"When did you become a vegetarian? You ate chicken last night." Taija scrunched her nose up and asked Kaleia.

"I remember what I ate last night. I'm not a vegetarian. I just like the Veggie Lover's pizza. It tastes good to me."

"Oh," Taija shrugged.

"Did anybody want to come in with me?" Celia questioned the kids.

"I'll come with you," Caleb answered, opening his door.

Celia looked at both girls but they shook their heads no. "I'll leave the car running so you don't get cold, but keep the doors locked."

"Unh, huh," Kaleia replied before she and Taija resumed their conversation about the upcoming Teen's Dance-Off Contest at Taija's school.

"Lock the doors," Celia repeated before getting out of the car.

Kaleia reached over the driver's seat and pushed the button as Celia walked into Pizza Hut. The aroma of Italian spices filled the air, but Celia felt immune to the smell. Her appetite had jumped ship the minute she saw Khalil and it didn't feel like it was coming back any time soon.

Caleb had already placed the order before Celia made it to the counter. He stood waiting with his hand extended for cash.

"Did you get what everybody wanted?" She pulled a twenty-dollar bill from her wallet and handed it to him.

"Yes, Mom. I got you the Supreme with extra black olives." He told her as he gave the cashier the money.

The pizza was done quicker than she thought. She could feel heat coming out of the bottom as the cashier handed her the box. She sat it on the counter and opened the box to make sure everything looked the way it was supposed to. The steamy aroma rose up into the air. She sniffed the air but she still couldn't force her appetite to come back.

Caleb looked into the box from the side of her and licked his lips again. "I can't wait to eat. My stomach is growling. Can I get a piece now?"

"Um, no. You know better than that. You are not eating in my car," She said without hesitation as she envisioned greasy stains on her leather interior.

Caleb used his back to hold the door open while Celia picked up the box. Her heart jerked again when she saw who was standing by the car. Khalil leaned against the back door with one hand resting on the hood as he talked through the open window. She could see Kaleia and Taija's mouths moving as they smiled at him.

"Daddy," Caleb hollered as he ran and hugged his father. Khalil almost lost his balance from the force as he put the hand that was on the car around Caleb.

Khalil laughed, "Hey Caleb. I missed you too."

"It's so good to see you Daddy." Caleb wouldn't let go as he held Khalil in a vice grip around his waist. His head pressed firmly against his father's chest.

"What's up with the cornrows?" Khalil said disapprovingly as he touched the top of Caleb's head.

"Taija did them. She said she was making me a 'G' like Omarion. Ain't they tight? She hooked me up." Caleb stepped back and primped.

"Khalil, can I talk to you," Celia asked as her nostrils flared. "Caleb, please take the pizza inside the car before it gets cold."

"Okay." He hesitated as he got the box and walked to the passenger side of the jaguar.

"Daddy, are you going to Megafest with us? Mom said I could ride the kid's bus if it's chaperoned. You can chaperone like you did when we went up to Canada last year," Caleb said before getting into the car.

"I would love to, son." Khalil smiled at Caleb.

Celia tapped her foot on the pavement. Her hands were on her hips as she resisted the urge to slap Khalil. "What are you doing? Don't make promises you can't keep," she hissed.

"What do you mean?" he innocently asked as he looked into the car. All the kids were staring into their mouths as they spoke.

"Let's go inside." She turned and headed back into Pizza Hut without waiting for his response. It took every ounce of energy she had not to go off on him.

There were quite a few people dining in the restaurant area. Celia looked for an empty booth away from other patrons. She didn't want anybody listening in on her personal business. Khalil walked in right as she noticed a booth in the far corner of the restaurant. They went and sat down across from each other.

"I just wanted to talk to my kids. I saw you during service at church and wanted to approach you, but I didn't know how you would react." He unzipped his jacket as he sat down.

"So you're stalking me now?" She clasped her hands together resting them on the edge of the table.

He furrowed his eyebrows and shook his head before calmly stating, "I am not stalking you. Greatness in Faith is still my church too."

"Whatever." She was pissed that he took her joy away. "We were fine without seeing you at church or otherwise. Greatness in Faith does have two morning services. You should have gone to service during the 8:00 a.m. early celebration if church means that much to you. And furthermore, you do not have my permission to see those kids."

"Permission? I don't need your permission to be around our children. My keeping the distance is a courtesy to you. I will always be their father." He looked agitated as he used his thumb to gesture outside.

A waitress came over with a notepad and pen in hand. "Can I get your order?"

"No thank you. I already ordered take-out. We are just sitting here talking." Celia didn't bother to look up at the waitress with pleasantries.

"Sorry I bothered you." She walked off.

"I think we need to get some things straightened out," Khalil said.

"Whatever," she stated grinding her teeth, nostrils still flared. If she had real fire in her, he would be burnt to a crisp.

"I also want to apologize for the way I acted the last time we saw each other. It was inappropriate for me to touch you like that. I wanted you to understand how I feel about you, but I don't think it came out the right way. I love you, and well . . . it was wrong. My grabbing your hand, all of it was inappropriate. I apologize for making you uncomfortable." He solemnly looked at her as he put his hands atop her clenched ones.

"Don't touch me," she snapped.

Khalil released her hands and flattened his palms on the table.

"Oh, and you're apologizing for being inappropriate? Well, while you were outside did you apologize to Kaleia? Now that was somebody that you were for real inappropriate with. Huh . . . did you apologize to Kaleia? Huh . . . huh. That's all I want to know." She spat angry words at him.

"I don't have anything to apologize to Kaleia for. I know that. Kaleia knows that. You're the only one that hasn't figured it out yet."

Khalil's jaw set and his eyes narrowed. "In all the years we've been married, I've never given you one reason to distrust me. Not one. If I said I was going out, you knew where to find me. If I said I was doing something, you knew what it was. And now you want to play the *Diary of a Mad Black Woman* role over some garbage you think you saw." He leaned against the table. "I should get the benefit of a doubt from past experience alone." His tone was even, but his agitation still showed as the muscles in his jaw flexed after he clamped his mouth shut.

Celia leaned against her side of the table. "Say I did have it all wrong. My eyes lied and I entertain your version. It still wouldn't be okay for *our* teenaged daughter to be in *our* bed in her underwear." She leaned back and crossed her arms. "So I still don't trust or believe a word coming out of your mouth."

He looked at the napkin holder as he frowned, then he

stood up. "This conversation is going nowhere. I'm leaving."

"That's what I thought. Denial is a trip ain't it, Khalil?"

"One day you will see the truth, and when you do, you know where to come and apologize," he said as he walked towards the door.

She doubted there was any chance of that happening.

He turned around and came back to the table with a solemn but stern look on his face. "Celia, I am not a soft or weak man. When I get tired of playing by your rules, remember you did this to yourself." He walked out.

She got up and walked out afraid he might say something else to the kids before he left. He waved goodbye to them before getting into his Durango.

"Didn't I tell you to keep the doors locked," Celia snapped at the girls. She saw fear in their eyes.

Taija spoke up, "The doors were locked. I was the one that rolled down the window. I mean it was Uncle Khalil. I didn't realize . . ."

"I don't care if God himself knocks on the window. If I tell you to do something then you need to follow orders," Celia said as she sped out the parking lot.

# CHAPTER
# TWELVE

Celia wasn't able to secure an initial consultation to see the psychiatrist until more than two weeks after Kaleia's physical with Dr. Williams. Celia crossed her legs as she sat in the dark leather wing back chair. Dr. Malawi was directly across from her perched on the arm of the other matching chair. Celia was focused on moving forward without all the negative banter that had been playing in her head. Whenever she felt a bad thought form in her mind about Khalil she would start to pray. She didn't care where she was at, if the thoughts came, she prayed until they went away.

The other day Celia was in the produce aisle squeezing peaches to check for ripeness when the image of Khalil squeezing parts of their daughter he had no business touching popped into her head. She immediately dropped the fruit and began pacing and praying loudly, "No weapon formed against me shall prosper. I am more than a conqueror. Lord, I am going to thank you in advance for the powerful move you're about to make in my life. I praise you on sunny days and I praise you through a storm. I praise you despite my circumstances. I give you glory in my situation. Victory is mine!"

She didn't realize that her voice had drawn attention until she opened her eyes and noticed a small crowd of four people watching her. She got mixed responses from those standing nearby, but expected that in public places. One lady had said amen when Celia finished, while an elderly man turned his nose up at her and grumbled that prayer wasn't meant for the grocery store and the young couple simply walked off without comment. She had learned years ago that opinions varied just like the selections of fruits and vegetables displayed that she was trying to pick from. They may be physically in the same location, but from closer observation they were still very different. Anyway, her prayer was between her and God. If someone else got blessed in the process, then more better for them. If they didn't, so be it.

Celia stared at the tape recorder as Dr. Malawi began to speak, "You're probably wondering why I asked you here without your daughter."

"The thought had crossed my mind," Celia said as she relaxed her hands from around her purse.

"How are you doing in all this?" Dr. Malawi asked as she stood and walked over to her desk with the tape recorder in hand.

"Fine. I personally don't need counseling if that is what you are getting at." As far as Celia was concerned, she had learned to manage to the best of her ability.

"Actually, I wasn't bringing you in for psychological therapy. Instead, I want to discuss my goals and your expectations of my meeting with Kaleia. Ultimately, we both have to be in some kind of agreement that will benefit her. Child molestation is a serious issue. It is a prevalent problem. One in four children are victims of sexual abuse. Girls are three times more likely than boys to be victims of molestation. I would dare to say it is a hidden epidemic, especially in African-American families. Many children fall victim and never receive help because people don't want to admit that it happens."

Celia simply nodded her head. She could completely understand how someone would deny the existence of child molestation. If she hadn't seen it with her own eyes, she didn't know if she would believe it herself. Denial and ignorance can be stronger medicine than most drugs a pharmacist prescribes.

"I must commend you on coming forward and seeking help for your child. I realize that it was not an easy decision for you to come here. No parent wants to be put in this situation where they have to see me. Now, I have the referral from Dr. Williams, but the information is vague. I have one question for you that will help in the process." She paused as she pursed her lips, appearing to be deep in contemplation. "Do you know who molested your daughter or would you be more comfortable with me addressing the subject with Kaleia?"

Celia listened to the waterfall from the wall behind her. She expected to be asked that question, but still found herself tongue-tied in response. The sound of flowing water soothed her as she calmly replied, "Her father."

She expected surprise or shock from Dr. Malawi, but the woman didn't even blink an eye as she confirmed, "An incestuous relationship."

"You're not surprised? A father sexually touching his own child is incomprehensible to me." Celia raised her eyebrows at the psychiatrist's indifference.

"Unfortunately, it's not uncommon. I have had numerous cases with similar circumstances. Uncles, cousins, family friends, stepfathers and biological fathers are often unsuspected perpetrators. It's a matter of trust for many perpetrators. They pick a child that they don't think will tell, because there can be other emotional, social or physical issues within the family which makes a child an easy prey. They chose a family member or friend of the family's child, because they have already built up a level of respect and then they use different methods to pursue their victim. In Kaleia's case, who better to trust than her own father?"

Celia shifted her weight in the chair as she uncrossed her legs and then crossed them back again. She wanted to ask the right questions but didn't know where to begin. "Dr. Malawi, it seems that even though she trusted her father, she should have been able to trust me more. I can't bring myself to accept that something this big was going on underneath my nose, in my own home, and I didn't know. My daughter didn't display any unusual behaviors, and more importantly, she didn't tell me that her father was even looking at her inappropriately. She didn't tell me anything, even after I saw them. I mean, I'm her mother. I'm not a frigid parent. I don't fear talking about sex with my child. We've had the talks. You can't tell me that she didn't know allowing her father to touch her was wrong. It is sick." Celia felt slightly insulted by Kaleia's behavior.

"Yes. There is a serious degree of sickness involved with child molestation. Sometimes that sick mentality trickles down to the very ones being abused. They don't feel there is a benefit to speaking out. Kaleia could have thought it was her fault, a form of punishment for wrongdoing or she could have believed that was her father's expression of love towards her. Most kids are too ashamed or embarrassed to admit they have been violated; they may rationalize the assaults or dismiss the incidents as a coping mechanism. I really won't be able to know until after I've meet with her. Criminal intent, allegations and forced acts of sexual abuse can be confusing for adults, imagine the impact on the mind of a child. Of course it is still a serious crime, but most children are too busy blaming themselves to see the assault for what it is."

"I don't know." Celia inhaled sharply and tried to absorb the information. "It's a lot to take in. For over three weeks I've mulled over this whole thing in my head. There isn't an hour that goes by that I haven't tried to make sense of it all. Not only has my marriage vanished, but also my daughter and I are no longer close. She and I can barely talk without it being awkward. That's hard to handle. I've lost my husband and daughter all at the same time. I want her to get help so we can move past this. In a way I am disgusted that she still loves and respects her father. I can see it in her eyes when she has looked at him. The admiration is disgusting to me. Do you have any idea of how maddening that is for me? Sometimes I wonder if I even like my own child because of all of this." Celia stopped talking because she could feel her composure waning.

Dr. Malawi looked sympathetically at Celia as they shared unspoken words of understanding. Celia felt awful for venting about the child she had birthed. She didn't want to be persecuted for her anger. The psychiatrist handed several pamphlets to Celia across the desk. Celia read the headings then set them in her lap.

"Does that make me a bad person to say that I don't know if I like my own child?" Celia asked as if she was being judged.

"No it doesn't, but please remember it's not your daughter's fault that she was molested by your husband. I don't believe there is a child alive that wants that kind of trauma. Most people find comfort in initially blaming somebody. Over time you will feel a variety of emotions to cope with this and if you decide to get some therapy for yourself then I am here." Dr. Malawi and Celia stood up and shook hands.

"That won't be necessary, but thank you for offering. I think I will be fine with time."

"It's a matter of the wounds. Sometimes the inner wounds are so deep that regular time won't do. It's not enough."

"I believe God can heal any wound at any time regardless of how deep it is. It's something on the inside that he molds and shapes which allows us to get through."

"I don't doubt spiritual healing. Just remember that God gives us Himself through other sources too. Sometimes he sends us people to help us get through the rough times."

Celia shrugged her shoulders as she pondered that thought. "Maybe. Thank you again for talking with me. It did clear up some questions I had. I will make sure to read the information you gave me when I get home. When do you want to see Kaleia?"

"You can set the appointment up with my secretary. I believe I have a couple morning slots available next week. You have a good day and call the office if you have any questions before Kaleia comes in."

"You have a good day too."

Celia felt confident that Kaleia was in very capable hands. Dr. Malawi had earned her respect during their short conversation. It also gave Celia an opportunity to learn more about child sexual abuse. Hopefully the more knowledge she obtained, the better she would become at understanding what her daughter was going through. What she herself was going through.

# CHAPTER THIRTEEN

Celia pushed through the glass doors, excited to be heading back to her professional world. Even though she had used up all of her vacation time, she was far from rested. She could admit that she wasn't tensed up like she had been when she took the time off. She felt like she fell in the middle of a psychiatric chart that ranged from maniac depressive to euphoric. She wasn't in the best of shape but she definitely wasn't in the worse either.

Celia got on the elevator and pressed the button for the seventh floor. Celia watched the numbers of the floor change with a big smile. The elevator stopped at the third floor and a man got on from the accounting department.

She didn't recognize him, but she spoke anyway, "Good Morning."

"Morning," He glanced at her temporarily.

"Have you been working in accounting long?"

"No." He paused as he looked at her again. "I started

last week. I'm the new Financial Analyst. The guy before me was stealing company funds and got fired. They moved me from logistics."

"That's too bad," she said without thinking.

He frowned as he looked up to see what floor he was on. He scratched his scalp of short chestnut brown hair.

"I mean that's good you were promoted, but it is too bad someone else had to lose their job in the process."

"Unh, huh." The elevator door opened and he walked off.

She opened her mouth to say something, but immediately pressed her lips back together as the door closed shut.

The elevator stopped at Celia's floor shortly thereafter. She stopped at the reception area to pick up her mail.

"Welcome back, Celia." The administrative assistant smiled as she handed her the large pile of mail from the office bin.

"Wow," Celia mouthed as she fingered through her mail. She expected to have plenty to come back to, but one month didn't seem like long enough to accumulate the mountain of paperwork and envelopes she was carrying. "I see I have a lot of catching up to do," she said. Enough to keep her mind occupied.

Celia walked into her office, kicked the door closed with her foot and dropped the stack on her desk. It made a thud sound against the metal top as she sank into the comfortable cushion of her office chair. Celia wanted to relish in the uncomplicated space of her office, but knew the quicker she began to conquer her tasks, the better off she would be. She sat up and opened the center drawer in search for an envelope opener. It was stuck inside her tray behind the paper clips. She tugged it free and wondered if it was normal to be as enthused about getting back to work as she was. It kind of reminded her of her first professional job right out of college and sitting in a cubicle with her nametag on the side of a divider. A feeling of empowerment so intense, it made her giddy.

A newly discovered market of low management maintenance companies was finding interest in setting up accounts for the new iPod alarm system. It would take micro technology to a whole new level for SecureTech. Celia would have to schedule an immediate staff meeting with the sales team to discuss marketing strategies for the product line. Although she was sure her staff was more than competent to handle business without her micromanaging them, she didn't want to be out of the loop on current affairs.

She turned on her computer as she ripped open an envelope. The system seemed to be booting up slower than she remembered. The hardware was supposed to be upgraded while she was in Florida. She would definitely have to talk to Jose in the IT department about getting it taken care of.

"Oh well," she sighed as she waited to log into the system. Technology was technology. Advanced, but still inhuman. It was probably good that computers were a little faulty so people don't become obsolete. At least they had an IT department for such matters.

Celia finished reading through her mail, flicking each item in her desktop mail holder as she scanned documents. When she got to the bottom of the stack she sighed again. After the desk was clear she noticed a box of Godiva Chocolates and a rectangular present wrapped in metallic gold paper propped up against the side of the mail holder. She tapped her fingers on the desk before sliding both boxes towards her. There wasn't a card. She put the wrapped box next to her ear and lightly rattled it.

She couldn't tell what it was. Several staff members were notorious for giving out gifts for all kinds of occasions, from Valentine's Day to Christmas and anything in between. She unwrapped the gift as she wondered what holiday she could have missed besides April Fool's Day. Once in a while she got gag gifts like butt warmers and clock timers in mockery of the mandatory overtime, but it was all in good fun for the most part. She had learned to expect the unusual.

She uncovered a black velvet jewelry case. She ran her hand across the soft box before opening it. Nice. Inside was a tiny key attached to a gold necklace. She pulled the long chain out and curled it around her fingers.

"Definitely not a gag gift," she said to herself as she played with the emblem. At the bottom of the case was a gold card. She pulled it out and read the inscription on the back of the card.

*She who holds the key will forever have my heart. My love for you will surpass this lifetime. Yours Truly, Khalil.*

Celia tossed the card back into the box and slid the necklace inside with it. She pushed both boxes towards her mail bin. She sat back in her chair and sucked her teeth. Why do people assume redemption has a monetary equivalent, as if forgiveness can be purchased? It was enough to irk her. Khalil's peace offering wasn't acceptable. He just didn't get it and she wasn't entertaining his insanity. He could keep his jagged declaration of love and his tainted heart. Neither was of use to her.

"Alright, Khalil I'm not giving you my joy today. No offense, but I won't be keeping your stuff," She spoke like he was in the room to listen. She stood and grabbed both boxes as she dashed down to the lunchroom. She sat the box of chocolate on one of the tables for whomever to have. She didn't care who ate them. She just didn't want them in her office. She went to the trash bin intending to throw away the necklace, but she didn't have the heart to do it. That would be a waste of good jewelry. She walked down the back way to the mailroom as she loosely held the case in hand. She was going to stay in good spirits no matter what.

Celia had to scan her identification card to gain access to the room at the end of the hall. The lighted door module flickered red until it read her name and beeped open. The storage area was crammed with outgoing SecureTech packages. It was good for the corporation that the demand for alarm systems had increased significantly in the last couple of years. Celia could only imagine what the storage room would look like when the new product line gained more popularity. She almost tripped over a stack of packages as her foot caught on the rack's edge while she navigated her way around the cluttered mailroom. She felt her nylon snag and a thin line of frayed fabric creep up her leg. It probably would have been wise for her to use the main entrance instead of taking a shortcut.

The mail room workers looked busy as one crew stuffed alarm systems into boxes while the other crew separated mail into bins against the wall. She went into a cabinet and grabbed one of the smaller empty boxes and a label maker off a shelf. Celia quickly typed the address into the machine and stuck the printed label on the center of the box. She wondered what Khalil's reaction would be when he received the necklace back in the next day's mail. Celia wanted the message to be clear. His gift giving was like writing a bad check, null and void wasted imprint. He can't buy her back and he gets no love. Not after what he did.

"Morning, Mrs. Alexander. Is there anything that I can

help you with?" Jonathan, the shipping clerk asked as he shoved a mail bin across the floor.

"No. I think I got it handled," Celia replied as she tossed the box into the outgoing mail bin and sashayed out the room. She needed to get a new pair of nylons and get back to work. The day was just beginning after all.

# CHAPTER
# FOURTEEN

Celia lay on a patio chair on the two-tiered deck for the first time since spring began and enjoyed the sunrays as they beamed down on her skin. There was nothing like the sound of nature on a calm still day. All she wanted to do was bask in warmth as the elements did their thing.

"When are you going home?"

Celia could almost imagine that she was by herself on a beach of white sands in Montego Bay until her mother burst the mirage of her fantasy. She looked up into charcoal gray eyes and observed the exotic beauty of the woman standing in the sunlight. Her French Creole and Indian genes were obvious as olive skin glistened in the warm weather.

"I'm not," she dryly stated.

"And why is that?" Celia's mom, Patricia, asked as she sat a tray of lemonade on the patio table. Celia rolled her eyes beneath the sunglasses she wore. If she could lock up that subject, toss it into the Detroit River and watch it sink to the bottom, she'd give up her 401k plan and the next ten years worth of salary.

"'Cause I can't. It's complicated. A bad situation."

Her mother persisted, "What bad situation? Celia, Khalil loves you with a passion. He has called almost every day to talk with me about you. He wants you back home, and whatever happened can be fixed. Every marriage has its bumps and bruises. That's what makes the relationship stronger. You still have time to make things right. Do you know that he comes by every weekend to spend time with your father and me? Every single weekend?"

Celia knew her mother was exaggerating, because it had only been a month since she left Khalil. "Remind me not to come over on the weekends unless I call first."

Patricia ignored her. "That is time he should be able to spend with you and the kids. But no, he's here with us making repairs on our house. He patched the leak in the roof and did you see those lovely cherry cabinets and granite countertops in the kitchen?" Her mother asked even though she didn't expect Celia to respond. "He installed all of those. Khalil is a wonderful husband, an incredible provider and he's family oriented. Do you know how many women would like to be in your shoes right now? Woman that would kill to have your husband? I'll tell you how many; thousands of women out there would be clawing at each other to have what you are throwing away. You were blessed to meet and fall in love with a man like him."

"We can't claim everything as a blessing. Just because it came from God doesn't mean it is of God. We give God credit for things He never wanted us to have, but we were too blind to see. Didn't want to see. That supposed blessing may feel good and be all kinds of wrong. He knew before we knew that what we love so much would

bring destruction and pain. Sometimes what appears as
blessings are actually thickly veiled curses." Celia looked
at the horizon speaking to herself, because she knew her
mother wasn't listening.

"You and Khalil have been together way too long to let
a small blip or a bad situation wreck your solid marriage.
What kind of example is that to set for your children?
They need their father in their home raising them, especially Caleb. There's enough little black boys running
around fatherless and undirected without adding my
grandson to the batch. Khalil is a positive role model for
Caleb and he wants to be an active parent."

Celia spoke with a calm even tone as she avoided eye
contact with her mother, "Momma, please. No disrespect, but let me worry about my marriage and my kids.
Khalil is not made of gold and the last time I checked he
couldn't walk on water either. Maybe in your mind he's
the best thing to happen to me, but I have a totally different point of view regarding him."

Disapproval and disappointment laced Patricia's voice.
"Divorce is a sin. Is your bad situation worth going to
hell for? I thought Otis and I raised our children better
than to act like this. Otis Jr. still has his wife and they are
very happily married, even with the stress of his busi-
nesses in Japan and Australia. They are still keeping it together. Granted, Alicia has been wayward for more years
than I care to remember, but you had a level head. You
used to make us the most proud of all our children. I always hoped that Alicia would learn the value of a relationship from the example you were displaying. It looks like
her destructive habits are rubbing off on you instead of
the other way around. Maybe you shouldn't be staying
with your sister. She doesn't give the most responsible
advice. She will lead you straight to hell."

Celia shot up in the chair and turned to her mother. It

was unnerving how her mother hated on Alicia like that. She had too much respect to go off. "Mom! Now, is that necessary? My self-worth is attached to Khalil and that farce of a marriage. Why does it have to be like that? If I do go to hell, it won't be Alicia's fault, and it definitely won't be because I'm not with Khalil."

Once it hit the surface there was no turning back. She got up before she allowed the anger to get the best of her. The sliding glass door shut closed as she went searching for different company to keep within the house. She could hear laughter from down the breezeway. Taija and Kaleia had taken Caleb to get his hair cut, so she knew it wasn't them. Her father and twin sister were in the recreation room playing pool.

"Do you mind if I join you," Celia asked as she picked out a pool stick and cubed the tip.

"What would you do if we said no?" Alicia responded sarcastically as she bent down and closed one eye. She positioned her fingers with the pool stick between the circle of her thumb and index finger. She looked like she was concentrating hard on the balls in front of her.

Celia quietly watched the line form on Alicia's head as she struck the white ball and it knocked a red stripped one into a pocket. There was only the eight ball left. It was almost the end of the game and looked like Alicia was about to win. Her twin had a competitive nature that could match any man walking. Although she looked like a woman, she had quite a few male tendencies. Celia sometimes thought that Alicia was secretly pumping testosterone pills into her system.

Her sports drive went back to high school when she made up a petition for the creation of a female wrestling team after watching Glorious Ladies of Wrestling on television. Celia was competitive in her own right but not obsessed like Alicia. She sucked at most male dominated sports and was just learning a technique good enough to hit anything on the table, let alone knock them into a pocket. Everybody had their talents and she recognized which ones weren't hers.

"Daddy, you're gonna let Alicia run you like that?" Celia joked as she sat on a stool.

He looked up at Celia and smiled, "Baby girl, this is the warm up round. She can't handle me."

He poked Alicia in the side with his pool stick, breaking her concentration. "Ouch . . . quit messing around and take this butt whipping like a man."

He squawked at her, "We'll see how much butt whipping you can do after this round. I was going gentle on you before because I love you. I see the game has gone to your head. I see I'm going to have to bring you down a notch and show you a thing or two."

He was a master pool shark and on his best day could wipe the floor with Alicia in a game. Nothing could get him more pumped up than being challenged to prove his skill.

"Bring it," Alicia said, rolling her neck.

"Keep talking trash you can't back up, Baby Girl."

Their dad had been calling them both "Baby Girl" for as long as they had been alive. He would holler out that name and wait to see who came running first. Celia thought it was because he couldn't tell them apart when they were little and he didn't want to embarrass himself by calling one sister by the other one's name. After a while they were so used to his slackness that they couldn't see him calling them anything else.

When it came down to attention, he loved his girls equally. Their mother was a different story, constantly comparing and critiquing their every move. It was their father that kept them grounded. Alicia and Celia didn't have sibling rivalry because of Otis Sr. He kept them busy and was willing to take the girls and their older brother anywhere he went. Some fathers give more time to their sons but not Otis. If one family member learned to play basketball, then everybody learned to play basketball. The girls soaked their father's attention up. Alicia loved every activity their dad put forth and Celia loved having a father devote himself unselfishly and entirely.

As Celia thought about it, she realized the similarity between her father and Khalil. That was one of the things that drew her to Khalil. His devotion to family reminded her of her father. With men disappearing from households quicker than roaches fleeing at the break of light, Celia thought she had picked a gem amongst a haystack of thorns.

"Your game," Alicia said to Celia, putting her stick back in the chamber.

"I thought I was supposed to play the winner," Celia stated.

"Gurl, please. You don't want none of me. I'll spank you even worse than I spanked daddy."

Celia threw a cue across the table at Alicia.

Alicia ducked and laughed, "I'm just joking. I got to get me a drink."

Otis Sr. sent Alicia a stone-faced glare.

"Non-alcoholic," Alicia explained. Liquor was not allowed in their parents household and everybody knew if Alicia disappeared it was because she left to go get something with the word "proof" on the label.

"Daddy, alright, let's do this," Celia said, bringing her father's attention back to the game as she centered the balls inside the rack.

"That sista of yours is something else," he grumbled, shaking his head.

"I know Daddy. Believe me, I know."

"You want to break or do you want me to do it?" Celia

usually let somebody else break the balls because her aim was off, or rather too weak to move the balls any significant distance.

"I'll do it. I have to get some skill at this sooner or later. Can't keep passing the buck."

She angled her fingers several different ways before finding a comfortable level to hit the ball. She squinted her eyes as she leaned over the table and slowly pulled her arm back. She tried to keep the stick steady as her grip tightened at the back end. Playing pool was an art form and she was determined to perfect the craft. She channeled all her energy into her pool stick and struck the ball like she had a vendetta. The solid and striped balls scattered across the table with three solids and two stripes falling into pockets.

"Finally," Celia said with relief. "Now that's what I'm talking about."

Her father was astonished. "Baby Girl, you alright. You hit those balls like you mad at 'em."

"Yeah. Just a little bit. That felt good though."

"Well, it's your call. What do you want, solid or stripe?"

"Solid," she grinned as if the game was already hers.

"Fine with me. Let me see what else you got."

"Unh, huh." She bent over to take aim again.

Alicia walked back in sipping a glass of lemonade that matched the shirt she was wearing.

"What I miss?" She handed her father the other glass she was holding.

"Thank you. I am thirsty. Your sister hit some balls. More than one I might add. I've never seen her break balls like that before," Otis gulped down his lemonade.

Celia tuned them out as she aimed for a green one, slightly stroking the table with her stick. She didn't hit the ball until she felt it was centered just right and until she could see a clear picture of Khalil's face on her targeted ball.

BAM!

The green ball flew across the table on impact, zigzagging against the walls several times before settling in a left pocket near Celia.

Alicia shouted as her eyes got big, "What? She is bringing some fire. Go on girl and do your thang."

"See . . . I told you. I might be waiting a while." Her father sat on a stool and placed his glass on the wet bar.

Celia strutted around the table with focus. She had found a constructive way to vent her frustration. She pointed the stick, "Yellow. Right corner pocket."

Alicia and Otis Sr. watched in silence while Celia scrunched her eyebrows and focused on her mark. It was easy as long as she aimed at the tip. She envisioned Khalil smiling on the white ball and put as much controlled anger into the pool stick as she could.

"Got it," she said as it went in the pocket.

"That's my daughter." Her father gave her a standing ovation. Alicia put two fingers in the corners of her mouth and whistled. Celia knew they were only doing that to cheer her up, but she was glad they cared enough to exaggerate.

"Can all of you get any louder?" their mother scowled with one hand on her hips.

Celia had already decided on her next target while they were conversating. She wasn't enthused to see her mother, but refused to let frustration break her stride. "Blue ball. Center pocket."

She got back in position against the table as she angled the stick.

"Can I play?" Khalil walked in smiling with a glass of

lemonade in hand. He went to the pool rack and pulled a stick from the rack.

Celia's hand slipped and the ball barely moved as she scratched it. "Ugh," she gritted her teeth aggravated.

Alicia angrily stalked over to where Khalil was standing and pointed at his head. "What? Who let the stray dog up in here?"

Khalil smirked at her with his mouth and glared with his eyes, "You would know all about stray dogs, wouldn't you, Alicia? Stray dogs and Hennessy?"

WHACK was the sound of Alicia's fist as it collided with Khalil's face when she stole him in the jaw. It happened so fast that no one had time to respond.

"That's for my niece, you sick puppy," Alicia spat angrily.

"Alicia!" her father hollered, standing up from his stool.

Patricia shouted at her daughter, "What is wrong with you?"

Khalil looked stunned as he put his hand up to his busted bottom lip where a trickle of blood was forming. He glanced at his blood dipped finger then back at Alicia. He set his glass on the edge of the pool table and balled up his fist like he was about to hit her back. They had both spoken words of resentment that they'd held in for years and stood against each other like two trains on a collision course.

Their mother turned to Khalil and said, "Let me go get you some ice."

Celia jumped between the two before more blood was shed.

Alicia continued to talk over and on the sides of Celia as she tried to swing at Khalil again. "You can't say jack about me. You lucky I'm not Celia 'cause I would've taken a butcher knife to your stuff. See how many little girls you can screw with your jewels cut off."

Otis Sr. grabbed Alicia around the waist and began pulling her towards the door scolding her. "You know we don't act like that. You need to get a grip. Go outside and calm down."

"I don't need to calm down. You need to put this nut out of the house. I don't want him nowhere near my daughter or my family."

Alicia stopped talking when she saw Celia's mouth, "Don't tell them, please."

Patricia came back in with ice wrapped in a towel. She rushed over to Khalil, "Are you okay? I would have never invited you over if I'd known this would happen. Sometimes my daughter is like a bad apple; all rotten and ugly."

Khalil glared at Alicia once again as he put the towel on his lip before his expression softened. "Mom, I'm fine. I think its best that I leave. I appreciate you trying to get Celia and I back together, but we'll have to work it out on our own."

Celia was in too much shock to do anything but stand against the pool table.

"My sista don't want your nasty tail." Alicia spewed in Celia's defense.

"Let's go out to the deck," Otis Sr. instructed Alicia. She frowned but followed him out of the room.

After Khalil left, it was twenty minutes before Alicia and Otis Sr. came back into the room. During that time Celia had to repeatedly hear how she was ruining her life and that her mother only had her best interest in mind. Celia tuned her mother out, occasionally nodding her head to appear as if she was listening. Celia was concerned that Alicia would talk too much while they were outside. Celia didn't want to discuss Kaleia's molestation yet.

"I told Khalil to come over because my son-in-law

wants his wife. None of this would have happened if Celia would have been at home with her husband instead of here playing pool," Patricia told Otis Sr.

Celia wondered how Alicia's punching Khalil became her fault.

"That was totally out of line. Celia is a grown woman. She don't need you to dictate her marriage."

"I'm not dictating anything. I can't stand by watching my child destroy a good relationship and you shouldn't either. We both know her and Khalil belong together. She's acting childish."

"Here we go again," she mumbled as her parents argued.

Celia didn't know why it was so hard to break the news to her parents. Probably because they loved Khalil as much as they loved their own biological children. What family wants that kind of news about another family member? It was going to devastate them. She might as well get the conversation over with.

"Mom. Daddy. I have something that I need to say," Celia stated loudly to be heard over their arguing.

Her parents stopped talking and turned towards her.

"It's why I'm not going home. I have been keeping something from you. I wanted to avoid this talk, because I didn't want to hurt you. I know how much you love Khalil and there is no way that I can prepare you for what I am about to say."

Celia looked to Alicia for moral support. Alicia stood by Celia's side and squeezed her hand. "You can do it."

Celia rapidly blinked as tension prinked her skin. "Khalil has been touching Kaleia."

Her mother looked relieved as she said, "Tsk. Is that your reason? You mad because your husband is disciplining that teenage girl. Maybe she's getting out of hand and needs a tap on the behind."

Celia's father tuned into her struggle for words and his voice boomed as he interjected, "Patti. Stop and listen."

Her mother stilled her tongue, clamping her lips shut.

Celia resumed her confession, "Khalil has been molesting Kaleia."

Her mother gasped while her father held a somber gaze.

"That's not true. What an awful thing to make up," Patricia accused.

Celia couldn't hide her dismay, "Why would I make up a story like that?"

"I don't know. Maybe 'cause you don't appreciate what you have and you're trying to turn the rest of us against Khalil."

"Celia, are you sure about this?" her father sadly asked.

"As sure as I am standing here," replied Celia.

"How can you be sure? Kaleia could be seeking attention by making up this crazy tale."

Only God was keeping Celia from cursing her mother out for defending Khalil and insulting the virtue of her granddaughter.

"My daughter didn't tell me anything. I saw him molest her with my own eyes," Celia said

"Jesus," her father said, rubbing his salt and pepper head of hair.

Her mother stared at her stunned and speechless.

Alicia took over the conversation. "Stop, just stop. We need to unite as a family in all of this and ban that idiot from being around all of us. Celia and Kaleia need all of our support to get through this. Hurling insults at Celia isn't making the situation better. She didn't want to say anything and I see why. Mom, you know Celia is not prone to lying. How can you talk to her in that way with a clear conscience?"

"Khalil would never do that. I refuse to believe it." Their mother frowned defiantly.

"Whew . . . I need to get some more air." Otis jumped off the stool and stalked out the room.

Celia walked off right behind him. She had just about as much of her mother's disrespect and drama centered around Khalil as she could take in one day.

# CHAPTER
# FIFTEEN

Celia sat in the waiting area of Dr. Malawi's office and marked through the first ten pages of her staff's marketing proposals with a red ballpoint pen. Kaleia was in the room with the psychiatrist for her fourth therapy appointment. Kaleia had a standing appointment every Tuesday at five in the afternoon. The first two appointments didn't seem to yield any results or at least none evident to Celia. Dr. Malawi explained to Celia that Kaleia would need to become trusting of the doctor in order to talk about the molestation. It may take awhile so patience would be a necessity. Celia wanted to be patient, but she needed answers. She still didn't know how long Khalil had been violating his daughter or what made Kaleia allow it.

She glanced over at her son, who sat slouched in the chair next to her. It was the first time she brought Caleb with her. Usually Caleb stayed with Alicia or Otis Sr., but Celia was running behind schedule after she picked the two children up from school and went back to her office to grab the proposals she needed to revise. She didn't

have time to drop him off. Caleb knew his sister was seeing a doctor, but that was the extent of conversation
about that particular subject. With Kaleia not talking
about her molestation, Celia didn't know what to say to
her ten year old son.

Caleb looked bored as he read a comic book. "Mom, is
Kaleia crazy?" Caleb suddenly looked up and asked as
he rolled his comic book in his hand.

Celia was shocked by his question and inadvertently
slashed red ink through portions of the proposal that she
meant to keep. "What did you say?"

Caleb sat upright in the chair and pointed to the metal
plate on Dr. Malawi's door. "You told me we were taking
Kaleia to a doctor's appointment. We are at a psychiatrist's office. Psychiatrist only see crazy people. You can
tell me Mom, because Kaleia has been acting awfully
strange lately."

Celia didn't know how to respond. She had misjudged
Caleb's observation of his surroundings. "No, your sister
is not crazy. She is having some problems and needs help
I can't give her. Who told you that psychiatrists only see
crazy people?" Celia whispered to Caleb, conscious of the
woman sitting three chairs down. The thin brunette cut
her eyes at them obviously insulted by Caleb's words.

"In my class at school there was a boy named Dustin
that sat in front of me. Everybody picked on Dustin. He
always smelled funny. One day Mrs. Wilkes sent him to
the nurse's office, because he had this big red spot on the
back of his pants. Come to find out that Dustin wet the bed
at night and his mom made him wear diapers. The rumor
is that he had huge sores on his backside and his mom
was making him wear the same diaper all week long and
when he took it off he had to use the dirty diapers as pillows and sleep in a closet. Dustin stopped coming to
school and I heard that Dustin's mom was crazy and had

to go see a psychiatrist before she could get Dustin back. My friend, Ricky, said that Dustin's mom was a citified lunatic."

"Citified? No, he probably meant certified lunatic."

Caleb nodded his head as he quietly stated, "Yeah, that's it. He called her a certified lunatic. Ricky said only the craziest of the crazy would do something like that."

"Regardless of whether Dustin's mom was crazy or not, it's not nice to call people names or gossip. Kaleia is not a certified lunatic and I suggest that you don't go back to school talking about your sister like she is crazy. " Celia warned in a hushed tone.

"I won't," Caleb assured Celia.

At six o'clock on the dot, Kaleia emerged from Dr. Malawi's office. Celia looked into her daughter's face for a breakthrough. There was nothing there to lift Celia's spirits or take the anxiety away. Neither a smile nor a frown, Kaleia's face was a blank canvas. Kaleia looked at the ground as she shoved the straps of her tote bag onto her shoulder and walked to the exit door.

Caleb closed his comic book and jumped from the seat. "Are we leaving?" he said.

"Yeah, wait a minute though. I just need to talk to the doctor before we go," Celia told Caleb. Kaleia had already walked out and was probably standing in the hallway.

"Okay." He lingered by the door and opened his comic book back up.

"Any progress?" Celia asked with hope in her eyes.

Dr. Malawi responded, "I think she is coming around. As I've said before, don't rush her progress. It may be months before Kaleia breaks her silence."

*Months.* Celia didn't think she could endure months of Kaleia's silence; months of not knowing.

* * *

Caleb shot past Celia like he had a Hemi engine built inside his shoes. He looked adorable running with his little Superman fishing pole and tackle box.

"That boy is going to keep me busy all weekend long," Otis Sr. said as he walked towards her from the house.

Celia smiled. Caleb was obviously excited about his fishing trip with his grandfather. She watched him play like he was steering the wheel on her father's boat which was attached to his truck.

"He is staying in a house with nothing but other females. I think all that estrogen has been a little more than he can handle. He is dying for some male attention," Celia told her father as she stood shivering in the early morning cold. It was just after dawn and the sun was still hidden. She thought the sweater she had on would be warm enough to drop him off in. She had worn the wrong coat, a thin spring jacket instead of her wool coat and she was paying for it.

"You're welcome to come inside the house," her dad offered while watching her teeth chatter.

"No, I would rather not. I don't want to deal with your wife," she half-joked, nudging him as they stood against her car. It had been close to three weeks since she'd been to the house, not since her mother's verbal assault.

"Patricia had no business talking to you like that after she invited trouble into the house. When she thinks she's right about something it's hard to get her off the subject."

"She was mean."

"She used a poor choice of words," he defended his wife. Celia couldn't expect any different from her father. He had been dealing with her mother's insensitivity for so many years that he was probably immune. Even though her mother talked to Alicia any kind of way, she never got that ugly when speaking to their father. She hadn't gotten that way with Celia either, not until that night.

"It shocked me to hear her talk like that to me. I was used to her berating Alicia, but Mom has never insulted me. I don't know which hurts more; what Khalil did or my own mother's response."

"Despite what it looks like or what you may think, your mother loves you."

"I know she does. Mom held me at a different standard than Alicia. She has all these expectation of me and I've been trying to live up to them. I didn't realize how painful Mom's words could be until I got verbally burned by them. I can now see why Alicia gets so defensive sometimes."

"How are you holding up overall?" Celia knew he was referring more to Khalil than her mother's abrasiveness.

"I'm doing the best I can. Taking each day one at a time. Starting my mornings with a clear mind and trying not to think about it too much. I have to press forward. I have to do it for Kaleia and Caleb." Her arms felt like little needles prickling her as the cold whipped around her. She rubbed her hands up and down her arms to keep some warmth.

"You want to sit in the garage where it's warmer?" her father asked.

Celia hesitated. "I don't know."

"Your mother is still asleep," he answered reading her mind.

They walked up the driveway to the heated garage. It was where her father went to when he wanted to be alone. He had a beat up old couch sitting to the side next to his tool cabinet.

Celia sat on the couch and watched Caleb who was having a good time entertaining himself on the boat in the driveway.

"Has he been back over since I told you?"

"Yes, he has." Her father sat next to her, bending slowly because of his bad knees. "And I made it very clear that he isn't welcome in my home."

"What about mom? She doesn't believe it happened. Is she okay with that? With Khalil not coming around?"

"It doesn't matter if she's alright with it. Right is right. She still calls him though. Not when I'm around, but I know she still calls."

"That's messed up." Celia felt betrayed by her mother.

"Khalil has been in this family for over fifteen years. Your mother doesn't want to disown him no more than she would want to turn her back on any of you."

Celia needed answers from a male perspective. "Daddy, what makes a man do something like that . . . you know . . . something that awful?"

Otis furrowed his eyebrows and looked at Celia. "That ain't normal. It ain't right. I have you two girls and nothing like that has or would ever cross my mind. A real father wouldn't violate his children. A real man would seek help when the thought crossed his mind. My main job as your daddy is to protect you; protect you and provide for you. Any father that ain't doing those two things can't call himself a father."

"I had no clue, Daddy, I thought Khalil was a wonderful father."

"We all did. Have you decided what to do from here?"

That had been all Celia had thought about, but she still couldn't come up with a resolution. She changed her mind constantly on how to handle Khalil.

"I don't know what I'm going to do. As I said earlier, I got to keep pressing forward," Celia said.

"Paw-Paw . . . come on," they heard Caleb hollering. He must have gotten bored. Celia didn't see him in the boat, but she could definitely hear his high pitched voice.

"Daddy, take that boy fishing. Thanks for talking with me," Celia said.

They got up from the couch. One a little slower than the other.

"Baby girl, you don't need to thank me. That is what a real father is supposed to do." He hugged her hair and kissed her forehead.

Caleb had gotten into the passenger seat of the truck.

Celia hollered as the cold air hit her again and she headed to her car. "Caleb catch Mommy a big fish."

He held his fishing rod up and said, "I'm going to catch you a lot of fish."

She chuckled and jumped into the car, waving good-bye to her dad and her son. She turned the heat on and thawed as she drove.

# CHAPTER
# SIXTEEN

*Creed Tabarome.* That was the scent emanating from her car. She knew it well. It was Khalil's cologne. She bought it for him as a birthday present. The smell was faint, not strong enough for someone not familiar with its intoxicating fragrance to notice. Celia noticed because she used to love how it smelled on Khalil. Now it sickened and revolted her. Even the weakest hint disgusted her.

She inhaled the scent as her stomach turned and churned all the way to the gas station before work. It didn't click until she was in the parking lot of the gas station that she shouldn't be smelling Khalil. He hadn't been in her vehicle in close to two months.

She started to wonder what Khalil was doing in her car that the smell of him would be fresh. Had he been in her car the night before? Because that smell hadn't been in her car the day before. The image of him sitting in her car watching the house from Alicia's driveway during the late night hours made her uneasy. She threw her guard up and looked around. There wasn't anything inside the Jag worth taking. Nothing that he would value. Maybe she was imagining things.

Celia got out of the car and swiped her credit card to pay at the pump. She stood against the car waiting for the vehicle to fill up. She looked at the man two pumps down as he struck a match and lit up a cigarette. That was a hazard if ever she saw one. One flicker of a cinder from that cigarette hitting the fuel could blow the whole gas station up and a couple other city blocks right along with it.

After putting the nozzle back in the pump she smelled her hands. They faintly smelled like gasoline. She got into her car and reached into her glove compartment for the wet wipes she kept there. On top of her wet wipes was a long black box. It looked familiar. She pulled it out and opened the box.

*Not again.*

It was the necklace Khalil had sent to her office. The one she had mailed back to him. It was no wonder she could smell his cologne.

"Maybe mailing the necklace wasn't a direct enough approach for you Khalil. Maybe you need me to give it to you face to face," She thought aloud.

Celia swung the heavy glass doors open at Wilson, Alexander and Franklin Engineering Firm, walking past curved walls and contemporary furniture. The necklace case was clenched in her hand. She marched combatively past Tracy, the office manager, who walked her way with a cup of coffee in hand.

"How are you this morning?" Tracy smiled warmly.

"Fine," came the clipped response from Celia. She carried her foul attitude straight into Khalil's office. Khalil's head was bowed as he vigorously sketched on his drawing board. He didn't notice Celia enter.

"What's this?" she asked, flinging the case onto his pad, breaking his concentration.

He raised his eyes up to her then back down at the necklace case. He dropped the pencil he had been sketching with and picked up the case.

"It's the necklace I bought you," he said, staring at her.

"No," she rapidly shook her head as she used her right hand to point at the case. "What is it doing in my car? In my glove compartment?"

He looked baffled and spoke slowly. "Maybe you put it there."

Her mouth dropped open. "Wha . . ."

Irritation was rising. She placed her hands on either side of his drawing board and leaned close to him, letting her long hair cascade from her shoulders onto his desk.

"No, you put it there," she said, her words as slowly as he had.

He stared blankly at her.

She stood up straight realizing she was closer to him than she wanted to be.

"I don't like playing games, Khalil. I'm a grown woman and I don't play stupid mind games."

"I have no idea what you are talking about. Why would I put a necklace I already gave you inside your glove compartment?" He posed the question with arched eyebrows.

She put her hands on her hips and said sarcastically, "I don't know. Why would you put a necklace I sent back to you inside my glove compartment?"

"I didn't"

"You did"

"No, I did not"

"Yes. You did."

After going back and forth several times Celia exhaled. "Khalil, this is juvenile. I could smell you. The scent of your cologne is lingering in my vehicle as we speak. Don't tell me that I can't recognize Creed Tabarome. I know ex-actly what it smells like. Especially on you. I don't take kindly to being harassed. What is it you're trying to prove? What do you want from me?"

He didn't budge as he watched her ranting and raving.

"You," he said. His expression soft, his words emotion filled. "I want you. I miss you. I miss how you let me kiss your neck while you brushed your teeth in the morning. I miss how you slept with one leg bent over my stomach and your arm draped across my chest. Your mouth pressed against my ear. I missed the smell of mango in your hair when I lay my head on top of yours. I miss it all."

A small smile appeared on his face as he reminisced.

Her heart jolted in recognition, but she stood like he didn't affect her.

Khalil came from behind his desk. He intended to get close to Celia. For every step he took forward, she took one backwards. They did that tango until she was almost against the wall. She glared at him coldly, hoping he would get frostbite from her deliberate icy stance.

He got the message and went to sit back at his desk.

"Maybe you could smell my cologne because you miss me. Maybe you miss me and don't want to admit it. And coming here with the necklace, blaming me for some-thing I didn't do, was an elaborate ploy to see me," Khalil reasoned.

She tossed her hair back and said, "You wish. I don't miss you. I don't know you, so I can't miss you. You can keep your jewelry. I don't want it. I don't want anything you have to give."

She wasn't going to get a confession about the neck-lace no more than he would admit to molesting Kaleia. Fine, if he wanted to play games, he could play by him-self. She wasn't about to be a willing participant.

"I'm going to the police," Celia spat. She was tired of

his manipulation. Obviously he wasn't going to leave her and the children alone. If he thought she was easy prey then he had another thing coming.

He slanted his eyes and said dryly, "Really? And what would that prove?"

"I can show you better than I can tell you." She spun on her heels and walked out. With or without Kaleia's consent, the nonsense had to end.

# CHAPTER
# SEVENTEEN

It wasn't as dramatic as she expected. The inside looked like any other office building. She stood at the police department's entrance trying to figure out where to go. She scanned the room for a man or woman in blue uniform.

Celia walked up to a blond-haired officer at a desk. "Excuse me Officer Gibson." She looked at her name badge. "Can you tell me where to file a report?"

"It depends. What kind of report do you want to file?" The unsmiling officer said as she sorted a stack of files.

"Harassment," Celia said as she played with the strap of her purse, "I want to file a harassment report."

"You mean a stalking report?" The officer asked.

Celia didn't know if that was the right report, but it sounded good. If Khalil was leaving stuff in her car without her permission, then it must have been illegal somehow.

Officer Gibson pointed to a bubble glass window across the room. "Someone over there will be able to help you file a report."

Celia looked in the direction that was being pointed out. "Is there a bell or do I knock on the glass?"

Officer Gibson wasn't interested in all Celia's questions as she spoke in a monotone voice similar to a computer voice recording. "There will be a police aide at the window to assist you."

She hoped the next officer was a little more pleasant than Officer Gibson.

Celia stepped up to the bubbled window and sure enough another blond that looked barely out of high school came to the glass on the other side.

"Can I help you?" She asked with her mouth in a thin line.

Celia might as well forget the warm reception. This officer may be young, but no less unfriendly.

"I'd like to file a stalking report," Celia told her.

"Domestic?"

*What the heck was domestic*? "I guess," Celia said although she looked like she had no clue.

"Is the alleged stalker someone you know?" The police aide spoke to her like she was mentally challenged. Celia was starting to think going to the police was more of a hassle than she needed.

"Yes, I know him." Celia controlled the irritation quickly building in her voice.

The police aide explained the basic procedure for filing a report and handed one sheet of paper through a slit in the glass. "An officer will be out to take your statement after you complete this and bring it back to me."

"Here you go," Celia said pushing the paper back to the aide, after filling it out.

Celia sat down and waited for someone to come get her. She hoped they wouldn't be long. She needed to get to work.

As the police aide looked over the completed form,

Celia asked, "Is that it, do I need to do anything else? How long before the officer comes out?" She had a marketing plan to review for the new I-Pod line before the day ended.

"You said that your husband, with whom you are separated from, broke into your car?"

"Yes."

"That is called breaking and entering, not stalking. Were there any windows broken?"

"No."

"Items taken?"

"No."

Celia was starting to feel like she was wasting her time. All she wanted to do was get Khalil arrested without forcing Kaleia to admit to the molestation. Kaleia may not want Khalil locked up, but Celia felt that his being put behind bars would make him less of a nuisance.

"I don't think you will want to file a report based on the information you have written here."

"What if my husband molested our daughter? Can I report that?"

"Is your daughter with you?" The aide glanced around the almost empty room except for a Mexican woman with a badly bruised face and two men holding hands.

"No, she's not. Why does she need to be here? I witnessed it myself, anything she has to say I can say for her." Celia thought the aide was intentionally making things hard for her. She didn't know why, but that's what it felt like. The aide didn't want to deal with more paperwork so she was discouraging Celia from filing.

"You can't file for her. She has to be present."

"Why?" Celia didn't believe her.

"In the state of Michigan, a parent cannot file a claim on behalf of a minor child or children against another parent."

"What?" Celia couldn't have heard that right.

The police aide repeated it for her, in exactly the same way.

"That is the stupidest thing I ever heard of. You mean to tell me that if I see my underage child getting violated by her father, I can't do anything?"

"Yes, that is what I am saying."

"So the law isn't going to help me protect my child?" Celia's voice was rising.

The police aide didn't bother to respond.

"Okay . . . okay," Celia said, lowering her voice. "What is the procedure if I can get my daughter down here to file a claim?"

"At that time, your daughter will give a statement to a detective and receive a case number. Once the information is processed she will be instructed to the Family division. From there the appropriate course of action will be determined, but without your daughter's statement, there isn't much that can be done unless you were being raped, beaten or violated in some way also."

Celia was seething as she grabbed her purse and left. She didn't have anymore time she wanted to waste. She would protect her kids on her own.

# CHAPTER EIGHTEEN

"Excuse me. Pardon me. Oh, I'm sorry. Excuse me," Alicia said as she made her way down the pew, squeezing past people until she got to the center where Celia was sitting.

"We should have sat on the end of the row." Celia cut her eyes at Alicia. She had come back from the restroom for the third time since they got to church service.

"My nylons keep creeping into uncomfortable places," Alicia said apologetically as she fidgeted with her skirt. They had run to Walgreens right before church and Alicia grabbed the first pair of coffee brown nylons she saw. The first time she went to the bathroom it was to put them on. The second time was to adjust them because they were two sizes too small. Third time must have been to adjust them again. Celia didn't think Alicia had gotten any of the word with all the running back and forth. Service was just about over.

The church secretary walked up to the pulpit with a stack of announcements in hand. The rhinestones on her purple dress sparkled under the lights. For as long as

Celia had been going to Greatness in Faith, she had noticed that all of Sister Dorothy's clothes had rhinestones in them. She also wore a matching hat, handbag and shoes with each outfit. The lady believed in coming to church decked out. It was like watching the hostess at a runway show for Fashion Fair.

Sister Dorothy smiled at the congregation before pulling the microphone down slightly, "Good afternoon, church, giving honor to the Lord because he is so very worthy to be praised. It is a blessing to be standing before you once again. I have our weekly announcements."

She leafed through the stack and pulled out a card. "The Matthews family sent us a card and would like to send thanks for all the food, gifts, and support give during their time of grievance and asked that we keep them in our prayers."

Richard Matthews had been with the church since before the foundation was broke. It was sad to lose him. He was probably one of the oldest members of the congregation. A robust man with a hardy laugh, he stayed active in the church up until his final days of battling Alzheimer's or what everybody liked to call old timer's disease. It was interesting how he could barely remember the day of the week, but somehow still made it to church every Sunday with the help of his daughter, Margaret, and three grandsons Perry, Nathaniel and Marques.

"We have the annual Teen Sleep-Out in a few weeks. The kids will be spending the night in Zap Zone. The fare is ten dollars per child and we would like all the monies in by the nineteenth. If you wish to sign your child up, please see Brother Khalil Alexander. He will have a table set up in the vestibule following service."

Alicia put the church bulletin up and whispered out of the corner of her mouth, "Did she say what I think she said?"

Celia wished it was her imagination. "She sure did."

"Unh, unh." Alicia pursed her lips. She began to fan with the church bulletin even though the air was on full blast.

Celia felt her skin get clammy. Her stomach did somersaults like a foreign object was trying out for gymnastics in her body. Her ears seemed to plug up like she was descending from a flight and all she could do was watch the church secretary's mouth move.

"That is the end of the announcements. As service concludes can the church say amen?" Sister Dorothy finally requested.

"Amen," Celia mechanically repeated. She didn't think she could ever get unsettled in the House of God. Church was where she found peace. It was her sanctuary. Greatness in Faith was her retreat from reality. She looked down at her hands and realized she had unknowingly ripped the church bulletin to shreds and the remains lay in her lap. As everybody filed out of the sanctuary, Celia stayed glued to her seat. It reminded her of the time when Khalil took her for that ride to see his supposed new toy plane development project. She felt just as dirty sitting in the pew as she did parked in her car that day.

"Celia, get up. It's time to go." Alicia bumped her with an elbow.

"Huh?"

"Let's go," she gestured with her head.

"Oh." Celia stood and rubbed wetness from her hands onto her black dress pants.

"I got to get out of these nylons before my circulation is cut off. I can't take it no more." Alicia sped walked out of the pew tried to maneuver past congregation members waiting to exit, but the line seemed stalled.

"You alright?" Alicia asked as she looked back with concern in her eyes.

Celia knew she probably looked distraught. "He can't do this."

"He is tri-fi-ling." She sounded the word out like they were in three parts.

"Come on line, move it," Alicia commanded, twitching and pulling at the hem of the nylons that had rolled down her hips.

The church was large and even though they had three levels there was only one exit. She wasn't getting out quick enough. She squinted at the exit like she had powers and could part the crowd.

"Don't let him stress you."

Sure. That was easy for her to say. She didn't have a perverted husband that preyed on young girls.

Finally they made it out the double doors and Alicia rushed to the left towards the women's restroom sign.

Celia pivoted on her heels and made a beeline towards Khalil's table. He stood in his favorite cobalt blue three piece suit grinning at a member she didn't recognize with a pen in his hand.

"What are you doing?" she hissed, cutting to the front of the line.

"Hey Celia, did you need something?" Khalil smiled brightly at her like she was the best thing he had ever seen.

The unknown female member frowned at her as Khalil explained, "This is my wife, I'm sure she didn't mean to be rude and cut in front of you like that." He gently squeezed her arm and ushered her to the other side of the table next to him.

"You want to help me get these signatures?" he asked Celia.

"No, and you shouldn't be getting signatures either." She spat words with as much attitude as she could produce.

"We're in public, don't make a scene." He kept smiling

as he glanced at the bigger line forming of people eager to send their children away for a night.

"What business do you have supervising other people's kids after what you did?" she knew her voice was rising, but she remained oblivious to the crowd staring at her.

"Ssshhhh," Khalil said as he turned from the crowd pulling Celia with him. "Don't start this now."

"What? Am I embarrassing you?" She snatched her arm from his grasp.

"Celia, please." he pleaded, reaching for her again.

"You shouldn't be here. You shouldn't be allowed in nobody's church," Celia hollered.

"I'm not going to stop living, Celia. You act like you want me to stop living."

Khalil grabbed both of her wrists and tried to get her to calm down as she shoved him against the wall.

"Don't touch me." She jerked away and stumbled into the sign-in table. The table turned over and went crashing to the floor. She felt someone pulling her backwards.

"Gurl, you are showing out. We need to go before you embarrass yourself any further," Alicia pulled Celia from around the overturned table.

Utter astonishment, hushed conversation, captivated stares, and a few smirks, rippled through the crowd as Celia took her attention off of Khalil and observed her surroundings. All eyes were on her. Heat seared her cheeks from embarrassment. She saw Sister Elise and two of the armor-bearers, Joshua and Eugene, coming her way.

"Pastor Daniels wants to speak with you and you in his office now." Sister Elise pointed an annoyed finger at Khalil and Celia.

"Everyone, Brother Joshua and Eugene here will be taking down the names for the Sleep-Out. Please form two lines so we can speed up the process." She pushed Khalil from the area and replaced him with the two other men who picked up the table and some of the forms that were all over the floor.

"Go get the kids," Celia said calmly as Alicia tried to cover the big "O" that formed around her mouth. Luckily, children's church and the teen ministries were in a building adjoined to theirs. They didn't need to have any part in that atrocious scene that had just been displayed.

Celia walked towards the pastor's office making sure to keep at least three feet of distance between herself and Khalil. He waited for her before he entered the room and he let her enter first.

Celia felt like she was ten years old about to be disciplined by her father, which was rare because her father didn't feel she needed much discipline growing up.

They each sat in the chairs facing the pastor.

"I saw you two out there arguing. Would either of you like to explain what's going on?" Pastor Daniels asked, removing his glasses and folding his hands in front of him on the cherry wood desk. He had been the shepherd of Greatness in Faith for over ten years. He knew Celia and Khalil very well; neither of them had drawn negative attention to themselves at church before.

Celia looked at Khalil then back at the Pastor not able to think of something to justify her actions.

Khalil looked at her; he stretched his legs and shifted in his chair.

"Somebody tell me something," Pastor Daniels looked at Khalil.

Khalil coughed in his hands and adjusted the lapel of his suit.

"I don't think Khalil should be in a leadership position right now," Celia stated.

"And why is that?" Pastor asked.

"We are having marital problems," Khalil said.

"Is that the reason, Sister Alexander?" Pastor Daniels awaited Celia's response.

"That's putting it lightly." She closed her eyes because her head was starting to hurt. Soon her eyes would water.

Khalil turned to address Celia. "Baby, I love you. I want to work it out."

"There is no way in he . . ." she cut it short when she saw Pastor Daniel's eyebrows instantly rise. "There is no way on this earth that we will work out that farce of a marriage we had out," Celia rolled her head and eye-balled Khalil up and down before exhaling. She laid her head back on the chair closing her eyes again as her throat became scratchy and tears formed. "Pastor, he has been molesting our daughter." She felt a tear cascade down her cheek even while her eyes remained tightly sealed.

"That is an erroneous tale my wife plucked from her imagination. She won't listen to reason. It started from a simple misunderstanding and blew up into nonsense," Khalil calmly stated.

"I got your erroneous tale." Celia allowed the tears to spill on her camisole as she glared at Khalil.

"Sister Alexander. That is a serious allegation."

"I would never harm either of my children. I don't know why she is making up a story that sick. My kids are my world. We are very close. You can even ask Kaleia and she will tell you herself."

"Yeah, because you brainwashed her. Sniff . . . sniff." Celia used the back of her hand to wipe her nose.

Pastor Daniels handed Celia a Kleenex box from which she pulled several tissues and blew her nose into one.

"Kaleia knows the truth. I've never done anything to hurt her." Khalil was adamant.

"Khalil, how can you lie in a church like that?" Celia was flabbergasted and insulted.

"There is a lot of emotion in this room," Pastor Daniels said as he opened his Bible. He put his glasses back on and looked up. "You do have your Bibles."

Khalil pulled the marker from a bible page he was holding.

Celia didn't know if he was making a statement or asking a question. She scanned the floor for her Bible and purse. She patted her legs like that would make them appear. She looked up ashamed. "My sister must have mine."

"That's alright, I have plenty here. Why don't you go over to the bookshelf and grab an NIV version?" He signaled to a massive cabinet on the left.

Celia walked over and scrolled down until she found a Bible. "Got one." Celia held the Bible up in the air.

Pastor waited until she was back in her chair. "Could you go with me to Ecclesiastes chapter seven, verse nine?"

Khalil and Celia flipped through the Bible and stopped at that page.

"Read with me," Pastor Daniels said as he begun to read. " 'Do not be quickly provoked in your spirit, for anger resides in the lap of fools.' Now go down a couple of verses to fourteen thru eighteen."

Celia began to feel extremely uncomfortable. Was her Pastor calling her a fool?

Pastor continued. "And the word of God says, 'When times are good, be happy; but when times are bad, consider: God has made the one as well as the other. Therefore, a man cannot discover anything about his future. In this meaningless life of mine I have seen both of these: a righteous man perishing in his righteousness, and a wicked man living long in his wickedness. Do not be over righteous, neither be over wise. Why destroy yourself? Do not be over wicked, and do not be a fool. Why die before your time? It is good to grasp the one and not let go of the other. The man who fears God will avoid all extremes.' Do you see what I am getting at?"

Celia tried to understand the point Pastor Daniels was making.

He went on. "There will always be trials and wrong-doing, but as Christians we have to find balance for our lives. We can not let our emotions rule us, because our emotions will lead us astray even when we feel we have been wronged and want to retaliate. A wise man thinks before he acts and treads softly. Also, where there is darkness, light is not far behind. God knows all rights and wrongs. He knows the good. He knows the evil and will handle those that dishonor him or his children. The battle is not yours, it's his." Pastor pointed to the ceiling.

"Now, I won't comment on some of what was said here, because I have no proof, nor can I take sides. I'm here for spiritual guidance. I do realize that sometimes my members need other help as well. After you have prayed and sought the Lord's words, if you need legal counsel at that time, I will refer you to the right individuals."

Pastor Daniels turned to Khalil. "Brother Khalil, at this time I will have to ask you to step down from leading any axillaries until this matter is cleared up. Alright?" He came from behind his desk as Khalil stood.

Khalil protested. "Pastor, I don't think that is necessary."

"But it is necessary. I have to consider the safety of all my members when they are in this House of God. Get your house together and we will see about placing you back in leadership. Alright?" Pastor Daniels asked again.

"Alright," Khalil agreed as they shook hands.

"Well, I hope to see the both of you in bible study this Wednesday night."

"Yes." Celia hugged her pastor. She didn't have the heart to tell him she didn't want to breathe the same air as Khalil.

"I'll be here," Khalil said.

"Is there anything else I can do for you?" Pastor asked.

"No." Celia put the bible back on the shelf.

Khalil spoke up, "Could I have a few minutes of your time alone?" Khalil asked Pastor.

"Sure. Sure we can do that," Pastor Daniels agreed. He then escorted Celia from the room. "You have a blessed evening," Pastor said.

"You too," Celia said feeling much calmer than she had earlier.

She looked at the clock in the hall. They had been talking for over an hour. Celia walked out of the building and was relieved to see Alicia parked of the curb. Thank God for small favors. She jumped into the car.

"What happened?" Alicia asked.

Celia looked at the back seat and all three kids were sleep.

"We'll talk later. Let's go home."

# CHAPTER NINETEEN

"Hey, Ruben," Celia said as she sat Indian-style on the couch rapidly typing away on her laptop.

"Hi, how are you doing?" Ruben replied.

"I've been better."

"Alicia told me about what happened; the incident at the church."

"Alicia talks too much sometimes." She continued to click away. She refused to think about her peculiar behavior, let alone the humiliation it brought about. Her reaction was hot-headed and immature. She was a step above a mad woman. She didn't know herself anymore. It felt like someone out of control had invaded her body.

"It will be alright."

"That was a horrible mistake." Celia had given the church gossip mill enough to talk about for the next several months to come. Looking back, she acted foolish and embarrassed herself way more than she could have embarrassed Khalil. Even though Monique and Justice had called with words of encouragement, she knew their response didn't mirror the sentiment of the rest of the congregation. She shouldn't care what people thought about her, but in that particular case, she did. How could she show her face at church after that disgrace? Maybe she needed to find another church home.

Ruben stood bobbing his head like there was music playing. He had his hands in the pockets of creased black jeans. His black and gray stripped button down shirt was neatly tucked in. A small rope chain hung loosely around his neck.

She broke her typing stride and unfolded her legs. "You look nice." She smiled. Celia didn't want him to think she was so unhinged that she couldn't be civil. "Have a seat." She waved him over to Alicia's sectional.

"Oh, okay." He smiled back and removed his hands from his pockets as he walked over.

"You looked intense. I didn't want to bother you," he explained as he sat down.

Celia nodded.

"What were you doing?" he gestured towards the laptop.

"Oh, those are some reports I have for work. You know how that goes. Are you and Alicia going somewhere special?" She signaled to his appearance.

He looked down at his apparel.

"There is an exhibit at the African-American museum that I want to show her. She said she has never been there. I told her she was missing a treat."

Art. Seeing Alicia in a museum would be a treat alright. It was just a matter of what kind of treat he was expecting Alicia to embrace. Celia had invited Alicia to a gallery opening a few years back hoping to peak her creative side, but Alicia spent more time perusing the champagne buffet than enjoying the exhibits.

"What kind of art are you into?" Celia asked, a little

surprised. With his burly build, he didn't look like the artsy type.

"Actually, I'm not that big on most art. I like the museum because it tells a historical story," he admitted, clearing his throat.

"Yeah, I know. I do too. I especially love the expressionist view of Romare Bearden with his 'Family' piece, and have you seen works by Clementine Hunter or Henry O. Tanner's 'Banjo Lesson'? My favorite artist is Jacob Lawrence. I have a lot of his prints in my house. Let me take that back. I had a lot of his prints in my house," she corrected her statement.

Ruben gave her a blank stare. It was apparent that he didn't have a clue who any of the artists were by name. She wasn't in the mood to educate him either.

"Hope you two have an informative and fun time," Celia said cheerfully.

"I hope so too." He leaned over and whispered like he was about to divulge a big secret. "I really care about your sister."

She would swear he sounded like Antonio Banderas. Celia whispered back imitating his accent, "I can tell."

She chuckled on the inside. She missed that newness that couples share when they first get acquainted. The stolen glances. Slight touches. Knowing smiles. All the warm and fuzzy stuff that new love brought. Celia still believed in love. She just didn't believe in loving Khalil.

She hoped Alicia would allow it to blossom.

"I'm ready." Alicia came out with Taija and Kaleia in tow. She was strutting her hips in a red spaghetti sundress. She switched as she walked. Her short layered hair and makeup was flawless.

"Doesn't my mom look sexy," Taija asked, sitting on the armrest of the couch.

"Wow, you look nice," Celia said.

"Very nice," Ruben grinned sheepishly.

"Thank you, thank you and thank you. I do look hot don't I?" Alicia put her hands on her hips and struck a pose.

"Don't toot your own horn," Celia told her arrogant sister.

"Toot . . . toot." Alicia made a train sound.

"You're going to freeze your behind off. It's only April," Celia scolded Alicia. The spring season in Detroit was unpredictable, which was enough cause to at least have a light jacket on hand.

"It is the end of April and I checked the weather channel before I got dressed," Alicia quirked.

Ruben stood and shook his legs like they were going numb.

"Come on handsome, let's blow this joint," said Alicia.

He rushed past Alicia to open the door and hold it for her as she walked out.

"Aw. How cute," Taija cooed.

He continued to smile as Alicia brushed up again him.

"On second thought, let me grab a light jacket. It does get chilly at night this time of year." She doubled back to the closet. "Bye," Alicia waved with her fingers.

Celia turned to Kaleia and Taija. "Little ladies, I guess it is you and me. What do we have on the agenda today?" Caleb was spending more and more time with Otis Sr., since the fishing trip. It would be an all girls evening.

"Can we go to the mall?" Kaleia asked.

Celia was ecstatic about that idea. Not because she wanted to go shopping, but rather to spend time with her daughter. They hadn't done that in a long while. Even when Kaleia and Celia went to therapy appointments the conversation was minimal, like strangers. In fact, they didn't laugh. They didn't hug. They were too busy tip-

toeing around each other to be affectionate. It was long
overdue for a change.

Celia, Taija and Kaleia sat sprawled out on the sectional in front of the television fat and happy after leaving Fishbone's restaurant. Celia didn't know if she was
tired more from all the food she consumed or from the
trek around the mall.

"I'm stuffed," Kaleia moaned rubbing her tiny stomach.

"I don't think I will be able to eat for another week.
Those crab cakes were so good," Taija said. She out ate
both Celia and Kaleia combined.

Celia used the remote to flip through some channels
on the television. "What are we in the mood for? Com-
edy . . . adventure . . . romance? I take that back, I don't
want to do romance." She stopped at the sci-fi station,
but the movie looked horrific and she never did have a
stomach for blood and gore.

Nothing came on worth watching on a Friday night.
She didn't see why cable was so expensive with half the
junk that played.

"Auntie, can we watch videos? The new one by Chris
Brown is premiering. Kaleia, you remember that one song
"Run it.' " Taija began singing and snapping her fingers.

"They play it a lot on the radio," Kaleia said as she
continued to rotate her hand in circular motions on her
abdomen.

"He isn't one of those rappers that like to disrespect
girls, 'cause you know I am not about to watch some half
naked females parading across the T.V. oblivious to being
dogged 'cause they can be seen across the country."

Taija and Kaleia both giggled.

"Alicia doesn't mind you watching that?" Celia asked
her niece.

"My mom doesn't hide stuff from me. She said if you don't know, you can't grow. Besides, we like those videos," Taija answered.

"Why?"

"'Cause they are funny and entertaining."

"What's so funny about being called out your name?"

"I don't see it that way. I mean, I'm not an itch or ho so it doesn't bother me to hear any rapper says that in a song. I know they can't be talking about me. Besides, I am a beautiful young lady that demands respect."

Celia listened to her niece sounding so grown-up and self assured. Taija may have been the thickest girl in the family, but it didn't appear to be a problem for her. More young ladies should be that secure. As far as the videos go though, Celia still considered it planting seeds of negativity. All kids weren't as perceptive as Taija and tried to live up to what they saw. It was the reason certain things were restricted in the Alexander home. Celia thought she could protect them; keep her kids from growing up too fast.

"I will compromise with you. We can watch videos, but I'm turning as soon as they get too raunchy," warned Celia.

"Deal," Taija took the remote and quickly changed the channel.

Celia lived up to the compromise and the show ended after half an hour of broadcasting. They saw the debut of Chris Brown's song and the last three videos on the countdown. The movie that came on after that didn't look interesting.

"I think *Law and Order* is on," Celia said, getting the remote from Taija and turning the television.

Instead *Dateline* was on. "To Catch a Predator" flashed across the screen.

Celia sat up as her curiosity peaked. They appeared to be setting up men who pursued young girls. That was enough to keep Celia interested.

"Have you seen this before?" Celia asked the girls as they did a recap from a previous show.

Taija nodded. "Yeah, I think it comes on every week."

"Oh, really?" Celia wasn't an avid television watcher but she didn't know how she could have missed it before.

"Uh, huh. *Dateline* goes across the country catching men who use the internet to hook up with girls our age and younger. It's tripped out how they do it too. I think they were in Florida when they caught this one guy naked. He was stupid too." Taija got animated as she set up the storyline. "They have this decoy house where they use an undercover police officer pretending to be a kid. She acts like she is changing clothes after she lets them in and the men wait in the kitchen for her to get dressed. Then bam . . . Busted!"

"You said they caught one guy naked?" Celia questioned.

"Yes. He was stuck on stupid. He answered the door buck-naked. Who answers somebody else's door without clothes on? S-T-U-P-I-D. Just stupid. He deserved to get caught and locked up. That's nasty for grown men to be touching on girls our age anyhow. Ain't that right, Kaleia?" Taija looked to her cousin to co-sign the statement.

Kaleia mumbled a weak, "Yeah." She had a pained expression across her face. "I don't feel so hot," she groaned. "My stomach hurts really badly. I think I'm gonna throw up."

Celia put her hand to her daughter's forehead which felt cool.

Kaleia stood up holding her stomach. Her shoulders heaved; she doubled over and went running down the hall.

Taija and Celia both stood up worried.

"Should I go check on her? Taija asked.

"No, I'll go. That's my child," Celia said, heading down the hall.

Celia didn't believe it was just the food that made Kaleia sick, but thought the conversation was a contributor too. Kaleia hadn't told Taija about her father. Celia had been sure Kaleia would confide in Taija. For all the time they spent together it seemed inevitable. What could make her hold that in?

Celia knocked on the bathroom door, "Hey you okay in there?"

The toilet flushed.

"Uh, huh," Kaleia replied.

"You want some Alka-Seltzer?"

"Uh, huh."

Celia knew Alicia didn't keep any in the house, but she had a few packets in her purse. Taija, can you bring me my purse?" She shouted into the living room.

"Sure." Taija's bare feet flapped against the floor as she went and grabbed the purse from beside the sectional. The noise of her steps followed her down the hall.

"Kaleia, honey can you open the door?" asked Celia.

"Unh, unh."

"Alright, I'm going to slip a packet of Alka-Seltzer under the door." Celia bent down and shoved the packet in the slit under the door.

She heard the water tap go on, run for a second and go back off. Celia stood by the door and waited for Kaleia to emerge. Kaleia finally opened the door with a flushed face.

Celia brushed the hairs sticking to her forehead back

and looked into her child's puffy eyes. "You can talk to me about anything and I do mean anything. No matter what it is, you can talk to me."

"Okay, Mom," Kaleia responded lowering her eyes and nodding her head.

Celia didn't know if she would take her up on the offer, but at least she put it out there.

# CHAPTER TWENTY

"Do not be quickly provoked in your spirit for anger resides in the lap of fools *wisdom is a shelter."*

Those words played in Celia's head as she sat parked in a rental car down the street from her old residence. She had to think smarter to get justice. Khalil would be leaving for work soon and that would give her all day to snoop around. Staying angry and lashing out would get her nowhere fast.

Celia scooted down in the driver's seat until her eyes were barely above the dashboard as the garage door lifted. She watched the Durango roll back. She ducked down further. The armrest was sticking her in the side and she was anxious to get into the house. She repositioned herself and pressed her hip against the driver's side door only to realize she couldn't see a thing out the window. Nothing except clouds. She listened for the acceleration of his vehicle to drive by. After waiting for what felt like hours she quickly glanced up to see what was taking so long.

The Durango was still parked in the driveway and Khalil was nowhere in sight.

Celia prayed that he hadn't seen her. She lay down uncomfortably in her seat and grimaced in anticipation of him knocking on the window. A car zoomed by. She recognized the sound and thanked God.

Celia turned the gray Mazda back on and pulled into the driveway only to pull back out and park on the street.

"Just in case he comes back for something else," she thought out loud.

A wave of nostalgia overwhelmed her as soon as she entered. Fresh lilies sat in the vase on the glass entrance console. The marble floors glistened like they were freshly mopped. The dining room table was adorned with gold-etched chinaware and set for a family of four. Everything was in place. It was almost eerie.

Celia walked through the house touching all that was once hers. She passed the great room where their family portrait hung above the fireplace. She swallowed sorrow as she walked in and stared at it.

They looked so happy.

Khalil sat on the carpet behind her with one arm draped over her shoulder. Kaleia and Caleb kneeled on either side of them. They all had on blue jean outfits and white tennis shoes.

Khalil wanted them to look casual and to represent an average family. He was tired of taking formal, stiff pictures. He said the formal ones looked artificial.

But they were living an artificial life. Celia just didn't know it at the time.

She pulled herself away from the portrait. She had a purpose and reminiscing wasn't part of that plan.

Celia walked into Khalil's office and settled in the leather swivel chair.

"There has got to be something. Something here I can use against him." She sat her purse alongside the keyboard and reached down to the modem turning the computer on.

She examined the room with its dark moss walls as she waited for the computer to spring to life. She felt claustrophobic. She always felt claustrophobic in that room. She and Khalil had argued for months about the color. She hated the color and insisted it made the room look dark and depressing. He called it a manly room. He said it wasn't supposed to be bright and cheery. Although she continued to bring home other color swatches after it was painted, he stood firm in keeping his masculine domain.

The computer clicked on requesting a password. She was grateful that was one thing he shared with her. The code was Kaleia's and Caleb's initials and the day of their birth.

She typed in kaca317 on the keyboard, hopeful that the code remained the same like everything else in the house.

The main page appeared and Celia sighed with relief.

She opened up his "My Documents" folder and scrolled the extensive list. He kept back-up files for all his work. He had so much that it was hard to decipher what wasn't work related. She continued scrolling down.

She clicked into a picture folder marked "Special Demo." She almost passed by it thinking it was something else from his job, but he normally didn't take pictures for work.

Celia's hand trembled as she hesitated before clicking the mouse.

The first picture seemed to be innocent enough with a dark-skinned teenaged girl wearing a "Happy Birthday" hat and dressed in a khaki short outfit. The girl grinned happily into the camera. She was sitting legs crossed with a brown paneled wall backdrop. Celia didn't recognize her. The next photo was of the same girl, in the same poise except she only wore the birthday hat. Her arms were folded over her bare breast.

Celia clicked again.

The picture was disturbing.

Although she couldn't gage the child's ethnicity, she looked young, maybe ten or eleven years of age. Dark red lipstick smeared her partly opened thin lips. Pale green shadow covered haunting eyes; sad eyes that appeared almost lifeless. She wore pink bunny panties and a white training bra over her ghastly frail frame.

"Oh, Khalil," a guttural moan escaped Celia's lips.

Celia was revolted but couldn't stop herself as she clicked again and again. Each picture became more graphic than the one before.

Suddenly the computer asked for a pass code.

Celia typed in kaca317 and pressed enter.

*Access Denied*

She tried it again, typing the code in slower.

*Access Denied*

"What's wrong with you?" she said to the computer.

She turned the caps lock off thinking maybe it was case sensitive.

A white line flashed across the screen, and then it went black. The computer had shut itself down. She turned it back on as she tried to shake off the horror of it all. Khalil was twisted beyond her comprehension. She didn't know what she had expected to see, but the degradation of those photos reached beyond her imagination.

The ring tone to "So High" by John Legend went off on her cell phone. It was her sister.

"Where you at?" Alicia asked after Celia answered the phone.

"I'm at the house," Celia asked.

"Well, why didn't you answer the house phone? I just called."

For a second Celia was confused. The house phone hadn't rung. She realized that Alicia thought she was at the other house.

"I'm in my house. Or rather what use to be my house a few months ago."

"What are you doing over there? I thought you said you would never enter that house again. Is something going on? Please tell me that Khalil is not there with you."

"No, Khalil is gone to work. I made sure I saw him leave before I came in. I thought if I found evidence that I'd have a better chance of seeking justice. With Kaleia not talking about it, it's his word against mine. I figured I had nothing to lose by coming to do a little investigating. I just wasn't prepared to actually find something." Celia bit the inside of her cheek. "Alicia, Khalil is a very sick and disturbed man."

"You already knew that."

"Yes, I know." She entered the pass code for the login. "I just didn't know how disturbed."

"Of course you did. He molested your daughter. It doesn't get anymore depraved than that."

"Alicia, he has these pictures on his computer. It's . . . it's . . . it's. It's terrible. I don't know how else to describe them but to say sadistic. There are pictures of little girls younger than Kaleia. Little girls that are half clothed. In some of them the children had nothing at all on."

*Access Denied. Please enter new code.*

The computer wouldn't let her login.

"No!" Celia hollered at the screen.

"Celia, what's going on?" Alicia screamed timorously.

"Stop shouting. I didn't mean to scare you. The computer won't cut back on!"

"Oh," she sounded relieved. "I thought something bad was happening."

"Something bad is happening," Celia said. "I'm seeing Khalil in his true form; the full twisted version."

"Celia, you need to get out of that house."

"I got to try and get this computer back on so I can print these pictures off. They're the only evidence I have."

"Khalil is dangerous. Get out of that house!" Alicia demanded.

"Stop worrying. I'm here alone. Nothing is going to happen to me. I'm not going to let Khalil keep me scared, no matter how crazy he is."

"Well, keep me on the phone until you are safely back in the car."

Celia walked into the living room and looked out the window. Alicia was making her paranoid.

"I just looked out the window, and as I said before, I'm by myself. Get a grip. Why did you call me?" She roamed back into the family room.

"Celia, please be careful."

"I am. Now why did you call me again?" Celia repeated the question, wanting to change the subject. Thinking about Khalil was making her skin crawl.

"My car won't start. I was planning to go grab something to eat for lunch, but the car wouldn't crank. I need you to pick up Taija after her dance practice."

"Got any idea what's wrong with it?"

"No. I just know it won't start. Ruben's picking me up after work and we're having it towed to a mechanic."

"Oh. Hope it's nothing expensive. But yeah, I'll get Taija." Celia brushed her fingers around the frame of the family portrait.

"I hope it's nothing expensive either. I can't afford major repairs. Why couldn't this happen three months ago when I still had my warranty?" Alicia paused. "Hey, I got to go, my lunch break is ending and the boss is looking dead in my mouth. Are you sure you going to be okay?"

"Stop worrying about me and get back to work," Celia said before she ended the call.

"Why should someone be worried about you?" a voice came from behind her.

She jumped and spun around. "Khalil."

He was leaning against the doorframe.

"Hey . . . uh, hello. I wasn't planning on seeing you here . . . today." She stumbled through words. "What are you doing here?"

He folded his arms and continued to lean. "I live here."

"Well, um I know that. I mean, what are you doing home now?" Her legs were going to cave any minute. She walked over and sat on the sofa.

He frowned. "Mike and I are going to the gym after work. I came to get some extra clothes. What are you doing here?"

"Me? Well, um. I came to get some stuff."

"Stuff like what?" He continued frowning.

"Caleb's basketball uniform. You know he plays for the junior Gods Men League this summer. It's coming up soon. I figured that while I was here I would get some of our clothes. I just got caught up in the moment when I got here." She glanced back at the portrait.

His eyes followed hers. "Those were better times for us." He persisted to question her. "What about the rental car?"

"The Jag stopped on me and I'm having a mechanic look at it," she lied quickly. She subconsciously twirled hair between her fingers.

"Why are you doing that?"

"Doing what?"

"Playing in your hair. You only do that when you're upset or nervous."

Celia placed her hands in her lap.

He came and pushed the plant centerpiece down the coffee table as he sat directly in front of her. "Celia, am I making you nervous?"

"No . . . of course not. I have a lot on my mind."

"When are you coming home?"

Her skin was crawling, "I thought we discussed this already."

"And we are discussing it again."

She sighed.

"Celia, you and my kids need to come back. I don't know how many times I have to say it before you understand. All the drama needs to stop."

"I agree with you there."

"Then come home," he pleaded.

"Time. All I'm asking for is time." She was buying time as she spoke to him, hoping to get out of there before he did something to her . . . before she did something to him.

"Let me apologize for acting juvenile at the church too. I shouldn't have acted that way," Celia apologized.

He nodded his head. "I know you haven't been yourself lately."

She kept her eyes downcast. She tried to focus enough to stop trembling.

"I'm worried about you." He stroked her face tenderly.

Her mind told her to slap his hand away, but she couldn't compel her body to respond.

"How are things going with Dr. Malawi?" he asked.

She gulped stunned that he knew about Dr. Malawi. He knew an awful lot to not be stalking them. He needed to get his facts correct though.

"How do you know about Dr. Malawi?" Celia wondered how long he'd known about Kaleia going to therapy and who told him.

He placed his hands on her cheeks and rubbed his fingers across her lips. "It's my responsibility to know what's happening with my family."

There were other responsibilities that should have been more pertinent than him stalking them.

"You have such soft lips. I miss how soft your lips are. I want to kiss you." Desire flickered in his eyes. Celia didn't understand how he could want her one minute and have the same yearnings for their daughter the next.

"Stop!" She jerked her head back.

A shadow crossed his face as he stood and jammed his hands in his pants pockets. He walked over to the picture window looking out. "I think you're ill."

"Ill?" She didn't think she heard him right.

He turned around with concern back on his face. "Have you talked to the doctor about pharmaceutical treatment for your disorder? You've been having hallucinations lately. First with that nonsense about me and Kaleia, the necklace and then your episode after service two Sundays ago. I think your unusual behavior is a symptom of deeper issues, but whatever is wrong with you, I'm sure it's curable with the right medication. I want us to work through this. I'm willing to support you anyway I can."

Celia furrowed her eyebrows and looked at him hard as her jaw clinched. She didn't know if she wanted to laugh or cry; be mad or hurt. She was no longer shocked by what he did. Surprised by the things he said. Yet emotions still slapped her silly. It drained her energy.

He would like her to believe that he was a protective father consoling his daughter through teenage blues when she found them. He would like her to believe the

necklace and its case sprouted legs and hands, then un-
locked her car door and placed themselves in her glove
compartment. He would like her to believe she was suf-
fering from schizophrenia or a nervous breakdown or
God only knew what other illness he could conjure up. If
she was honest with herself, she would admit that in her
heart she would like to believe it too, because her being
crazy and have to be prescribed Prozac for the rest of her
natural life would be much more tolerable than the reality.

She stared at him hard because she couldn't believe
the man she had loved all of her adulthood was trying to
play her crazy. Not with the sadistic child pornography
he had stored in his computer. He might be able to fool
other people with his fake sincerity and docile appearance, but Celia had seen enough to know the real Khalil.

She wished she could tap into the recesses of his brain
and figure out where the wires crossed. Where he could
switch from her sweet and sexy Khalil to the deranged
manipulating man before her.

"I'm not crazy," she said with assurance. "I am many
things right now, but crazy ain't one of them."

"I didn't call you crazy. I said you are ill. I don't want
you getting upset again thinking I called you crazy." His
words dripped with sympathy. "You may not want to
admit it, but I'm not the only one that sees it. We have a
whole church congregation that witnessed your episode.
You need to come home so I can help you. Otherwise . . ."

She straightened her back listening.

His demeanor turned cold, "Otherwise I will be forced
to take extreme measures. Maybe the kids would be better off in my care."

She stood and calmly walked over to him. She stroked
his face like he had done to her earlier. Then she stared

deep into his eyes. "There will be ice caps floating in hell and you will be standing on one before I give you my kids."

They both stood there glaring at each other. Neither blinking.

His cell phone rang. He turned the phone on and lifted it to his ear, still staring at Celia.

"The meetings about to start?" He broke his stance to check his watch. "Give me ten minutes. I got held up."

"We will continue this conversation later," he stated as he bound up the stairs.

"No we won't." She watched him disappear into the bedroom, her purpose lost in an emotion she couldn't place. She snatched her purse off his desk, glanced at the login request and walked out the house leaving the door open.

# CHAPTER
# TWENTY-ONE

"I'm glad you came," Ruben told Celia as she swayed in her seat after Alicia excused herself to the ladies room.

"I'm glad you invited us," responded Celia. It had been a long time since she had been out for an evening of enjoyment. "Thank you. You didn't have to do it."

"It was my pleasure. I get the company of two lovely ladies." He grinned, tapping his glass of champagne in sync to the beat of the jazz ensemble.

Celia pulled at her ringlet of freshly pressed hair. She had been to Kaboo's Natural Hair Salon early that morning. She was Sabrina's, her stylist, first appointment for the day. Celia wanted to get in and out before the shop got too busy. Sabrina had scolded her waiting so long to come in. Celia had been pressing her hair every other day and damaged it from playing in it, plus adding too much heat. Her ends were fried. Sabrina fussed while she cut off four inches of dead hair. Celia's mane was still at the center of her back, but Sabrina told her to never try maintaining her own head. Leave it to the professionals.

She turned in her seat to inspect her dimly lit surroundings. The jazz club had a relaxing ambience. "How
long have you been coming here?" Celia asked.

Ruben lifted his eyebrows and put a hand to his ear.
He couldn't hear her as the tempo of the music became
louder. The band was playing an instrumental version of
Maxwell's

"Ascension".

"I said how long have you been coming here?" she
spoke louder.

He lifted two fingers. "Two years. That's when it
opened. My best friend is playing the sax." He pointed to
a pecan-colored stocky brother in the band. "I come here
probably once a month, just about every time I can get a
weekend off."

"I like; didn't know the place existed."

"A lot of people don't. It got this crowd from word of
mouth."

Celia surveyed the room again. There had to be over
two hundred people. All well dressed. Some were in the
bar area or in the restaurant, while others roamed around
on one of the three floors.

Alicia came and sat back down. "Whew, that line was
ridiculous. Why is it that I'm always stuck in a line when
I need to use the bathroom the most? They need more
bathrooms in this place. What is the cost of that in con-
struction? It can't be much. Waiter!" she hollered, waving down one of the uniformed attendants.

"What can I get you?" He pulled out his pen and pad.

"I want to order a bottle of Cristal to celebrate my
birthday."

The waiter took the order and headed towards the bar.

Ruben didn't look happy, but he didn't say anything.
He turned his attention back to the band playing.

"I was telling Ruben that this is a nice spot." Celia leaned towards Alicia to make sure she could hear her.

"I didn't think you would be into this sort of environment, Ms. Bible-Tottin'." Alicia playfully nudged her, laughing.

Celia didn't take offense. She was used to Alicia's jokes.

"You act like I sit in a corner singing old church hymnals on a daily basis. The only reason I didn't go out before was because of my busy schedule. I like any environment where adults can act civilized while they enjoy themselves. You won't catch me in a regular club, but this here is nice," said Celia.

The waiter brought the bottle of Cristal and set three glasses down in front of each of them. "Happy Birthday," he said as he poured.

"Thank you, but no thanks." Celia smiled pleasantly as she covered her glass with her palm. "Can I get a Virgin Daiquiri?"

"What's the difference between a Virgin Margarita and a Virgin Daiquiri?" Ruben asked.

"A regular Daiquiri has rum in it. A Margarita has tequila. I don't think there is much difference without the alcohol," Alicia answered.

Celia folded her hands and waited for her drink.

"Come on, Celia. It's our birthday." Alicia pushed the bottle towards Celia.

"Unh, Unh." Celia put her hand up.

Alicia was determined to convince her. She downed most of her drink leaving a small amount and holding it out to Celia. "Here, try a little bit."

"Is that supposed to convince me? I don't know where you're lips have been." They hadn't shared cups since they were toddlers.

Ruben chuckled and sipped his drink.

"I know where you're lips ain't been." Alicia finished her glass off.

Celia ignored her as she searched for the waiter and her Daiquiri. If she didn't acknowledge Alicia's jabs, then Alicia would find something else to talk about.

Ruben continued to enjoy the band, glancing at Alicia each time she took a swig of her drink. Alicia had finished a second glass when Ruben asked her to dance.

"We're going to the next floor," Alicia said scooting her chair back.

"I'll watch your drink," Celia responded before Alicia could ask.

Ruben held Alicia by the waist from behind as they walked off. They made an attractive couple even with him towering over her.

The waiter finally brought Celia's Daiquiri. She took a few gulps, wiped a spot in front of her, then set her drink atop a napkin.

Celia put her elbows on the table and cupped her chin as a jazz vocalist came to the stage.

The cinnamon-colored vocalist had a statuesque elegance that Celia couldn't describe. The burnt orange shrug she wore over a multi-colored wrap dress added to her commanding but subtle appearance. The vocalist stepped to the microphone and began to sing with such soulful intensity that Celia's eyes began to water.

"Hi, beautiful why are you so sad?" she looked up and a handsome mocha colored man in a tan suit stared back at her.

She took a napkin and patted her eyes. "Hello."

"You shouldn't be sitting here by yourself."

"I'm not alone. My sister and her friend are upstairs. They went to dance."

"Do you mind?" he gestured to the chair.

"No . . . no go ahead." She was overwhelmed with a sense of loneliness. "Have a seat."

He seemed relieved as he pulled the chair up next to her. "My name is Tyrese. Tyrese Munroe. And you are?"

"Celia. Celia Alexander." She extended her hand.

He took her hand and gently squeezed it. "It's a pleasure to meet you. What you drinking?"

"Daiquiri. Virgin."

"Want anything stronger?"

"No. I'm good." She hoped he wasn't looking to intoxicate her in preparation for a one night stand. He was at the wrong table for that.

"Can I at least buy you another one of those?"

"It's your money." She shrugged.

He ordered the drinks.

"What brings you to 'The Set'?"

"I guess you could say it was a birthday present."

"Today's your birthday?"

"All day." She nodded, smiling.

"Happy Birthday." He glanced down at her empty ring finger. She felt self-conscious without the wedding band on.

"What brought you here?" She hoped her voice didn't tremble.

"I own it."

"Yeah, right." She threw back her head and laughed profusely. He wasn't laughing with her.

"Oh, you're serious." Her cheeks warmed.

"Yes."

"I'm sorry. I didn't mean to offend you. I don't know what I was thinking. This is a nice establishment you have here."

"Thanks." He looked at the stage. "It took a long time to get it off the ground, but I'm definitely proud."

"What made you want to open up a jazz club?" Celia's curiosity was peeked.

"I didn't see a lot of options for entertaining the mature, discriminating adult in this area. I wanted to bring something with a more unique flavor. I kind of checked out a few spots of similar interest on the West Coast that offered 'jazz elegance' as I like to call it, made some major investments, connected with the right people and here we are now."

"That was fun." Alicia and Ruben came strolling back to the table. "If you thought this floor was nice, you should the second floor. It is decked out," explained Alicia.

Alicia realized Tyrese was sitting there. "Oh, hi." She poured another glass of Cristal and downed it before taking her seat. "I'm so thirsty. Dancing can take a lot out of you."

"What's up with you, Tyrese, man?" Ruben gave him a handshake and half hug as Tyrese stood.

"Chillin'." Tyrese sat back down.

"I take it it's your birthday too," he joked with Alicia.

"All day." She poured her glass half full.

"That's exactly what . . ." Tyrese stopped.

Alicia was paying him no attention as she locked lips with Ruben.

Celia was surprised too, for the way Alicia claimed not to be attracted to him.

"Are you originally from Detroit?" Celia asked Tyrese to cut the awkwardness.

"No, I was born in Houston. My mom moved up here many years ago after her and my father divorced. I stayed in Houston until I graduated from high school, then I moved up here to go to the University of Michigan on a football scholarship. You?"

"We were born and raised in Dearborn," Celia answered.

"Oh yeah? Did you like growing up here?" Tyrese inquired as his thick eyebrows rose in interest.

"It was alright. I've never lived anywhere else to know a difference."

The waiter brought the tab.

Ruben picked up the bill and choked. Tyrese plucked it from his hand. "Kenny, it's on the house," he told the waiter.

That got Alicia's attention. "Why you paying for all our drinks?" she eyed him suspiciously. "My sister is no ho." She was drunk.

Tyrese frowned, clearly shocked by Alicia's comment. He looked at Celia, then turned to Alicia stating, "I would never treat her like she was one."

"I'm just letting you know. Don't mess over my little sister. Anybody mess with her they got to go through me first. She's been through enough crap with you men already. You no good trifling men. Ain't none of ya'll worth the sperm you come from." She tried bringing her glass up to her mouth but couldn't hold her hand steady.

Ruben took the glass from her. "That's enough."

She snatched it back. "What cha mean enough? This man paid for a whole bottle and I'm gonna drink the whole bottle."

Ruben tried to wrestle the glass away. "Alicia you're drunk."

"I can be drunk. It's my birth . . . day."

Celia set the almost empty bottle on the floor between herself and Tyrese while they argued.

Ruben finally pried her fingers from around the glass.

"Fine! I have to pee anyway." Alicia stood and wobbled.

Ruben reached out to help steady her balance and Alicia slapped at his hands.

"I'll go with her," Celia volunteered.

"We should leave," Ruben said.

"Let me get her to the bathroom first." Celia hoisted Alicia's arm around her neck and dragged her towards the restroom area.

The line snaked around the corner.

Alicia looked up. "I told you they need more bathrooms." Her words continued to slur.

Celia was not about to drag her to the next floor. "Where are the elevators?" she asked Alicia.

"I don't remember."

Celia asked a few of the ladies standing in the bathroom line. Nobody seemed to know.

"Think you can make it up the stairs?" Celia asked her twin.

"I'll hold it."

"You'll hold it?" Celia questioned. She could barely understand any of the words coming out of Alicia's mouth.

"Yeah." She held her head up to talk. Her eyes barely open.

"You sure you don't want to go use it now? I'll help you up the stairs. I'm not carrying you. You need to put forth some effort."

"I can wait."

"Alright, we're going to get Ruben so we can leave."

"Ruben's a punk. He stole my drink."

"Okay, but he's our only ride home."

"What . . . ever," Alicia said as they slowly made their way back to the table.

Celia handed Alicia over to Ruben. He effortlessly swung her up into his arms and carried her out the club.

Celia turned to Tyrese apologizing, "She's not always

like that. She's a great person to be around when you get
to know her."

"Don't worry about it. Go get your sister home."

She turned and started walking away.

"Can I call you?" he asked.

She absently scribbled her cell number on a napkin,
too caught up in the moment to think, and rushed to
catch up with Ruben.

Alicia was laid out in the back seat when Celia got inside Ruben's Platinum Infiniti.

"Ruben, I'm sorry you had to see her like this. I don't
know why she feels the need to drink until she gets
sloppy. It's an ugly habit."

"I've seen her drunk before. Not quite like this, but
I've seen her drunk. What she is doing is out of control.
Sometimes I don't know what to do with her. I have
strong feelings for her, but I can't take her acting like
that."

Celia's heart skipped a beat for Alicia. He really cared
for her sister and Alicia was messing things up. Celia
wanted Ruben to stay around though. He was the first
man that Alicia respected even a little bit.

"Alicia feels the same about you too. She's just got a
problem."

He shook his head as he drove. "She's going to kill herself if she keeps drinking like that. She's self destructing.
I wish I could get through to her."

"You and me both."

They rode the rest of the way to Alicia's house in silence.

He pulled in the driveway and Celia held the back
door so he could get Alicia out. Ruben tossed her over his
shoulders.

"What the . . ." he looked at his hand as he held her
with one arm.

"What's wrong," Celia asked as they approached the steps to the house.

"She's wet," exclaimed Ruben.

"Oh, no." Celia jammed the key into the door and swung it open. They walked in.

Celia scrunched up her nose to a repugnant odor that reminded her of dirty diaper pails. "Do you smell that?"

"Yes, I do. I think Alicia did more that pee on herself."

"Oh my goodness," she covered her nose and mouth as the scent hit her and she recognized it. "Let's get her in the tub." Her voice was muffled through her hand as she shut the front door and rushed through the living room.

Ruben was already ahead of her as he gently dropped her in the tub. His dress shirt had wet streaks running down the side he had been carrying Alicia on. He held his shirt away from his skin and twisted up his face.

"I'll take it from here." Celia bent down by the tub and took off Alicia's shoes.

Ruben washed his hands in the sink.

"Are you leaving?" Celia asked.

"No, I want to stay until we get her into bed. I'll go make some coffee, while you get her in the tub. Maybe we can get her sobered up some." Ruben said solemnly.

Celia was grateful for the assistance, because she didn't know how she was going to get Alicia down the hall and into her room unconscious without him there. She also didn't know how Alicia would live this one down.

# CHAPTER TWENTY-TWO

Celia hesitated as she knocked on Alicia's bedroom door. Alicia's head must have been pounding after consuming all that alcohol.

She waited for a reply before entering.

Alicia mumbled, "Come in."

Celia sat a tray with saltine crackers and chamomile tea on the bed. "I didn't know what to give you for a hangover." She walked over to the curtains and pulled them open letting light stream into the room.

Alicia threw her hands over her eyes almost knocking the tray off her lap. "Can you please close those back?"

"Sure" Celia pushed them back closed.

Alicia looked at the tray, grimaced and put the tray on her nightstand. "I can't do nothing with that right now."

Celia shoved Alicia's feet over as she sat on the bottom of the bed. "Ruben called and said he was on his way . . . to check on you."

"Umm, hum." Alicia laid her head against the headboard and began to rub her temples.

"Alicia are you alert enough for us to have a serious conversation?"

"What about?"

"Your drinking. I think it's a little out of control." Celia had thought for a long time that Alicia needed to slow her love for the liquid poison down.

"What can I say? I like a good time. I'm a social drinker."

"Social drinker's don't pass out and loose control of their bowels."

Alicia stopped rubbing her temples and squinted at Celia like her eyes hurt. "I used the bathroom on myself?"

"You sure did." Celia felt bad for Alicia.

"In front of other people?"

"Yes."

"I don't remember that." She looked confused.

"You probably don't remember a lot of stuff that happened last night, but I can guarantee you did. I was the one that cleaned you up. Which I'm not to happy about I might add."

"Ughhhhhh." Alicia groaned.

Celia hoped it was a wake up call.

Embarrassment registered on her face. "Was Ruben there?"

Celia nodded her head. "You wet up his shirt."

Alicia gasped in horror. She covered her mouth and spoke, "No, I didn't!"

"It's not cool to get that drunk Alicia. It is not cool," Celia explained, shaking her head disapprovingly. "I don't mean to lecture you, but I had to say something."

Alicia stared blankly at the dresser mirror behind Celia's head.

"You remember when I first got here and I was so depressed that I couldn't think?" Celia waited for some kind of response from Alicia.

Her eyes went from the mirror to Celia's face. That was enough for Celia to keep talking. "Here I was over-whelmed with devastation. So much so that I didn't want to breathe. I didn't want to move. I could barely make it from the bed to the bathroom. And what did you do to help me in my time of grief? You pulled me out of the bed. You told me to get it together."

A small smile formed on Alicia's lips, but she didn't say anything.

Celia began speaking with her hands, moving them back and forth to get her point across. "You said I have two kids that need me to be strong. All I want to know is . . ." she paused trying to pick her words carefully, "Doesn't that same statement apply to you too? Don't you think you need to get it together? Is it necessary to get that drunk? Is the high you get from that alcoholic buzz worth it? What example is that for Taija?"

She fired questions at Alicia not expecting her to an-swer all of them, but to at least think about them.

Alicia tilted her head and twisted her mouth to the side. "If you want me to be real about it, I have to say I don't know. I don't even know anymore. I've been drink-ing so long that it's a habit. I don't get the same high I used to, not like I did back in the day." Her eyes glazed over. She seemed to be daydreaming about days long gone.

"You want to keep that kind of habit?"

Alicia shrugged and said bluntly, "The feel good feels familiar so I keep doing it."

"There is a verse in the Bible that says something like 'Don't get drunk on wine it leads to debauchery, but in-stead be filled with the Spirit," Celia quoted from mem-ory.

"I appreciate your quote from the Bible, but I don't know what debauchery is and there isn't anything wrong with my spirit." Alicia looked disinterested.

Celia didn't let Alicia's lack of enthusiasm deter her. "Debauchery means wickedness and . . ."

Taija poked her head in the room. "Hey mom, Ruben's here."

"Tell him to have a seat. I'm coming out in a sec." Alicia nudged Celia with her legs from beneath the covers. "Move. You're lying on the covers. I can't move until you move."

Celia rose up.

Alicia threw the covers back and asked, "Do you have any Tylenol? I'm all out."

"No I don't think I do, but I saw a bottle of Excedrin in the cabinet under the bathroom sink. You might want to look down there."

Alicia walked into her closet and pulled clothes from her rack. She threw the outfit she picked out over one arm and then fished through her dresser drawer.

Celia could tell by Alicia's puffed-up demeanor that the conversation about her drinking was headed to a dead end. She didn't want it to become an argument because she wanted to push her point. If the shoe were on the other foot, Alicia would have pushed it, but Celia didn't have the energy to force the issue; not with all the other drama in her life. She stepped around Alicia and went into the living room.

Ruben was sitting on the edge of the sectional flipping through one of the magazines he picked up off the coffee table.

She walked over and sat by him. "Good Morning."

"Morning," he said back. He looked tired and had dark circles under his eyes.

"Didn't sleep well I take it."

"Nah." He tossed the magazine with the pile of other magazines accumulating on the table. "How is she doing?"

"She's hung over."

"I bet she is."

"I tried to talk to her about her alcohol consumption before you came, but I don't think she is really listening. She let me talk, but I don't think she heard me."

He nodded with eyebrows scrunched, worry lines on his forehead.

Alicia cleared her throat. Celia and Ruben looked in her direction.

He stood.

"I'm so embarrassed." Alicia came and stuffed her face in his shirt.

He wrapped his arms around her. He held her tightly and placed his head on top of hers. "*Miaja*, you scared me." His accent was thick.

Celia felt like she was invading a private moment. "Do you two need to be alone?"

Ruben glanced over at her. "No. You should stay." He tried to pull away but Alicia held onto his shirt with her head still lodged in his chest.

"Alicia."

"I'm so embarrassed," she murmured again.

Celia didn't know what to say. She wasn't used to seeing Alicia humble and unassuming. Alicia didn't bow to no one, not even when she was in the wrong.

Ruben was able to get her to sit on the sofa with him.

"Can you open this?" Caleb brought in a jar of grape Smucker's jelly and held it towards Celia.

"Did you speak to everyone?" Celia asked her son.

"Good morning everyone." Caleb threw his hand up and waved.

Celia twisted the lid but it didn't budge. She turned the jar upside down and hit the bottom a couple times with her palm, giving it good whacks before trying to open it again. Either the lid was sealed tightly or she was weaker than she remembered because a jar of jelly shouldn't have been that big of a challenge. It still didn't budge and her hand was starting to hurt.

She gave up. "Ruben," she said in a pleading tone.

Ruben reached over Alicia and took the Smucker's jar from Celia. The sill instantly made a popping noise. Ruben handed Caleb the top and the jar. "Here you go little man."

"Caleb, whatever mess you create, you clean up," Celia said as Caleb left the room.

"Yes, Mom." He pattered to the kitchen.

"Oh my head is killing me." Alicia put her head on Ruben's shoulder.

"No, your drinking is killing you," Ruben stated flatly.

"Oh no, not you too," she moaned. "I said I was sorry about pissing on you. What more do you want?"

"I want you to stop drinking." Ruben's tone was even and firm.

Alicia lifted her head off his shoulder. "Fine. I will try not to drink as much. I won't drink until I pass out." She conceded.

"How about you stop drinking entirely?" he asked. His eyes set with determination as he stared at Alicia.

"Now you're asking for too much." She cut her eyes at him like he was asking her to give up breathing.

Celia sat in silence. She wanted to save Ruben from the verbal assault he was about to get, but didn't want to get caught in the crossfire. When Alicia was pissed, she spared no mercy. She would spit the ugliest words that popped into her head out her mouth and keep firing until she ran out of ammunition or whoever she was telling off decided to vacate the premises. It was like watching a rattlesnake rear back to attack its prey. Lethal and unrelenting.

"Maybe you didn't see how you were acting last night, but I did. We can't go anywhere there is alcohol being served without you drinking yourself under a table and I can't handle watching you act like that. I care too much." Ruben's face softened and looked like he was in agony.

Alicia sucked on her teeth. She was fuming.

"I won't be coming around anymore if you don't stop drinking." He jutted his chin out.

Alicia stood with attitude and began rolling her neck with her hands on her hips. "So what you are telling me is, you won't be with me if I don't do what you say? If I don't submit to your demands?"

He stayed seated as he tried to explain. "It's not like that."

"It is like that," Alicia raged.

"Okay then, if that's the way you want to take it." Ruben was starting to get mad as the veins in his neck began to pulsate.

"Well, I got news for you. No *man* has ever controlled me and no *man* will start now." She said the word man like it was a disease.

His jaw clinched and unclenched. "I don't want to control—"

She cut him off. "Shut up. Just shut up." Her words were curt. "Drinking has been my friend and comforter for a far longer time than you have. And to be quite honest, I get a bigger thrill from drinking than you probably could ever give me. I'm going to stick to what I know and if you don't want me just as I am . . . You know what you can do for me."

He stood knowing the answer, but asking anyway. "And what is that?"

"You can go buy a canoe with all that money you've been trying to buy me with and row your high yellow

Spanish talking Big Bird tail back to Puerto Rico." She went and held the door open.

He sucked air through his teeth and walked up to Alicia, "Call me when you calm down."

He left and Alicia slammed the door.

# CHAPTER
# TWENTY-THREE

"Mom, you know how you said I could talk to you about anything?" Kaleia asked as they walked up the sidewalk path to Dr. Malawi's office.

"Of course you can. You can talk to me and I promise to listen no matter what you have to say." This was the moment Celia had been waiting for. She hoped that Kaleia was ready to open up. She hoped that her daughter felt she confide in her and was comfortable enough to talk about her father's wicked ways. Then they could file a junction to keep Khalil at a distance. Celia would finally be able to breathe easier. She had come to the decision that he needed to be locked up. He needed to be kept from harming another child. He should never be able to put his nasty hands on somebody else's daughter.

Kaleia shaded her eyes to block the sun and stopped on the sidewalk. "I hate coming here," she confessed taking her lavender tote bag off one shoulder and placing it on the other.

Celia stopped with her. "I didn't realize Dr. Malawi was that bad."

"It's not Dr. Malawi. She is nice and all. I don't have anything to say. We spend an hour eating cookies and staring at each other while she asks me the same questions over and over again. It's boring. A couple of times she let me do my homework for session, but I don't need to come here to do math."

"I thought you might need someone to talk to outside of the family with everything that is going on. You haven't been saying much lately. Dr. Malawi . . . she is trying to make you comfortable."

"But I'm not comfortable. I will never be comfortable here." Kaleia waved her arms like she was frustrated.

"Kaleia, I'm sorry. I thought this was helping. You don't have to come back if you don't want to."

"I don't want to."

Celia and Kaleia began walking side by side again. "Then that's that. We have to go up and let her know you won't be back, but you can sit in the lobby. I'll go talk with her. Okay?"

"Okay. You won't tell her that I said I hate coming here will you?"

Celia squeezed her daughter's shoulder as they continued walking, "No, I won't tell her that you hated it. That will stay between you and me."

Celia thought about how far she and Kaleia had come and how much further they still had to go. Their relationship had been damaged but not destroyed. Celia held the door open as Kaleia walked into the building. She continued to steal glances at her beautiful daughter as they made there way down the hall to Dr. Malawi's office. Kaleia set her bag full of school supplies in the empty chair next to her. Celia walked up to the receptionist desk and typed Kaleia's name on the computerized sign-in board. She sat down and waited.

"Kaleia, are you ready?" Dr. Malawi came out to the lobby and asked.

"Can I talk to you in your office for a second?" Celia stood and walked towards her.

"Sure Mrs. Alexander I don't see why not. Come with me."

"I'll be right back," Celia told Kaleia who had pulled out a book and was writing in a notepad.

Kaleia briefly glanced up and nodded.

Celia stepped into the psychiatrist's office and waited until the door was closed before speaking. "We are going to discontinue your services."

Dr. Malawi seemed puzzled. "I'm sorry to hear that. I was just getting to know Kaleia."

"It's not your fault. I know you tried to get her to talk, but we can't force her to talk about something she doesn't want to share. Kaleia told me she wasn't getting anything out of therapy. I was hoping time with you would make it easier, but it's not working. I'm wasting money here, and seeing I don't have as much disposable cash as I use to, I think it's best we don't prolong the inevitable."

"I'm here to help, and obviously if it's not working then just like with any other medical services, you have the right to stop coming. Would you like for me to refer you to another psychiatrist?"

"That won't be necessary. It wouldn't matter who we went to. Kaleia doesn't want to talk about being molested. I have to come to terms with that. I should have asked her how she felt about getting therapy before I dropped her off in your lap. I automatically assumed you would be able to fix her, but it's not that easy. She's not like a car in need of a tune-up. She's a living breathing human being with a mind of her own. And evidently in her mind it is better that she remains silent, at least when it concerns her father or what he did. We are finally talking to each other, which is an improvement. I didn't think we would ever have a whole conversation again."

Dr. Malawi sat on the edge of her desk. "I've been doing this job for a long time and I find that each case is different. How one patient handles situations can be completely contrary to how another does. Everybody's coping mechanisms are unique. The only thing predictable about therapy is that it's unpredictable. Be mindful that it usually takes incest victims years to get over the trauma. It is great to know that you and Kaleia are communicating. That is a tremendous milestone. You would be surprised at the number of families that don't talk. Most of my business was created from families that didn't know how to or didn't want to communicate. If you find a need to continue on with therapy at a later date, please feel free to call me."

"I seriously doubt that will be necessary, but I appreciate the offer." Celia stopped with her hand on the door handle. "Can I ask you something before I go?"

"Certainly."

"Do you think that the pedophiles and sexual predators . . . do you think they can be cured?"

"I don't think they can be cured. It's not that simple. They can get better if they acknowledge that they have a problem and seek help, but it's just like with drug or alcohol addiction. They have to keep putting forth effort for a lifetime to manage the urges for whatever led to the destructive behaviors." Dr. Malawi looked at Celia curiously. "Why do you ask?"

"I guess I was wondering if I have to spend my life worrying that he will touch Kaleia again."

"That is a valid concern. I wish you well."

They walked back out to the lobby together. Kaleia still had her head in her notebook.

"Ms. Kaleia. From what I hear this is the last time I will be seeing you." Dr. Malawi addressed Kaleia.

"Yeah," Kaleia smiled shyly.

"Do you mind if I give you a couple things to take with you?" Dr. Malawi was holding several items in her hands.

"Unh, unh"

"This book is called *The Teen Trip*. This one is *I Know Why the Caged Birds Sing* by the very famous Maya Angelou. *A Daddy's Apprentice* is about a young girl's struggle because of incest and lastly here is a journal with a key for you to write all your personal thoughts." She handed over each book as she read the titles.

"I don't think I will be needing this one." Kaleia handed back *A Daddy's Apprentice*.

Dr. Malawi shook her head and insisted, "How about you keep it. It is a really good read and if you don't like it you can give it away or throw it the trash, but I want you to have it."

"Okay. Thank you." She stuffed the books and journal into her backpack with her homework.

Dr. Malawi touched Celia's shoulder. "My invitation to return, if need be, will remain open indefinitely."

Her commitment was honorable. Celia respected her for it. "I have your card if need be."

Celia turned to Kaleia as they left the building. "We got a little time to waste, before we go get your brother. Want to pick up those shoes you were eyeballing the other day at the mall?"

Her face brightened. "The baby blue Invisible Air Force Ones?"

"You got it." Celia's couldn't help but grin as they got in the car and headed to Lakeside Mall.

Celia could hear her phone ringing in her purse as she

drove down Highway 102, but she didn't have her ear set with her.

"Kaleia, can you reach inside my purse and answer that for me?"

"Sure." Kaleia pulled the phone out of her purse and flipped the phone open.

"Hello . . . she's driving right now can I take a message?"

Kaleia pulled the phone from her ear and asked, "Tyrese wants to know when a good time to call you back is?"

*Tyrese.* She had forgotten that she gave him her phone number.

"Tell him that I will call him back a little later," Celia said uneasily.

Kaleia relayed the message. "He said you don't have his number."

"It's on the caller ID."

"Mom, he wants me to write down a different number. He said he is leaving work shortly and wants to give you his home phone number."

"Get a pen out of my purse and write it down on the back of that car insurance bill envelope."

Kaleia took the information from Tyrese and wrote it down. She repeated the number back to him to make sure she had it right.

"Alright, I'll tell her." Celia could hear Kaleia say. "He said he is looking forward to your call. Mom, who is Tyrese?" Kaleia looked at Celia curiously as she ended the call and put the phone back in Celia's purse.

Celia knew that question was going to come, but she didn't know how to answer without it sounding bad. "He is an associate of mine."

"You work together?"

"No, not that kind of associate. Just somebody I know.

He isn't anymore special than the other people that call me."

Celia had never made a personal call to any man other than her husband.

"Go with the flow." She told herself as she dialed the number Kaleia wrote down earlier that day.

"Hi, Tyrese. It's Celia returning your call." She used her professional voice as she pulled a pillow from behind her back in bed and rested the pillow in her lap.

"I was hoping you'd call me back," Tyrese said warmly.

"Yeah."

"That's good to know. How's your sister?"

Embarrassment at how Alicia acted at the club rose up in her. "She is doing a lot better than she had the night you met her. That was ugly. How are things at the club?"

"They're good. Real good. Listen. Can, I take you out this weekend?" Tyrese got right to the point.

Celia played with the pillow, conflicted. "Well, sure . . . No, I can't."

She initially thought in would be a nice distraction before calling him, but as soon as Tyrese asked, the idea seemed less appealing.

"No?"

"I have to say no. My life is complicated. I'm married, my husband and I separated a few months ago and I want to move on. I need to move on, but I don't think moving on like this, the trying to date thing is for me," she explained.

Celia didn't know how much she wanted to share with Tyrese about her situation. "Although we aren't getting back together, my head isn't right. I'm not in any condition to even perpetrate like I 'm ready to date."

She didn't think she would ever be ready to date again, but she didn't tell him that.

"It's all good. I appreciate your honesty," Tyrese said.

She felt the need to explain her decision further. "I think you're a nice man, and under different circumstances, I would love to take you up on your offer, but I really need to decline."

"Well, I still hope to see you at the club again."

"You will as long as you keep playing live jazz." Celia smiled into the phone.

"I can assure you that we will keep playing live jazz," Tyrese chuckled. "You have a good night."

"You too," she responded, positive that she was doing the right thing.

Celia knew that starting a relationship, even a platonic one, was dangerous for the wounded. It was like putting an Ace bandage over gangrene. Decay had to be cut out, not covered up. Pain was synonymous with hurt; one could not exist without the other. She had a past full of pain to reconcile. Celia had to allow the hurt to heal from it. Nobody, including another man could give her the healing she needed. Nobody, but God.

# CHAPTER TWENTY-FOUR

There was a small hill of clothes on the floor next to the sleeper sofa in the basement. Celia picked up a pair of Caleb's jeans amongst the pile.

"Caleb you know better," Celia mumbled to herself.

She went on the hunt for more articles of his clothes. One pair of underwear was under the bed. A shoe laid along side the television cabinet. The other shoe was by the bathroom door. Fortunately for Caleb, that was the extent of his sloppiness, but she would still have to talk to him about being tidier.

She tossed the pair of underwear on top of the clothes she was taking to the laundry room and picked up the shoe by the television. She walked over to retrieve the other shoe from by the bathroom. There was water running behind the closed door.

"Caleb, you are getting too irresponsible," Celia spoke to herself again. She had a mind to walk down the street to his friend's house and make Caleb take care of his clothes and the bathroom himself. She wasn't raising up a lazy man.

She opened the door to find the water source and saw a man standing at the sink looking at himself in the mirror. He was naked. She quickly closed the door and stood there stunned for a second.

There was a man in the bathroom. There was a strange man in the bathroom. A naked strange man in the bathroom. She processed all of that, and then she knocked.

"Yeah," he said.

"Who are you?" She wasn't accustomed to anybody making themselves that comfortable without her knowing it.

"Phillip, Alicia's friend," he replied.

'Oh.' She dropped the shoe she was holding and went in search of Alicia. She found her in the kitchen making a sandwich. "Alicia . . . um . . . why is there a naked man in the downstairs bathroom?" Celia scratched her head then pointed her thumb at the doorway leading downstairs. "He said he was your friend."

"Yeah, that's Phillip," she said, grinning while she bit into her sandwich.

Celia looked her sister up and down. "What is he doing here?"

She hoped that man hadn't slept in the house without her knowing it. Alicia hadn't been bringing men home. Celia didn't expect for that to change now, not while she was living there. It was Alicia's home and she had the right to do what she wanted to do, but they were going to fall out if this is what she had to look forward to.

Alicia explained, "Phillip cleaned out the drain in the laundry. The water was running slow and he found were it was blocked at. He got dirty while he was down there. I told him that he was more than welcome to use the shower and laundry unit to get cleaned back up. I didn't know you were going downstairs, otherwise I would have told you."

"Don't you think I should have known there was a man in the house I didn't recognize no matter where he was at in it?" Celia was annoyed at her sister's lack of consideration.

"True. Promise it won't happen again," Alicia apologized.

"I'd appreciate that it didn't."

"You got to see him naked?" Alicia grinned lustfully biting her bottom lip. "Maybe I need to go down there. Check it out. Um, he gets me hot with his clothes on. I can't wait to see him without them. Rub my hands all over that dark chocolate smooth skin. Um . . . um . . . um."

"I don't want to hear that!" Celia exclaimed, shutting down the image in her head.

"I'll be back," Alicia said, dropping the crust from her sandwich onto the plate and sauntering from the kitchen.

"Where you going?"

"Downstairs." Alicia looked at Celia like she was asking a stupid question.

Celia debated whether she wanted to go back down and do the laundry or wait until later, after Alicia's friend was gone.

Before she could think about it too long, both Alicia and Phillip appeared from the stairs. He was dressed in a dingy white t-shirt and a ragged pair of jeans. Besides his being dark, Celia didn't see what was so special about him.

The doorbell rang as soon as they got into the kitchen.

"I got it." Alicia said, walking down the hall and leaving Celia with Phillip.

"So you're Alicia's twin?" He came up and reached behind her, grabbing an apple out of the fruit bowl. He stood a little too close.

"Yeah," Celia said flatly.

"You just as fine as she is." He grinned as his eyes stayed lowered and he talked to her chest.

Celia crossed her arms over, instantly feeling uneasy.

"Double my pleasure." He licked his black lips then bit into the apple.

Celia rolled her eyes disgusted. That kind of comment was old, straight out of high school old.

Alicia came back into the kitchen. "That was Mercedes looking for Taija. I told her they were down the street watching the boys play ball."

She looked from Phillip to Celia smiling. "Are you two getting acquainted?"

"I'm going to go clean my car out," Celia said. She didn't need to clean her car, but she did need an excuse to remove herself from their company.

"It was nice meeting you, Alicia's twin," Phillip's syrupy voice called out after she walked down the hall.

"Ugh." Celia had to shake it off. "Must be his car," she said to herself when she noticed the big bodied brown Buick sitting in front of the house.

She used her Dust Buster to clean invisible dust particles from beneath her seats while she waited for Alicia's friend to leave the house. When she had been over the Jag three times and no Phillip had emerged from the house, Celia decided to go to the auto store and pick up leather polisher for her seats. If he was still there when she came back, she would pull out the polisher and shine her leather until he left.

She breathed a sigh of relief when she drove back from the store and his rust bucket was gone. She couldn't wait to ask Alicia who dropped her on her head.

Alicia was folding the laundry that Celia had started to wash earlier. Jamie Foxx's *Unpredictable* CD was playing in the background.

"Did seeing Phillip naked scare you off?" Alicia asked joking.

"No, it was seeing Phillip with his clothes on that scared me," Celia said, picking up a shirt and starting to fold it as she sat next to Alicia.

Celia couldn't resist saying something about him. "Your friend is slimy."

Alicia set an article of clothing in the folded pile and responded, "He is not slimy. He is cool peoples. You just met him. I don't see how you can call him slimy."

Evidently Alicia wasn't looking at the same man Celia was.

"He was stripping me down with his eyes while you were answering the door."

Alicia shrugged, "He likes to flirt. He's harmless."

Celia didn't think he was harmless. "His lips are black. That is unnatural for a man's lips to be that black."

"A lot of real dark-skinned men have black lips. That don't mean nothing."

"You can't possibly be attracted to him." Celia scrunched her nose.

"Yeah, I am. You saw him in his work clothes. When he gets dressed up he is fine. Sexy and fine. And what I like even more than him being fine and sexy is he regular. An average round the way brotha."

"Ruben is regular." Celia wished Alicia and Ruben would work it out.

Alicia frowned. "No. Ruben is a busta."

Celia frowned too. "What! How can you say that about Ruben? Ruben was the best man I have ever seen you hook up with. He treats you like a queen. He respects you. Alicia, the man is in love with you."

Alicia turned her nose up. "Pul-lease. Ruben ain't in love with me. He is frontin'. Any man that nice is frontin'. He spent all his time trying to please me. Trying to wine and dine me all up and down Detroit. He paid to have my car fixed. He didn't even press up on me to give up the goodies. All the men I know want the goodies, unless they gay or frontin'."

Celia couldn't believe her sister's logic. Any man worth the time of day would show some affection that didn't revolve around sex. She wouldn't have a man that didn't treat her with respect. If they weren't twins, she would be sure Alicia was adopted by the way she was acting.

"Did you think that maybe he is nice because he genuinely thinks you are worth his time and he wants to show his affection? Ruben doesn't look at you like a man who is frontin'. Plus, Daddy is nice and does that kind of stuff for Mom and he's not fake."

Alicia was determined to prove her point as she folded socks and threw them in a laundry basket. "Dad probably had his fake and frontin' days too. The only reason Ruben is going out of his way to please me is so I will let my defenses down. Then he will try to control my every move. He would start expecting me to report to him for everything I did cause he had me sprung. You should be able to tell that from how he told me to stop drinking. That showed me all I needed to know about Ruben."

Celia wanted to shake some sense into her sister's head. It's no wonder she never had a relationship last more than a few months, with the exception of Taija's daddy. Eric and Alicia had lasted over a year, but their relationship was so dysfunctional, it shouldn't even count.

"Ruben wanted you to stop drinking because he was worried about how you act when you get some alcohol in you. He wouldn't have said anything if he didn't care. You can't want to trade that for Phillip. Phillip looks like he can't even spell respect let alone do it."

"I know what Phillip's about. There are no surprises with him. I like it that way. I like for a man to be real about his intentions. No assumptions. No expectations. No games. Ruben can find another female to front with."

It made Celia sad to see her sister miss out on a good man. "Alicia, someday you are going to regret throwing Ruben's affection and attention away. No matter what you say, I can tell you for sure that Ruben is not frontin' about how he feels about you."

"Celia, this world is a cruel place with everybody using one another for various reasons. Ruben included. If you had taken off those 'Perfect Christian' bi-focals you like to wear, you would have saw how your husband had been frontin' while he slept with your daughter."

Celia winced.

Alicia immediately apologized, looking at the wounded expression on Celia's face. "I'm sorry. That came out the wrong way."

Celia went cold. "Don't apologize. You were already thinking it. You just spoke it out loud."

Those words hurt. Hurt like she was jabbed in the heart with a steak knife. Hurt enough that she wanted to hurt back. Celia paused as she thought of a retort, but the angry words she'd come up with would only infuse Alicia to say something even more nasty until they both were spewing negativity for the sake of their egos.

"I should have known," Celia agreed with Alicia. "I think about that everyday, but I can't step back into the past and try to see Khalil's deceit. There are no perfect Christians and my eyes work just fine. I know this world is corrupt and jaded, but that doesn't mean I have to be corrupt right along with it. I do not believe that everybody is out to mistreat or use each other. People choose to do wrong. People choose to live jaded and everybody in this world ain't making that same choice. Ruben is a good man. You may not want to see it, but I know a kind heart when I see one. Ruben is a *good* man," she repeated for extra emphasis.

Alicia wasn't moved. "You have a right to your opinion. I have a right to mine and as far as I am concerned . . . Ruben is a busta."

Celia wasn't going to waste her breath anymore as she picked up a laundry basket of folded clothes and went to put them away.

# CHAPTER TWENTY-FIVE

Celia sat in the floor of her new condo and relished in the silence.

Quiet . . .

She welcomed the quiet of her own place. The space was half the size of her house, but it would do fine for the three of them. If she could survive living in Alicia's small home then the new place would be more than manageable. As much as she loved Alicia it was time to go. The fact that Alicia allowed a man, a naked man, to be in the home without considering Celia or the children spoke volumes. That conversation about Phillip yielded one conclusion. It was time for Celia and her children to move out. Alicia could live however she wanted. Celia and Alicia weren't going to be able to live together, especially not on a long term basis. Their views on life were too different. Alicia sought comfort in a bottle. Celia sought solace in the bible. Celia and Alicia found it difficult to respect their contrasting views without adding judgment. They needed to give each other space to grow at an individual pace. Celia had to focus on improving her own life and encouraging Alicia by her own actions. Stop talking faith and start walking it. She already had to live without one person she had loved wholeheartedly. She didn't want to loose Alicia too.

Celia had learned a great deal about her sister and learned even more about herself. She knew she couldn't walk through life blindly anymore. She knew she couldn't take people at face value. She knew that perfection was to be aspired yet not attained. And she knew most importantly, that regardless of how she tried to control her life, things would only go smoothly when she turned the power over to the Lord.

Celia had filed for divorce earlier that morning. She forced herself to accept it as a necessity for her transition. Surprisingly, it hurt to severe those ties. As much as she hated Khalil's actions, it was hard pressing pen to paper. Dissolving her marriage with a few strokes of ink.

She still dreamed about him and occasionally tingled in her sleep. Once when dreaming of them making love she awoke and spent the next three hours crying. Not only because he was unworthy of their intimacy, but also because she didn't want to share her love, her body, her joy with another man. She always believed that her and Khalil would mirror the love her parents had for each other. As she sat on the carpet she found herself wandering back to a time before she knew what Khalil was capable of.

*Celia dumped the remainder of collard greens into a container on the counter. She looked at the mountain of dishes and the buffet table full of food and didn't know how they would get it all cleared out and cleaned up before the reception ended and she hoped to have time to enjoy her parent's 40th anniversary party. She shouldn't complain though, she had volunteered for kitchen duty.*

"Ce-Ce? Give me those rolls on the counter by you," her Great Aunt Lessie requested, calling her by her nickname.

Her Great Aunt Lessie was one of her dad's three siblings that had driven up from Mississippi for the celebration. She hadn't seen any of them since she had gotten grown. They rarely came to Michigan because they didn't like the cold weather. Khalil and herself had never been to Biloxi together because Khalil believed they were still lynching black people in the Dirty South.

Celia pulled the rolls from between a baking pan of corn muffins and a plate of fried chicken. She wiped her brow with the bottom of the apron she wore. The kitchen of the hall in which they were having the celebration was hotter than an incinerator. She felt like a broiled chicken in all that heat.

"Whew." Celia fanned herself with her hand.

Her nice silk dress from Neiman Marcus was about to be a sweaty mess of material. She patted her hair. It's a good thing she let Taija practice her micro braiding technique, because that would have been a sweaty mess too.

Her cousin, Carmelle, Aunt Ernestine's daughter bumped into her carrying a pot of boiling water to the sink. Hot water splashed on the floor and Celia jumped back to avoid getting scolded.

Aunt Ernestine yelled, "You all better watch what you doing . . . and somebody hurry up and get that water before I fall and break my neck."

"I don't know where the mop is. Ce-Ce can you get it?" Carmelle asked as she poured the pot of water into the sink.

Celia stepped over the spill and went into the storage room to retrieve the mop. She broke a perfectly manicured nail as she pulled the mop from the wall holder.

"Ouch." She sucked on her finger as it began to bleed.

*There were too many people in the kitchen.*

*She quickly cleaned the water from off the floor as family members walked all around her with trays of food.*

*Uncle John, Celia's father's oldest brother, came into the kitchen. He was a large, extremely wide man. "Where's the aluminum foil at? I got four plates I need to cover and take with me."*

*"What you need four plates for? It's only one of you," Aunt Lee May asked. She was the only other family Celia's dad had that lived in Michigan and she was the most out-spoken of the bunch.*

*"Lee May, wasn't nobody talking to you. Don't you worry about how much food I got. Give me the aluminum foil before one of them folks out there see my stash and take my food."*

*"We only have one roll of foil left with everybody making themselves to-go platters. You would think we were at Ponderosa," Aunt Martha said. "John, you will have to bring your food in here for us to cover up your plates. Can somebody run to the store up the street and pick up a few more boxes of foil?"*

*"Ce-Ce?" Great Aunt Lessie called out.*

*She hoped she wasn't planning to ask her to be the one to go. She had been filling requests all night and thought it was somebody else's turn to be the running man.*

*"Can you go get the roaster with the turkey knuckles and dressing? That's my good pan and I don't want it to end up missing," Great Aunt Lessie stated.*

*"Where is your sister Le-Le at and why are you in here and she ain't? I tell you Otis should have put his foot up her tail when she was younger and she wouldn't be so messed up now," Aunt Ernestine complained as she shook her head. Her wig was on sideways.*

*Aunt Lee May piped in, "Leave my Le-Le alone. You just jealous because she got sense enough to be out there having fun* and your crusty behind back in here with us. And fix your wig. Your hair is on a gangsta lean."

Celia laughed to herself as she went into the dining area to get the roaster. She watched everyone dancing and scanned the room for her husband.

She saw Alicia dancing with their dad. Taija and Kaleia were in a corner talking with a few other relatives their age. Caleb had a huge slice of cheesecake in front of him that he was trying to cram into his mouth.

Celia stared longingly as she located Khalil twirling her mother around on the floor. A huge smile was plastered to his face.

Celia sighed. He looked so sexy out there.

She caught his eye and he winked at her. She mouthed "I love you" as she lifted the heavy roaster and went back into the kitchen. They still had a lot to finish.

Uncle John was walking out with his four plates covered as she walked in. She stepped aside and balanced the roaster on her hip as she waited for him to pass. There was no way they both were going to fit in the doorway together.

"Good night, Uncle John." Since he had his food, Celia knew he was leaving for the night.

She set the roaster down and peeled a lid off one of the Tupperware containers. She spooned what was left of the dressing into it. A hand went around her waist and Khalil peeked over her shoulder.

"Come dance with me," he asked.

"I can't. I have kitchen duty," Celia said, sadly scooping up dressing and slinging the spoon into the Tupperware bowl.

"Not anymore you don't." He untied the strap to her apron and removed the spoon from her hand. "I paid Whitley to take over your duties." Whitley was the great niece of Celia's mom, Patricia.

"How much did you pay her?" she asked as he escorted her from the kitchen.

"Fifty dollars."

Celia gasped, "Fifty dollars? You could have given Whitley a twenty dollar bill and she would have been happy with that."

"That's the smallest bill I had on me," he explained. "Besides, you my lady, are worth every little dime."

He pulled her onto the dance floor.

"I feel so special." She kissed him softly as the crowd seemed to disappear and she focused on being in his arms. Celia locked her fingers around his neck and bumped her newly bruised finger.

"Ouch." She put the finger in her mouth.

"What happened?" He frowned.

"I got a boo-boo." She pouted showing him her index finger.

"Awww, my poor baby. You want me to kiss it and make it better?"

"Yeah," she said in a little girl voice as she continued pouting.

He kissed her fingertip, then slid her whole finger into his mouth gently sucking on it. He was heating up the core of her insides. She pulled her finger out of his mouth.

"Stop that. You're making me horny," she joked.

"Oh, I would never want to do that." He feigned innocence.

"You're funny."

The song, "Forever My Lady," by the male group named Jodeci, began playing over the speakers.

"Oh, Khalil, I love this song," Celia said, encircling his neck as they swayed to the music.

"Look at them." Khalil gestured to her parents who were also on the floor slow dancing cheek to cheek.

"You think we'll be like them, still in love, on our 40th anniversary?"

"No doubt about it, I couldn't live without you if I tried.

*You are forever my lady." He kissed her, slowly drinking in the moistness of her lips and they continued swaying.*

Celia popped back into the present and looked at her bare condo. She looked at her bare wedding ring finger. She stood up brushing wrinkles from her clothes.

No. She would never feel like that again. She would never let a man get close enough to love her again. She would never let a man touch her or her daughter. Not knowingly. No, not never.

# CHAPTER
# TWENTY-SIX

There was a twenty car pile up on the expressway and Celia was stuck in traffic. A car jam stretching three miles long. Her car hadn't moved at all for over fifteen minutes. She knew because she kept looking at her watch. The radio said there was at least one casualty. They were still in the clearing stages. Celia sent up a silence prayer for the family of that victim.

She glanced at her watch again. Kaleia had been let out of school five minutes ago and Caleb would be getting out in twenty minutes. She wasn't worried about Kaleia 'cause she knew to wait, but Caleb was another matter all together. He would be running to the main office and ringing her phone off its clip as soon as he stepped out the building and didn't see her car.

Maybe she should call his teacher and have her keep him in class until she could get out of traffic.

She looked at her watch again as the car inched forward a few feet. At least they were moving. She strained to see over the other cars; to see if the exit sign was near.

She decided to go ahead and call. There was no way she'd make it in time.

She put her earpiece in and requested Greater Grace Elementary on the voice activated system.

"Can I have Ms. Wilkes room?" she asked the office secretary.

"I believe she is getting some of the children on the bus. Would you like her voicemail?"

"Yes, please."

Celia waited while she was transferred to voicemail. She checked her watch yet again. "Hello, Ms. Wilkes. This is Mrs. Alexander, Caleb's mother. I am stuck in traffic. If you could keep Caleb in your room until I get there I would greatly appreciate it. The time is now 3:20. I should be there in about fifteen minutes. Please give me a call on my cell phone if you have any questions."

She set her phone in the clip on her visor and rest her head on the driver's side window as traffic inched forward.

Her phone rang.

She unclipped it and checked the caller ID.

"Hey Justice, how are you doing?" Celia asked.

"I'm blessed. The question is how are you?"

"I'm pressing through," Celia said with honesty.

"Celia, I have Monique on the other line, hold on while I click her in."

Celia listened to the double click of the phone.

"My Sista in Christ, we miss you at church. We want you to know you are loved despite whatever you are going through," Monique said.

A small smile crossed Celia's face. She hadn't been back to the church since her and Khalil's altercation. Celia was too ashamed of her behavior to go back.

"You are a divine daughter of the highest king, don't

let the devil have the victory. We just wanted to let you know we are here, and when you need to talk without fears of judgment, please call one of us. You don't have to press through by yourself," Justice said.

Celia phone beeped as another call came in. "Somebody's on my other line. Ya'll hold on."

"Mrs. Alexander?"

"Yes. Please hold for a second" Celia said clicking back to the other line. "Justice . . . Monique. This is my son's teacher. I'll have to get back with you."

"We're still praying for you," they said in unison before Celia clicked the phone.

"Are you still there?" Celia asked.

"Yes, this is Ms. Wilkes returning your call."

"Thanks, were you able to get Caleb? I didn't want him worrying when he didn't see the car."

"Your husband picked him up half an hour ago."

"He did?" A sense of dread covered her.

"Yes, he came to my class and got him. Caleb was very happy to see him."

"Oh . . ." she said flatly, "Thanks for letting me know."

She hung up and quickly dialed Kaleia's school with trembling fingers. She misdialed twice before getting it right.

"Could somebody go see if Kaleia Alexander is standing outside by the front entrance of the building? This is her mother and I am running late to pick her up." Classical music began to play as they put her on hold. She prayed, "Lord, let her be there. Please Lord, let her be there."

Traffic was still inching forward but it seemed to not be moving at all.

Celia hollered at the cars in front of her. "What's taking so long? I have to get off this expressway."

The person on the other line came back to the phone.

"I'm sorry, there is not a student named Kaleia Alexander standing at the front entrance."

"Are you sure? She is light brown, about five two, and petite. She is very petite. And her hair is dark brown . . . shoulder length."

"I'm sorry, ma'am. There is no one at the front entrance that fits that description."

"Okay," Celia inhaled deeply. "Thanks anyway."

She had to get to that school and check for herself.

Laying her hand on the horn she yelled, "For God's sake move!"

The couple in the gray car on her driver's side stared at her like she had lost her mind as they conversed about her. The driver of the blue sedan in front of her flipped her off. She didn't know what she was doing. Shouting at traffic wasn't going to make it move any faster.

"Don't panic. Kaleia probably went to the bathroom. That's why she wasn't where she was supposed to be," Celia tried to convince herself.

The only thing to do was wait.

"Alright, Lord, you're word said don't worry about life. So you are going to have to help me, because I can't stop worrying." She closed her eyes and tried to relax.

She was still practicing a breathing technique with her eyes closed when the car behind her honked their horn. Traffic had picked up speed and she was holding up a lane. The car that had just honked at her pulled alongside her, mouthing obscenities through the closed window before whizzing down the expressway.

Celia punched the gas and veered off at her exit. She flew through yield signs and barely paused at stop signs. The jag screeched to a halt in front of the junior high and she went running up the steps two at a time.

Kaleia was no where in sight and the building was void of other people. She pulled at the front entrance door, but it was locked. Celia pressed her face to the glass of the entrance. There wasn't anybody visible in the school that she could see.

"This is not happening," she said as she walked back to her car. The driver's side door was wide open and the keys still in the ignition. "I'm trippin'."

She gunned the Jag and headed to her old house. It was barely a five minute drive. She used the garage door opener as she pulled into the driveway.

The Durango was gone.

Celia went through the side door inside the garage and entered the house not expecting to see the kids, but wanting to make sure their clothes weren't missing.

Celia charged into Kaleia's bedroom and flung open her closet door. She combed the racks inspecting every outfit that she knew belong there; that should be hanging in the closet. She opened the totes on the bottom shelves and checked her dresser. There was no rhyme or reason to her search. Celia went down to Caleb's room and inspected his closet and drawers in much the same way. There wasn't anything missing in his room either.

Kaleia had a key to Alicia's. Celia hoped that maybe he had dropped them off over there. Her cell phone was still attached to the clip in her car. She used the house phone in the guest room to dial Alicia's number.

No answer.

That didn't mean anything. The kids were always letting the phone go to voicemail, especially if they were in the room listening to music or Caleb was in the basement playing his games. Taija wasn't there. She hadn't gotten out of dance practice yet. Alicia was still at work. Who was she fooling? Khalil wouldn't purposely take the kids to her sister's, especially not with what was going on. That would be the last thing he willingly did.

She dialed his cell phone and it automatically went to

voicemail. Evidently he either was on it or had shut it off. She didn't want to leave a message. Not yet anyway.

"Where are you at Khalil?" Celia talked to the air.

The master bedroom's door was slightly ajar. The scene of her worst nightmare. The room that ended her blissful life. It represented evil beyond measure. She would rather drink a gallon of battery acid than step into that room. She didn't want to rehash memories subdued in the back of her mind, but she knew she had to.

She pushed it open with her fingertips and looked inside from the doorway. It looked the same as it had on all the days she came home from work. It even smelled the same. The scent of plumeria hung in the air. Instead of walking into that closet as she had planned, she walked to the nightstand. Her NIV Bible was still sitting atop the ebony wood furniture. She picked it up and flipped to the index where she found the word fear. Isaiah 41:10.

Taking a deep breath she began to read aloud to combat the heavy palpitating of her heart, "So do not fear, for I am with you; do not be dismayed, for I am your God. I will strengthen you and help you. I will uphold you with my righteous right hand. All who rage against you will surely be ashamed and disgraced, those who oppose you will be as nothing and perish. Though you search for your enemies, you will not find them. Those who wage war against you will be as nothing at all. For I am the Lord, your God, who takes hold of your right hand and says to you, do not fear. I will help you."

Celia closed the Bible and held it to her chest as she calmed. "I hear you Lord. I hear you."

Headlights.

She had never been more overjoyed to see a pair of headlights as Khalil's Durango pulled into the driveway.

It was past ten at night when they finally showed up.

She had done everything she could imagine to stay busy.
Busy doing nothing. She spent time meditating. Then she
rearranged the closets in all their rooms and cleaned invisible dust from countertops. After awhile she turned
on the television in the family room. Watched reruns and
old movies. Dozed in and out of sleep. She didn't want
her mind wandering. Imagining the worse.

She stood at the driveway door apprehensive as Caleb
jumped from the back seat.

"Hi mom," Caleb greeted her.

"Are you okay?" she asked Caleb, giving him the once
over. She inspected him from head to toe, then made him
turn around and checked his backside. The only thing
different on him was the new Piston's cap covering his
head.

"Mommy, stop." He pulled out of her grasp.

She wasn't listening though as Kaleia approached the
door. She had gotten out of the passenger side after talking with her father for a moment.

"Now, are you okay?" Celia asked, looking for any
sign to the contrary.

"Yeah." Kaleia gave her a puzzled look.

"Are you sure?"

It wasn't like her daughter had been forthcoming with
information before now.

Kaleia laughed at her. "I'm good. Can I go upstairs and
get my MP3 Player?"

"Go ahead."

Caleb rattled off excited as they walked thru the kitchen. "We got to sit courtside this time. I could see everything. Those players are really tall up close. I mean really,
really tall. Mom, you should have seen Big Ben. He
dunked and it was off the hook. He was killing 'em on
the court. We had so much fun. I'm so happy Daddy took
us."

"I'm glad you had a good time," Celia said calmly, as she fought the anger at Khalil rising in her.

"Are we staying here?" Caleb asked with hopeful eyes.

"No, we're not. How about you go find some clothes to take with you?"

Celia looked at Khalil, because she didn't want to see the disappointment in Caleb's eyes. She could see Caleb turn and head up the stairs out of the corner of her eyes.

She lifted her hand to slap Khalil. He caught her wrist before it touched his face.

He pulled her to him and whispered close to her ear, "Quite the temper you have developed. Perhaps that ignorant sister of yours is rubbing her bad habits off on you?"

The warm air from his breath might as well had singed her skin. She snatched her arm from his hand and hissed, "What's wrong with you? What are you trying to prove? You didn't think I deserved a call after you decided to take the kids?"

"You didn't think it was a priority when *you* took the kids?," he countered as he walked to the other side of the kitchen island.

"Are you thirsty?" He reached into the refrigerator and poured himself a glass of juice.

"You've got to be kidding me." She glared at him.

"I don't know if you noticed, but the kids were happy to be with me," he said putting the pitcher back in the refrigerator. "I'm done entertaining your delusions. Either you come home and we try to pick up the pieces, or you send my kids back to me. There are no other options. Take it or leave it."

"And if I leave it?"

"Then you leave them . . . with me. I will do whatever it takes to get my children back in this house. Whatever it takes, Celia." Khalil's cold gaze scared her.

He tossed that ultimatum at Celia and she had nothing to throw back. He could forget about her compiling. He may be willing to do whatever it took to get their kids back with him, but she was willing to do anything necessary to keep him away.

Kaleia came into the kitchen with her head set on as she lip-synced to her music. Caleb followed behind her with his duffle bag in hand.

He dropped the bag on the floor sulking. "I don't want to go. Daddy can I stay with you?"

Khalil straightened his son's cap on his head. "Caleb, you will be back home before you know it. I promise you that. Me and your mom are working it out."

# CHAPTER TWENTY-SEVEN

Celia listened to the vice president, Mitchell Paulson, drone on about cost analysis, projections and marketing strategies as she started doodling on the annual report given to her earlier. Her body was in the conference planning for the future of the Detroit division of the company. Her mind was planning for the future of her family.

Khalil and his ultimatum were foremost in her thoughts. The kids had three more days of school and she was on edge every time she dropped them off, afraid that Khalil would make good on his threat to take the kids and keep them. She felt powerless. Powerless and trapped.

The kids obviously had little problem moving back in with their demented father. Celia tried to convince herself that maybe she should do the same; reside with Khalil and keep a close eye on his actions. She could sleep in the guest bedroom because sleeping with him was not something she could stomach. She could do it for the sake of the children. Then she wouldn't be constantly on guard.

Who was she fooling? Her guard would stay up as long as Khalil had breath in his body and his limbs were moving. She would never be able to let her guard down. Even if Khalil never attempted to touch Kaleia again, he was still capable of molesting another parent's child may have already molested other children become somebody else's worst nightmare.

"That concludes our meeting today. I am excited about the direction in which this division is heading. We need to continue putting forth exceptional efforts to exceed our local goals and move ahead of the competition becoming number one in production of alarm systems." Silver haired, wiry Mr. Paulson turned off the Power Point Presentation.

All the directors filed out of the conference room and Celia headed back to her office.

"Celia," called Shannon from behind her.

Celia stopped and turned. "Hey Shannon, how are things going?"

"Great. I have so much to tell you. Come to lunch with me so I can bring you up to par."

"I'm not—" Celia hesitated.

Shannon cut in pleading with her blue eyes at Celia, "We haven't been out to eat or out at all for that matter, since we were in Florida."

The Florida trip was four months ago and Celia hadn't been spending time with any of her co-workers.

Celia gave a half-smile surrendering. "Where are we going to eat?"

"Friday's of course. That is my favorite restaurant." Shannon stopped at her office door. She glanced at her watch. "We can leave at about 11:30 to beat the lunch crowd. Otherwise, we will be waiting all day for our food to make it to the table. How about I meet you downstairs at around that time? We can take my car."

"Works for me," Celia agreed and then turned the corner to get on the elevator

"So who died?" Shannon asked as she cut her medium well steak into tiny bite sizes.

"Excuse me?" Celia asked, confused, as she squeezed a lemon quarter into her raspberry tea.

Shannon jogged her memory. "The death in your family. You took time off a while back because somebody passed. I was asking who it was."

Shannon speared a piece of her steak and savored the taste.

"Oh that. Well there wasn't an actual physical death," Celia confessed. "More emotional. I'm going through a divorce and certain things transpired that took their toll on me. I couldn't focus. I wouldn't have been any good at work. I'm still trying to bring myself up to full speed so I can adequately do my job the way I'm suppose to." Celia popped a shrimp into her mouth.

Shannon sipped her root beer. "You're getting a divorce? Your husband is very handsome and he looked like he was very much in love with you. Especially at the Christmas party. He couldn't keep his eyes or hands off of you. I remember the day of the award ceremony. You were homesick. I assumed you wanted to get back home to your man."

Celia remembered. "I was homesick. Very, very homesick. But that was before I knew what I was going home to."

"Did you catch him with another woman?" Shannon asked.

"No. I've gotten that question before. I think that is an automatic assumption when people break up. It's much more complicated than that. I really don't want to get into the specifics. At least not regarding how it happened." Celia bit into her garlic potatoes, surprised she still had an appetite. Usually when she thought about her failed marriage, she found it hard to eat. Maybe she was getting better at accepting her circumstances.

"Wow." Shannon looked astonished. "That goes to show you that no relationship is guaranteed to last. People change and grow apart all the time. I'm glad I never married. I never had the desire to marry. It's heaven in the beginning and hell in the end. That's a roller coaster I can do without riding. I learned from my parents' marriage. My father cheated on my mom and she put up with it for twenty years. She waited on him hand and foot. Made excuses for every time he went missing. Then he left her for a female younger than all three of his daughters. Then on top of that he took our mother to court to fight alimony. He said he had to pay for his new family and that mom needed to get a job and take care of herself. It's a good thing we were all adults when that happened, because he probably would have fought paying child support too and left my mom to fend for herself and five children."

Celia gulped her raspberry tea.

Shannon continued, "My father treated my mom so bad after they separated, that half the kids stopped talking to him. It took our mother years to get over it. She had taken all kinds of crap from our father only to have him act like she was nothing in the end. That was devastation for her. I knew at that point I would never marry and have that happen to me," Shannon said frowning.

Celia twirled her straw inside her glass as she watched the ice cubes clash against one another. "I loved being married. I loved having Khalil. We did family activities together and I was never overtly disrespected. I lived for my family. I will admit that things are very strained between Khalil and me now. Extremely ugly." Celia bit on her bottom lip thinking. "I look at him and feel all this disdain. I used to love him with a passion and that has dwindled."

Celia ate another fork full of potatoes, washing it down with her tea.

"He can't be the man I married. I want to ask him, 'Who are you and how did I end up sleeping with you all these years and still not know you?' I used to love Khalil like I loved living, and now that's gone. When I look at him or hear his name, I feel anything but love. I feel anger and sadness and contempt, but no love. I remember that I used to love him but I don't feel it at all."

"I'm sorry that you had to go through that."

"Me too, but let's change the subject. I didn't come to lunch to be depressed. Tell me something good. You said you had news. What's going on in your life?" Celia waved her fork.

A huge grin appeared on Shannon's face. "Well . . . You know how SecureTech has been kicking tail in profits?"

"Right."

"We are opening up two international divisions this year. One in Tuscany and the other in Sydney, Australia."

Shannon pushed her plate to the side as she bubbled over with excitement. Her blonde hair bounced as she spoke. "I get to head up the Tuscany operations. I'm talking my own company car with a thousand dollar a month car allowance, a quaint little villa already paid for and so many perks that I will be sitting like a fat happy rabbit until I retire."

Celia shared in her joy. "That is exciting. I've only been to Tuscany once, but now I'll have an excuse to go back. You are going to love living there. It's nothing like American culture. I don't think they have Friday's restaurants in Tuscany. How are you going to survive?"

Shannon lifted her eyebrows in mock surprise. "They don't have Friday's in Tuscany? Well that's going to have to change."

Celia burst out laughing. She took a sip of her raspberry tea and laughed again. Tea went down her windpipe and tears sprang to her eyes. She patted her chest between coughs and laughs.

"Are you okay?" Shannon looked worried. She stood and came around the table.

"Sit," Celia coughed out with a raspy voice as she waved Shannon back to her seat and took several long breaths. "Detroit's division of SecureTech is not going to be the same without you," Celia said sincerely. She wished she hadn't secluded herself. She missed out of so much because of it.

Shannon squawked at her, "I won't be missing Detroit. No offense."

"None taken."

Shannon had never made it a secret that she didn't care for the Motor City.

"When do you leave?"

"Middle of July."

"July? That's right around the corner. Shannon, I wish you the best of luck."

Shannon smiled and picked up the dessert menu.

"How about we split a chocolate brownie with ice cream?" she asked.

"Um . . . Sounds like a plan."

Celia sat back and listened as Shannon shared more plans for her life and for once in a long time, Celia was distracted from her own problems.

# CHAPTER
# TWENTY-EIGHT

Alicia dropped the heavy box onto the bedroom floor of Celia's recently purchased condo. Both sisters and their children were trying to get the new place organized. "Tell me again why you have me helping you move furniture on a Sunday morning, instead of your being at church?"

"I did go to church. I watched T.D. Jakes preach this morning at 7 a.m." Celia bent down and used the box cutter to open the box Alicia had brought into the bedroom.

"You know that ain't the same thing," Alicia said, standing and doing nothing.

Celia pulled her comforter set from the box. "How would you know whether it was the same? You only go to church when I beg you to."

"I'm not church bound like you are. Church is a big part of you."

"Wrong. God is a big part of me. Church is where I fellowship."

"Yeah, when you decide to go back."

"I will go back when I am ready to go back. Now we have to put this bed together."

"Fine. It's your soul."

"Why are you worried about my soul instead of your own?"

"I don't have a soul." Alicia twisted up her face.

"You can keep playing if you want to. Stand behind the headboard." Celia pushed the bed frame up to the headboard.

"And explain to me again why the movers didn't set all your furniture up yesterday?" Alicia questioned as Celia used her fingers to screw her headboard to the bed railing. It was the forth time Alicia had questioned her actions.

"As I said before, it was late when they got all the furniture in here. It was after nine at night. The movers were tired. I was tired. They said they could come back on Monday to set everything up, but I don't want to wait."

She almost had it tight even without tools. "Alicia, hold the headboard up. You're letting it lean."

Alicia pressed her body between the wall and the headboard as Celia made demands from beneath the bed.

"Almost got it." Celia dug her nails around the screw washer and gave one last turn.

Celia rolled from under the bed and surveyed her handiwork. "Not bad if I do say so myself."

Celia looked around her new bedroom to see what they would conquer next. She pointed to the dresser. "Let's get that over to this wall."

Alicia looked from where the dresser was to where Celia wanted it to be. "Oh heck naw. I'm not moving nothing that big. I'm here for light duty only. Dishware, clothes, maybe an occasional television, like the thirteen inch that Caleb has; I'll pick those up. The dresser ain't gonna happen. I just got my nails done." Alicia admired her nails with their glistening rhinestones and butterflies.

"I thought you said you were bringing Phillip with you to help," Celia said, although she was happy that he didn't come.

"He said he had to go pick up his boy from Jackson and he didn't know what time he would be free. They had business to go take care of. Besides, you didn't want to see him over here," Alicia said.

"You're the one that said you were bringing him. I don't have to want to see him and I don't have to like him; that is your friend. I respect your right to choose. No matter how bad the choice is," Celia responded as she tried to push the walnut dresser by herself. She got on her knees and shoved her weight against it, but it didn't budge.

"You want me to call the kids in here to help with that?" Alicia asked as she lay back in the chaise lounge watching Celia struggle.

Celia stood breathing heavy. "I'll leave the dresser where it's at. Let's do something simple like hang curtains. Besides, the girls have all those boxes of kitchenware to unpack."

"Why is it again that you bought all new furniture, appliances and decorating items when you have a house filled with the same stuff?" Alicia took a box cutter and opened a packet with one chenille curtain panel.

Celia came and snatched the box cutter out of Alicia's hand. "What are you doing? You don't need a box cutter for plastic. You're going to cut into the fabric."

"Sor . . . ree." Alicia pulled the panel from the bag and examined it for cut marks. "As I said before, why did you buy all the stuff when you have it already?"

Celia sighed as she opened the other packet with her cranberry chenille panel to accent her saffron color scheme.

"That's Khalil's furniture now. I'm starting over. I need new memories to go with my new life. Khalil doesn't even know I have this place. At least I hope he doesn't know. It would have looked awfully suspicious for me to go take furniture out of the house to put in your place. Khalil would have been all over that like a hound dog sniffing out blood."

Celia had pulled close to twenty-five grand from her 401k plan to fund the move into her condo. Her retirement monies weren't exhausted, but taking the money out put a nice dent into her savings. She didn't want to think about the penalties she would have to pay at income tax time.

"Mom, I'm done hanging up my clothes. What else do I need to do?" Caleb looked pitiful as he walked into the bedroom. He had been sulking since they got to the condo. Celia had explained that things would get better once he got used to their new place.

"How about you help your sister and Taija in the kitchen?" Celia suggested to him.

He sloshed off with his head held low, like he had lost his best friend.

"What are you going to do when Khalil finds out where you live?" Alicia asked.

"I guess I will cross that mountain when I get to it." Celia was playing it by ear. Since the kids were out of school for summer vacation, she didn't have to worry about Khalil snatching them up expectedly. When they weren't with her, they were with Alicia or her parents. Celia and her mother barely talked, because Patricia still believed Khalil was innocent of wrongdoing, but Celia knew her father would keep Khalil away from Kaleia and Caleb. Granted it had only been two weeks, but everything seemed to be going alright without incident.

When Khalil called on her cell phone, Celia would let

the kids talk to him. She didn't tell the kids they were moving into the condo until the morning of the move, to keep them from accidentally telling Khalil. It was a small sacrifice when she considered the other option.

"Hand me that curtain rod by your leg," Celia asked Alicia.

"Don't you need to iron those first before you hang them up?" Alicia said as she bent over on the chaise lounge and picked up the rod from the floor.

Good. Alicia had changed the subject. Khalil wasn't a conversation allowed in her new space.

"No, I'll use my steamer," Celia said

Alicia inspected the room from the chaise. "It's starting to look real elegant in here."

"Yeah, it's starting to look like a home," Celia said and smiled.

# CHAPTER
# TWENTY-NINE

Celia placed the bag of Chinese take-out that she had just gotten on the kitchen counter. Celia and the kids had fallen asleep after moving and unpacking. It was nine at night when they woke up hungry. Celia wasn't cooking that late and she had a craving for some egg rolls. Kaleia and Caleb opened up each container and began spooning fried rice, sesame chicken and beef with broccoli onto paper plates. They were missing the egg rolls. Celia checked the receipt.

It was on the list.

The doorbell rang.

"Must be the delivery guy with our egg rolls. Kaleia could you fix my plate while I go answer the door?" Celia pattered to the door barefoot. "I knew I was missing egg rolls," she swung the door open saying.

The one person she least wanted to see stood before her.

"Khalil," she said with her mouth in a straight line.

"Celia," he said, equally unenthused. "Can I come in?"

"No. I see it didn't take you long to track us down.

What do you want?" she said, crossing her arms as she stood in the doorway.

"Daddy!" Caleb hollered, excited as he rushed to the door.

Celia stopped him with her arm. "Caleb, go eat your food."

"No. Caleb you can stand right there."

Celia tilted her head and glared at Khalil.

"This is going to be a grown folks conversation," she said, making her words clear to both Khalil and Caleb.

Caleb could see the tension between his parents and went back into the kitchen.

"Khalil, why are you here?" Celia asked.

His eyes burned with anger. "I should have been told before that you were moving into this condo. You keep doing things behind my back. Things that involve our children. Why do you insist on acting like I don't exist?"

"Because, as far as I am concerned, you don't exist," her voice was laced with disdain.

"I'm sorry to hear you say that." He pulled a paper from his pants pocket. "I got your papers. The divorce papers." He threw them at her feet.

Celia looked down but didn't pick them up.

"You played your last card, Celia. Serving me with papers wasn't very smart on your part. But that's okay, you can divorce me if you want to, but you can't keep my kids. I'm taking them with me back home tonight."

"And you thought I was going to be okay with that? I'm not going to let you come in here. You can't have my kids, you pervert. I'm not giving them to you. So unless you plan on going through me, I suggest you leave my premises." Celia stood erect and steadied her weight in case he did try to move her.

"Fine. If that's the way you want to play it." He grabbed her, penning her arms to her side and lifted her up.

"What are you doing?" she shouted as she tried to free herself from his grasp.

"I'm going through you," he said with a determined scowl as he dropped her on the floor.

He rushed into the kitchen, while Celia picked herself up.

"You can't do this," she said running behind him.

Khalil ignored her. "Kaleia . . . Caleb, get your shoes on and go get in my vehicle. We're going home."

Both kids sat at the kitchen table wide-eyed. "Let's go," he said firmly.

They scooted out of their seats and scurried to the hall closet like scared mice.

Celia used all her weight to shove him back as he walked towards the doorway.

"Stop . . . Stop. You can't do this," she cried as her feet slid on the floor from him continuing to walk.

He was much stronger than she was, and no matter how much force she used, he was still going to pass her.

"Watch me," he said, looking at the open door and not at her.

Kaleia and Caleb stood staring at them fight from the dark outside doorsteps. Celia ran and shut the front door, leaving the kids standing outside.

"Please, Khalil, you don't want to do this." She tried to barricade herself against the door and get him to listen to reason.

"I'm done. Celia, I'm done playing the nice guy with you." His voice boomed with rage. It echoed off the walls as his eyes pierced a hole right through her.

Celia flinched. She had never heard him raise his voice at her before.

Khalil shoved her aside and threw the door open. He wasn't going to listen to anything she had to say. He stalked out of the condo and Celia ran to her bedroom.

She dug underneath her bed and tossed the gun case on top of her mattress. She quickly put the code in and opened the gun case.

She palmed the revolver as tears rolled down her face and she raced back to the door.

Khalil was just about to get into the Durango when she hollered, "Stop. Stop now!"

The night was pitch black but she could still see the stunned look on Khalil's face.

She walked slowly, gun drawn with one hand on the trigger as she watched Khalil and moved towards the passenger side of his vehicle.

She opened both doors and said with a shaky voice, "Go in the house, kids, and close the door.

She then went and stood in front of Khalil, gun raised to his chest.

Caleb began crying as he sat still in the back seat. "Mommy, don't kill Daddy. Please don't kill Daddy."

Kaleia got out of the car and went to Caleb. She pulled on his shirt, "Come on, Caleb. It's going to be okay."

He stumbled from the vehicle and Kaleia dragged his little body back into the house.

"You are a sick man, Khalil. You raped your own daughter. I will kill you before I let you take those kids. So leave before I have to make good on that and put you out of your misery," Celia began to step backwards towards the house.

Khalil slammed the Durango's door with a pained look on his face. "Is that it? You hate me so much you want me dead? Huh . . . You want to kill me. He began to walk towards her.

She tightened her grasp on the gun, pointing it at his head as she stood ten yards from him.

He stopped in his tracks. "Alright, you want me dead. Here let me make it easier for you. We wouldn't want you to miss skin." He unbuttoned his shirt and pointed at his heart. "Hit me right there."

Celia's eyes were tear soaked and she used the collar of her blouse to wipe her face.

Khalil stood before her with a bare chest. He held his shirt in his hands like a sacrificial lamb ready for slaughter.

Celia felt overwhelmed with exhilaration and dread. Her emotions collided. Her will against God's will. Her thoughts began battling in her head.

*Do not repay evil with evil but do what is righteous*
*Kill him he doesn't deserve to live*
*The battle is not yours but Gods*
*This is the only way to stop him, to get justice*

Khalil moved towards her again and she fired the gun. Knocking the shirt from his hands.

A look of horror covered Khalil's face as he threw both hands in the air and stood with his mouth open.

*Greater is he that is in me than he that is in the world*
*Protect your kids from him*
*For God cannot be tempted by evil, nor does he tempt any-*
*one but each*
*One is tempted by their own evil desire*

Celia held the gun steady at Khalil's head and calmly said, "Khalil please leave before I do something that I regret."

He reached down and grabbed his shirt without mumbling a word. He backed up until he reached his door and jumped in. His eyes never left Celia's face.

Celia lowered the gun and took in gulps of air like she was dying for oxygen. She stood in the middle of her yard sobbing until she saw his Durango disappear down the street.

When she got into the condo the first thing she heard

was Caleb's high pitched shrill and Kaleia's soothing voice.

"My daddy's dead," Caleb whined.

"No he's not. Mom wouldn't kill Daddy," Kaleia assured him.

They were on the floor in the living room. Kaleia held Caleb's head against her chest as his body shook.

Celia walked pass them into her bedroom where she dropped the gun back into its case. She slammed it shut and fell against it as her heavy heart pulled her down. "Oh, my God." She closed her eyes. "Oh my God."

The doorbell rang, then there was a rapid knocking on the door. Celia pushed her body into an upright position, put the case back under the bed and shuffled her feet forward until she made it to the door.

Two police officers stood at the door. Ruben was one of them.

"Ma'am, we got a call that there was shouting and possible gunfire at this residence," the other officer said as he looked inside.

Ruben reached down and picked up the divorce papers that still lay on the ground in the doorway.

"We're fine. Just a little argument," Celia said as she took the papers from him and attempted a smile.

"Celia, may we come in and check things out?" Ruben asked.

The other officer looked at Celia and then at Ruben. "You know her?"

Ruben spoke softly. "Yes, I know her."

"May we come in so we can see for ourselves that everything is okay?" Ruben asked again.

Celia moved aside. "Sure. Come on in."

She closed the door and walked to the living room. She stood against the wall as she watched them search the house.

"Do you need to file a report?" the officer asked.

Celia almost laughed at the irony. When she wanted to file a report she was told she couldn't.

"No, I don't need to file a report. I'm tired officers, is there anything else I can help you with?"

"Everything appears to be in order. I guess we can go," Ruben said.

The other officer spoke, "Feel free to come down to the station if you decide to file charges or you have any questions."

"I'll do that." She walked back with them to the front entrance. "Bye Ruben."

"See ya, Celia." Both officers walked down the stairs.

Celia shut the door and went to check on her kids.

# CHAPTER THIRTY

Celia was summoned to her lawyer, Dylan Wilburn's office. The divorce wouldn't be final for several months so she was wondering why her presence was requested.

"I got a visit this morning from your husband's attorney and it appears we have a little problem in your case."

Celia cleared her throat. "What kind of problem?"

"Did you recently have an altercation with Mr. Alexander?"

She knew that would come back to haunt her; she just didn't when. "Well yes, we did have an altercation this past Sunday." She spoke cautiously.

"Can you give me the details of what occurred?" he asked as he looked at her file.

"Khalil came to my condo late Sunday night. He was upset about the divorce papers and my moving without telling him. He demanded that I give him the kids and I told him that he couldn't have them and things went crazy from there." Celia stopped talking.

"How did they go crazy?" he peered up from the file.

"Didn't his attorney give you a full account?"

"I am your counsel. I need to hear it from you."

Celia pursed her lips then said rapidly like a guilty person, "When he tried to take the kids, I shot at him."

She uncrossed her legs and crossed them again, feeling antsy. "Isn't that what you wanted to hear, I shot at him?"

Dylan puckered his lips as he shook his head disapprovingly. "That was not a good idea. Not a good idea at all. Celia, you put yourself at a disadvantage."

"I shot at him. I didn't shoot him. He is still alive."

"Shooting at people is a crime, Celia. It doesn't matter whether the bullet hit him. You committed a crime. They have a shirt with a bullet hole in it as evidence."

The blood drained from her face as the reality hit her. She hadn't really thought of it that way. Not as a crime. She didn't feel like a criminal.

"Is Khalil pressing charges?" she asked.

"That is a possibility. His attorney wants to cut a deal with you."

"What kind of deal?" she asked with dread, knowing it was going to be something she didn't like no matter which way they sliced it.

"Mr. Alexander wants custody of the two children."

Celia squawked, "He can't have the children." She stood up from the chair and began walking nervously around the room. She stared at the stark white walls and the three small windows. "What kind of deal is that? I don't gain anything from that. If that is the 'deal' than we can take it off the table right now. He molested my daughter." Her blood pressure was about to shoot through the ceiling.

Celia began to grasp for solutions. "There has got to be another way. What about the child pornography on his computer? Can't you get a subpoena to search the house and seize the computer as evidence? You can't expect me to just turn my children over to Khalil? He is crazy."

"During your initial consultation, I asked if you wanted to pursue criminal charges against your ex-husband for incest and for child pornography. You told me that you just wanted to get on with your life. You didn't think he would leave incriminating evidence in the house after he caught you snooping." Dylan reasoned with her. "Celia, you don't have a lot of options. You have children that witnessed you commit a crime. If you don't take the deal, you are looking at years of jail time and he will end up with your children anyway. We can try to take it to trial, but I don't think you want to put your children through a lengthy trial. From what you told me before, your daughter won't even admit to anything happening, let alone press charges. As your counsel, I suggest you seriously consider the offer." Celia had told him all the sordid details of the molestation when she filed for divorce, including Kaleia's response to the sexual assault.

Celia dropped back into the chair and crammed her head between her knees as a wave of nausea hit her.

Dylan continued talking, "If you go ahead and give him the children, the charges will disappear. It will give us time to come up with a plan to get your children back to you before the divorce is final."

Time. That was what Celia had been going off of since the drama started. She didn't want to hear anymore about time.

She lifted her head and covered her mouth with one hand. "When does he want them?"

Dylan scrunched his eyebrows. "What did you say?"

Celia dropped her hand to her chin and spoke more clearly. "When does he want Kaleia and Caleb?"

"By six o'clock this evening."

Her whole body went numb as she stared at those stark walls. It was starting to remind her of a morgue.

"This evening?" Celia repeated to herself.

Time.

This evening.

She closed her eyes and inhaled deeply.

"You think I have a chance of getting full custody back?" she asked her attorney.

"I'm going to put my all into trying," Dylan said. He didn't hype her up.

"Okay." She felt so defeated. "I'll do it. This evening." She looked at her lawyer and stood up.

"Before you go there is one more thing."

Celia didn't know if she could handle anymore.

"He requested a mediator. He is concerned about his safety. You will need to bring the children here where I and his attorney will be present and the mediator will transport the children to Mr. Alexander."

Celia gave a disgruntled snort. *Khalil was concerned about his safety.* "Fine. I will bring the children here. Is that all?"

"That's all. Celia don't be discouraged. We're going to fight this. We're going to fight this hard," Dylan tried to reassure her.

"Uh, huh" Celia left the room like the walking dead.

Celia sat in her car in front of the law office at a quarter to six. Her heart ache. She couldn't allow herself to feel anything, because the grief would destroy her. She failed her children. She failed to protect them from a monster.

She had thought about not showing up or running away with the kids, but common sense prevailed. That was no way for her to live. It was no way for the kids to live. She didn't pack either of the kids a bag because she believed they would be back. And when they did return, all of their belongings would be exactly where they left them.

At five minutes to, she got out of the Jag.

"Alright kids, we have to go inside," Celia said as they each closed a car door.

She talked mechanically. She walked mechanically.

The two lawyers and a caramel brown lady with short curly hair and a casual sundress stood in the lobby.

"Good evening gentlemen . . . miss," Celia said addressing all that were present.

Dylan spoke. "Celia, this is Amanda Gibson, she works for the mediator's office."

The young lady extended her hand and Celia stared at it before giving a weak handshake.

"I'll take good care of the children in transport. We may see a lot of each other once visitation rights are established."

Celia nodded, looking off into the distance. She hugged both her kids as she choked back tears.

She gently squeezed Kaleia's face with both hands as she stared into her eyes. "This can stop now. Nobody has the right to touch you. Not even your dad." Celia inhaled sharply, "You . . . be . . . careful and look out for your brother. Okay?"

"Mom, please come home with us. Everything will be okay if you live with us. We can all be a family again," Kaleia pleaded with her. The tears began to well.

"I can't . . . I can't." Celia wiped tears from her eyes. Celia composed herself.

"I love you. I love you both," she looked over at Caleb who was wearing his Piston's hat.

"Kaleia and Caleb it is time for us to go," Amanda instructed them. Amanda Gibson and the kids walked out the building.

Celia ignored both lawyers as they said goodbye. She was too busy watching her life walk away.

# CHAPTER
# THIRTY-ONE

"You smokin' crack?" Alicia said as she stormed through the door of Celia's condominium like a hurricane. "You have got to be smokin' some serious crack to give that nut your kids. Why didn't you call me before you did something like that?"

Celia didn't call her first because she knew how Alicia would have responded. Alicia would have tried to talk her out of it.

Celia lay back on her recliner and balled herself up after letting Alicia in.

Her sister slammed her purse down on the glass table and began pacing the floor. "We can't be sisters' cause there is no way in hell he would have gotten mine. What were you thinking?" Alicia tried to get Celia to look up at her, but Celia kept her eyes closed.

"How could you let him manipulate you like that?" Alicia continued going off.

"Alicia, I didn't want to give him Caleb and Kaleia. I committed a crime. I could go to prison if I didn't. I can't do nothing for my kids locked up," Celia said weakly. She didn't have the energy to argue with Alicia.

"You could have taken that mess to trial. Kaleia would have talked if she thought you were going to prison. It would have forced her to say something about her father being sick and nasty."

"I wasn't going to do that to Kaleia. I didn't want to put her through a long trial."

Alicia put her hands on her hips and frowned down at Celia.

"Oh, I see. You would rather let Khalil do whatever he wants to Kaleia instead? What if he molests her again? Then what? The guilt will gnaw at your behind until you are old and crippled. Talking about you wasn't going to do that to Kaleia." Alicia shook her head as she mimicked Celia's words.

Celia had already thought about all of that. Alicia wasn't saying a thing that she hadn't already thought about.

"Book some tickets out the country or go to an underground women's shelter . . . but you don't give a pervert your children."

Celia got up off the recliner and went to the door holding it wide open.

Alicia looked stunned as she stood staring at the open door. She stomped over to Celia. "I'm not done talking."

"I'm done listening." Celia laid her head against the door waiting for Alicia to leave. She wished she hadn't called Alicia. Her twin wasn't about to be understanding.

"You are going to regret giving those kids to him," Alicia spat as she snatched her purse off the table and stomped out.

"I already do," Celia said to the closed door as she went back to the recliner.

\* \* \*

She should have shot him. She should have lodged a bullet between his sick depraved eyes. She may have gone to prison, but he would be dead. Kaleia and Caleb could have been raised by her parents. He didn't deserve to live no more than he deserved to have her kids. Those thoughts lingered strong as she lay in her bed wrapped in her sheet. Her babies were living in the home of a child molester.

Every night she came home from work, she went straight to bed and cried herself to sleep. She let the pain mingled with anger consume her. She didn't fight it. She didn't have any more energy to fight what was already a part of her.

Celia looked at her Bible on the night stand. She needed some words of encouragement before she hurt somebody. She flipped her Bible open and let the pages fall where they may. Her eyes fell on a chapter she had highlighted in neon green.

*Do you not know?*
*Have you not heard?*
*The Lord is the everlasting God,*
*The Creator of the ends of the earth*
*He will not grow tired or weary*
*And his understanding no one can fathom*
*He gives strength to the weary and increases the power of the weak*
*Even youths grow tired and weary,*
*And your men stumble and fall;*
*But those who hope in the Lord*
*Will renew their strength*
*They will soar on wings like eagles*
*They will run and not grow weary*
*They will walk and not be faint*

\* \* \*

She knew what she needed to get out of her funk. Celia looked at her clock and unwrapped herself from her co-coon.

Wednesday night Bible study had just started and if she got dressed quick enough she could make it in time to get some more guidance. It had been two and half months since she had stepped foot in church. But she needed to go.

She took off her wrinkled suit and quickly put on a short outfit and rushed out the door.

When she got inside Greatness in Faith, she sat in the third row from the back.

Celia listened to Pastor Daniels speak as Monique and Justice sat on either side of her. They didn't speak and neither did she.

"James verse one chapters two thru six says 'Consider it pure joy, my brothers, whenever you face trials of many kinds, because you know that the testing of your faith develops perseverance. Perseverance must finish its work so that you may be mature and complete, not lacking anything. If any of you lacks wisdom, he should ask God, who gives generously to all without finding fault, and it will be given to him. But when he asks, he must believe and not doubt, because he who doubts is like a wave of the sea, blown and tossed by the wind.' See, the Lord didn't say you weren't going to face trouble. Trials come to us all and sometimes even more when you are faithful to him."

Pastor Daniels began walking up and down the carpet, holding his Bible in the air. "But oohhhhhh, if you begin to wear the word of the Lord, like you wear your favorite suit or your best dress, wear His word even in your frustrations, pain, anger, through all of your troubles, the devil can't destroy you. He can attack you, but the devil can't destroy you. 'Cause the Lord is your father. He will protect you when you're mad. He will protect you when you're sad. He won't fail you."

Celia watched Pastor Daniels parade around the church and go back into the pulpit. A sense of calm came out of nowhere. It was the calm she needed and at that point she knew things were going to be alright. She reached to her left and squeezed Monique's hand. She reached to her right and squeezed Justice's hand. They both squeezed back.

Everything was going to be alright.

# CHAPTER
# THIRTY-TWO

Five months had passed since Kaleia and Caleb moved back with Khalil. The children were with her every other weekend. Their mediator, Amanda seemed to be a permanent fixture in their lives as she transported the children from one home to the other and relayed messages for the parents. Khalil and Celia had no other verbal communication. She didn't want to talk to him and evidently, he felt the same way.

Celia was still not adjusted to the transition. Her attorney, Dylan, had been true to his words and he was fervently fighting for her to regain full custody before the final divorce hearing in two weeks. There wasn't much evidence in her favor. Khalil made more money and worked less hours. At least she didn't have assault charges floating above her head.

Celia found herself examining both children for signs of abuse each time they came back from their father's house. It wasn't that she suspected Khalil of touching Caleb, but she could never be sure. Much of her speculation had never been validated. She would try to question Kaleia, but was concerned that the lawyers would catch wind about the conversation and think she was planting ideas of molestation in her daughter's head for custody purposes.

Celia was at her kitchen island eating waffles with strawberries and reading the latest edition of her favorite gospel magazine when the phone rang.

"May I speak with Ms. Alexander?" a stern voice asked.

"Speaking," Celia said as she put her fork down.

"Are you the mother of Kaleia and Caleb Alexander?"

Celia felt her stomach drop, not from the question, but from the tone of her caller's voice.

"Yes," she said cautiously.

"This is Detective Andrew Powell of the Detroit Police Department and I am going to need you to come down to the police station immediately."

Celia felt a new dread rising in her but kept her voice calm, "What is this in regard to Detective Powell?"

"I'm not at liberty to say over the phone, but if you come down I will explain everything here."

Celia had a bunch of questions to ask, but she wasn't going to try and pry information out of the detective.

"I'll be right there."


"I need to see Detective Powell?" Celia asked at the same bubble where she had tried to press charges against Khalil.

"That is on a different floor. Have a seat please," the police department clerk said.

A wave of dread and déjà vu hit Celia as she nervously took a seat and waited for the detective. She unzipped her winter coat and looked down at her pajama top and jeans. There was no time to change clothes. If it wasn't the middle of November, she wouldn't have bothered with grabbing a pair of pants.

It wasn't long before a thin white man with reddish brown hair approached her. "Ms. Alexander, can you come with me?"

She nodded and followed obediently while she prayed in her mind that her kids were okay.

Detective Powell took her into a room and had her sit at a gray metal table. She instantly felt like she was about to get interrogated.

"Could you please tell me why you had me come down here?" Celia pleaded.

"We have your children here, and in a little bit I will take you down to them," he said with a blank expression.

"Thank you, Lord," Celia said gratefully.

"But I wanted to let you know that your ex-husband," The detective looked over a sheet of paper he had, "Mr. Khalil Alexander has been arrested on molestation charges."

Celia's stomach dropped.

"We have a videotape in our possession as evidence showing Mr. Alexander attempting to molest your daughter Kaleia."

Celia's eyes fluttered as she listened.

"From the video it doesn't look like he was successful at his attempt, but the tape coupled with Kaleia's statement gives us enough to prosecute your ex-husband."

"Wait a minute. How did you get a videotape?" Celia asked as she let it all sink in.

"From what we were told, your daughter kept her computer's webcam on at night when she went to bed. She is a very brave and intelligent young lady. I don't know how many incest victims that would have had the courage to do that."

Celia clamped her hands in front of her and gulped, "Where is my ex-husband now?"

"He is in a holding cell."

"May I see him?"

"I don't know if that is a good idea," The detective said hesitantly, shaking his head with a scowl.

"Please." Celia needed to look in his face now that everything was out.

"I will see if he wants to see you, and if so, I will bring him down to this room," Detective Powell told her as he picked up the sheet of paper he read from and left her alone.

Celia stood and paced around the room. "Finally . . ." She looked up at the ceiling, completely relieved. She could bask in relief.

The door opened. Detective Powell and a muscular guard escorted Khalil into the room. He placed his hand-cuffed hands on top of the table as he sat down. Celia sat opposite him.

She looked intensely at him as she asked one question. "Why?" She knew she wouldn't get any solace from his answer, but she wanted something.

He wouldn't look up at her as his downcast eyes glistened. His face was rough and unshaven. His voice was filled with regret as he spoke. "I have these urges. I know they aren't normal. I tried to fight them. I've been fighting for years and I couldn't stop myself. I thought if I ignored them, denied them, they would go away. I . . . I . . . I'm sorry."

His lips trembled as he glanced up with red eyes. "I never meant to hurt you. Or Kaleia. "

"Instead of all that denying you were doing, you should have been getting help. You wouldn't be headed for prison if you would have got some help. God could have helped you. God can still help you. His power can deliver you from this sickness. I hated you for what you did. I despised how you tried to manipulate me. But you know what, Khalil? Hatred is bondage and I refuse to be bound. " She stared at the man she had built a life with for fifteen years and she felt nothing. Neither love nor hate. There was nothing there to connect her emotionally anymore.

Celia looked over at Detective Powell, who was standing by the door and said, "I'm ready to go see my kids. I don't have anything else to say to Mr. Alexander."

"You can take him back to the holding cell," Detective Powell instructed the guard.

Celia focused on the detective instead of watching Khalil leave.

"Your children are down the hall. I will take you to them now," the detective said.

She braced herself as apprehension overtook her while she stood outside the room that held her kids.

The detective swung the door open to a room that looked like a play area.

Caleb ran into her arms with a runny nose. "Mom, the police took my daddy away."

"I know they did, but it's going to be okay," Celia told him.

Kaleia came and stood by Celia. "I told him 'no'. Mom, I told him no."

Celia didn't comment, but instead squeezed both her kids to her body and hugged them like only a mother could.

All along, Celia trusted that God's strength could see her through and God was consistent in carrying her when she couldn't stand on her own. All her choices weren't the best as she struggled for understanding, but God always had the answers. She had to learn to be patient and wait on Him. Now it was time to start their lives anew with that burden lifted. Celia knew that it wouldn't be an easy journey for her and her children, but there was something on the inside where she knew they'd make it . . . she just knew.

# Readers Group Guide Questions

1. Celia was deeply in love with her husband. Did that lead her to ignore signs?

2. Do you think Celia is partially responsible for what happened to Kaleia?

3. What is your opinion about Celia's decision to leave the house instead of immediately calling the police?

4. Kaleia refused to help Celia press charges. Do you think that was out of loyalty for her father or fear?

5. Celia and Kaleia's relationship was strained. Should Celia have put forth more effort to communicate with her daughter?

6. Celia lied to several people about her situation. As a Christian, was her dishonesty inexcusable? Is it ever okay for a Christian to lie?

7. Khalil remained active in church ministry even though his life was deplorable. Should people with serious problems step down from church leadership?

8. Pastor Daniels refused to take sides between Khalil and Celia after their public argument. Should their pastor's reaction had been different?

9. What do you think about Alicia and Celia's mother, Patricia, and her relationship with her daughters?

10. Celia and Ruben tried to talk to Alicia bout her drinking habit. Were their efforts in vain? Should

Celia have been more aggressive in ministering to Alicia?

11. What were the similarities and differences between Alicia's addiction and Khalil's?

12. When Celia's lawyer suggested she give up Caleb and Kaleia, do you think she should have sought different counsel?

13. Under those conditions, would you have let the children go live with their father? If not, what would you have done differently?

14. During the ordeal, Celia stopped going to church. Did that seclusion from her church family increase her emotional turmoil?

15. Which character(s) could you relate to the most? Why?

## Ten Facts About Sexual Abuse

1. One in four women report that they were sexually abused as a child.

2. Statistics show that blacks are just as likely to be sexually victimized in their childhood as other ethnic groups.

3. Abuse is more likely to be reported by low-income families.

4. African-American women are less likely than other ethnic groups to involve police in cases of child sexual abuse, because of distrust of authorities and "the system."

5. 66% of all victims of sexual assault reported to the police were under 18 years of age.

6. In 95% of those cases, the offender was a family member or acquaintance.

7. In 14% of sexual abuse cases males are the victims.

8. African-American women are sexually abused with greater force.

9. Adolescents commit 23% of all sexual offenses.

10. Few pedophiles or predators tend to be violent. Child sexual abuses operate in silence and isolation.

For more information on child sexual abuse in minority communities, please go to the following resources:
www.childmolestationprevention.org
www.way2hope.org
www.robinstone.com